"The book takes you on car chases, shooting, great locations around the world all in the hopes of finding a missing friend and lost artifact. I read the book three times enjoying each time."

— Book Him Danno

"To save the day, Laurel takes you with her every step of the way on subways, planes, fast cars, and motorcycles all while being in danger. This book is truly a keeper, jump in and go for a ride!"

— Destiny's Book Reviews

"Incredible attention to detail. The author creates a world that you truly can get lost in. The book is also a fast-paced, fun read. I'm looking forward to reading book two."

— A Girl and Her ebook

"This fast-paced, action-filled whodunit was enjoyable and hard to put down...it was fun to watch the pieces come together in this well-written drama. I'm looking forward to the next book in this series."

— Dru's Book Musings

"Takes off as fast as a speeding locomotive...The twists in this story will keep you reading until the amazing end...Have a great deal of fun while delving into the art trade filled with betrayal, old secrets, greed, and some extremely strange gifts."

— Suspense Magazine

"This third book in the Bodies of Art Mystery series is as engaging and entertaining a worldwide romp as the first two books, and I highly recommend the entire series. Ritter Ames has penned a marvelous story with Laurel Beacham continuing to show her cleverness and intuition portraying a strong character...I was thrilled!"

— King's River Life Magazine

FATAL
forgeries

**The Bodies of Art Mystery Series
by Ritter Ames**

FATAL forgeries

A BODIES OF ART MYSTERY

RITTER AMES

HENERY PRESS

FATAL FORGERIES
A Bodies of Art Mystery
Part of the Henery Press Mystery Collection

First Edition | June 2017

Henery Press, LLC
www.henerypress.com

Trade Paperback ISBN-13: 978-1-63511-219-1
Digital epub ISBN-13: 978-1-63511-220-7
Kindle ISBN-13: 978-1-63511-221-4
Hardcover ISBN-13: 978-1-63511-222-1

Printed in the United States of America

To my husband, who realized pretty quickly that being married to a writer often means eating alone while she finishes up "just one more scene." And to my lovely dog, Honey, who didn't mind the fact that I had to change her name to Sugar to put her into this story.

ACKNOWLEDGMENTS

Every author needs a tribe as backup in all facets of the publishing game. From fans, friends, and the free advice that flows from other authors who've already walked the path I'm currently navigating, the number of people I could list here would be an entire book unto itself. Thank you, thank you, everyone!

I also have the greatest street team out there—Thanks, Readers— and several went above and beyond this time to help me proof this manuscript. A big thank you to Jeanie Jackson, Gail Sroelov, Andrea Stoeckel, and Eleanor Cawood Jones (in particular, thanks for the pictures, Ellie, so we could all travel vicariously to Hawaii with you while deadlines kept me chained to my chair). And thanks to all the reviewers and bloggers who give every author the visibility we truly need—in particular I'd like to recognize Jenna Czaplewski and Dru Ann Love who've been there for me since the very beginning.

I'd like to give a big round of applause to the Henery Press team. Laurel Beacham may climb buildings and mountains in my books like a pro, but the Henery editing and marketing teams leap tall obstacles in a single bound every day and always offer me a rope when I need one.

And reviewers...All you lovely readers out there who write even a short review for every book you love. As a collective group, you all are a key reason for every author's success. Thanks so much for each review—short or long—that shows readers see why they should try new series.

On behalf of myself and my characters, thank you, everyone.

ONE

The mid-January air was cold enough that I saw my breath, but I was too focused on my task to feel chilled. My uniform was a Lycra cat suit. A black hood covered my blonde hair. A coat would have created an extra obstacle I couldn't afford. Minutes ticked down, faster and faster. No time for anything that didn't contribute to the job at hand.

The narrow cable lay coiled beside the rooftop A/C unit. A quarter moon hung bravely in the night sky, casting little light for me to see—or be seen from my perch so high above the ground. I felt more invisible than I truly was. Excessive self-confidence was always the greatest danger in this kind of game. Still, I took advantage and leaned over the five-hundred-year-old golden-stone balustrade, stealing a second to re-gauge the distance between me and the darkened edge of the forest several hundred feet away. In the semi-darkness, I couldn't distinguish individual trees. I pulled the night-vision goggles down to hide my blue eyes and double checked on the due diligence I'd accomplished with subterfuge the week before. All to make my mental map see the targeted objective. I only had one shot. No time for mistakes.

My right hand freed the collapsed crossbow from the holster on my thigh. My left dragged the arrow from a long pocket I'd fashioned into the Lycra on the corresponding leg. Connecting the cable to the arrow was easy. The hard part came in trusting that every other piece of this last phase would go as planned.

I pulled at the sides of the crossbow, opening it to full size. Although I'd oiled the mechanism to keep it quiet, a rogue *snick* sounded when the parts snapped into sequence. A pause to see if the unexpected sound caught the attention of security personnel. Nothing. I closed my eyes for a moment, realized I'd been holding my breath, and forced the air slowly from my lungs.

One more risk. I removed a glove to run sensitive fingertips along the cool top of the balustrade, at the point where I'd carefully worked indentations into the stone. I located the first indentation, then the second barely there scrape. Easily confused with earlier battles the fortifications withstood since its medieval architects pulled artistic ideals together with security specifications. At least I hoped so. Too late to worry.

In a heartbeat, I'd lined up the crossbow, placing the mechanism atop the stone and triple-checking my marks with the base of the device. I squinted at the tree line, then spent another minute unfurling the cord from its coil so it fell haphazardly across the paved roof. Working almost on instinct at this point, one end went into a metal loop cemented into the wall that I'd discovered earlier. The loop had been the final detail to seal my decision on where to run this phase of the operation.

The moon broke fleetingly through the gathered clouds, but it was dim and small and basically useless for any needed illumination. Exactly as I needed.

I risked the seconds to put my right glove back on—before I closed my eyes to pray, to wish, or to will everything and everyone to perform correctly in the next few minutes. Then I pulled the trigger and let the arrow fly.

A distant gratifying *thunk* told me my calculations for weight and distance remained spot on. I gave the cord a tug, satisfied the arrow point was wedged deeply enough into the tree's trunk. Both ends now secure, I attached a silver carabiner to the loop of the black cylinder and then the metal clip to the cord. I let the "package" sail down the line and kept hold near the loop to feel the vibration en route.

Now came the waiting. My focus stayed intent on the objective. Suddenly, the vibration in the line stopped. I felt the cord move again, up and down this time. A sharp tug on the line told me Nico had it at the other end. I felt the line jerk hard and go slack. My turn again. I grasped the line with both gloves. Hand over hand, I pulled back the once-used cord. It still had yards to go and escapes to make before it slept.

My black leather gloves never lost their grip on the steel line. Less than a minute and I heard the arrow slap against the side of the stone far below, as it began its ascent back to the roof. I didn't slow down. The sharp fiberglass arrow rode easily up this windowless side of the chateau. It was all a matter of timing at this stage. Things were going almost too perfectly. Unless I heard a shout of alarm, I was past the first round of danger. The next security patrol wasn't due for another three minutes. I rubbed at the top of the stone to smudge any fingerprints I may have left behind.

My objective—what flew down the line in the large black tube—was the Caravaggio masterwork the facility's director had not meant for us to see. When Jack and I visited days ago, a panel that should have been closed wasn't. The director was waylaid by an assistant and let us enter his office on our own. A glimpse of the visible drapery in the painting, though I could only see an inch width, lured me like a siren's call. Jack was busy looking at the bookshelf and neighboring awards, but he turned when I gasped and pushed the panel open farther. The sharp light and dark contrasting technique was Caravaggio's bold statement and trademark, known by the Italian term "chiaroscuro." And the incomparable realism of key images like that drapery told me this was a find. Five men in the work, and the expected illuminated cameo of the artist. A knife covered in blood shone like Chinese lacquer. Typical Caravaggio genius.

Then the director came in and uttered a soft oath. He'd quickly moved around the desk to close the panel. "Only a copy," he'd said, his French accent heavy in his anxiety. "Made from a new secret digital technology using oils." Even without reading his body language I knew he was lying.

This painting had been on the Beacham Foundation's "lookout" list for years. I needed no research to tell me who was the true owner of the painting. In that instant, I made plans to reclaim it.

Startling news about how the painting would be picked up in a few hours had moved things up. I stepped up my plans and recruited Nico for assistance.

Then, as the reclamation was in play, while I scouted the painting's security parameters in the darkened director's office, looking for the best way to safely remove the masterpiece, I noticed a figurine in a locked case. Another stolen work on our list. It was small and I operated on impulse, letting it ride piggyback in the cylinder with the painting.

A chorus of barks from the direction of the kennels reminded me how everything must work perfectly from this point outward. If the guard made his last solo round too late or too soon, I'd be discovered. However, if anyone noticed the empty frame in the director's study or the lonely case without the tiny figurine, it wouldn't much matter that I no longer had the items on me. Laurel Beacham in the inky black cat suit would get hauled off by the local gendarmes.

I had one chance to get down and get away. One chance after the guard made his rounds and before the dogs were turned out to roam the estate as residents and staff slept. One chance.

We'd taken every possible precaution. Some pre-work was already completed, so we weren't flying blind: we had preliminary blueprints and schedules. Nothing giving us complete details, but enough to provide a framework.

Charcoal darkened my face, and I'd pulled up my collar and bottom part of the hood to cover my mouth and most of my nose. I hid by the stone wall and risked a peek around and down, watching for the guard's approach. The wind picked up, and I shivered. A strand of blonde hair was teased free from cover. I poked it back in, then shifted the elasticized black hood for better coverage. I pushed my left sleeve away from my glove to sneak a glance at my watch and swallowed hard.

As I waited, I disconnected the cord from the loop and ran the loose end through the ring instead, so the line was doubled with the metal loop as its apex. I slapped the arrow back into the ready position on the crossbow, then slipped the strap over my head and one arm to lay in cross-body fashion. Everything was now hands free, but the weapon stayed open on my back and ready to shoot if needed. I didn't want to have to use the device in defensive mode, but I was ready all the same.

In the next instant, I saw a flash of light cut the darkness and round the corner of the chateau near ground level. Just in time.

The guard swept his beam in a relaxed manner. Most of his shift was over, and his gait told me he was probably a shade self-satisfied by this point. I was counting on that complacency.

I switched sides as he passed below, and I braced against the other side of the stone impediment to barely keep him in sight. The task required me to lean out slightly to see him disappear around the next corner. As he vanished, I leapt into the next task.

Grabbing the doubled lines together in my right gloved grip, I used my other hand to drop the bulk of the line over the side. The loop got another preparatory tug to check it still held fast in the ancient mortar, and I prayed its load limit met the average weight of a healthy five-foot-nine female without popping free of the mortar.

"Final curtain, folks," I muttered, jumping up to lever myself on the stone block that offered an opening at the crenelated end of the balustrade.

With my first leap, I began my descent, rappelling down the side of the building. I'd dropped about a story when I heard two hoots of an owl. It was our warning signal. I looked toward the direction the guard had disappeared and saw the beam of light bobbing back, quicker than when he'd passed. He was returning for some reason. Why?

I grasped the cord above and below me to hang in midair, then used the doubled line and the wall to maintain height as I walked sideways, meeting the oversized chimney several feet away. My black Lycra could bleed into shadows, but no way could I hide openly against golden-brown stone. Cowering in the crook next to the four-story stack was my only option, and I pressed in close to the architectural crevasse. I pulled the cord along with me, running most of it down the shadowed corner. I tried to make myself as small as possible while dangling next to a medieval stone chimney several stories above the ground. If he looked up and shined the light he couldn't help but see me. At least the steel line no longer ran down the middle of the blank wall.

For the second time in almost as many minutes, I held my breath, trying not to panic. When he passed the chimney, I didn't risk exhaling and making any noise, but his steps slowed. Time was getting close for the dogs to take up patrol. I chewed my lip, worrying over the fleeting minutes.

A gunshot sounded back the other way, and the guard reversed direction. He vanished again around the other side of the facility's mansion house.

I resumed rappelling down the wall. As my feet hit the grass I heard running. Nico slid to a stop beside me and jerked one line from my hand. Working as my team's digital wizard was his forte, but his skills extended equally well into the field. His black stocking cap couldn't completely tame his dark curls, but otherwise he was dressed for the business at hand. As he pulled the line to get it running free from the loop, I stood behind him and used my left arm and shoulder to coil it again.

"What was that?" I whispered. "A gunshot?"

The line end dropped wiggling from the heavens and Nico caught it as he answered, "Insurance I prearranged. Just sound on a remote timer. Come on."

I dragged the cord as we raced across the open lawn. We dove into the tree line. Nico grabbed the coiled line from me and heaved it into the underbrush. "No fingerprints," he said. "No worries."

But I scooped up the heavy line and reset it onto my shoulder. "DNA. Always worry."

He shrugged, holding the black tube under his left arm and bracing one end with his hand.

The crossbow slapped my back as I kept a steady pace behind him. We'd come to the chateau from separate directions. If they found my earlier scent and followed, it would just lead to the train station. I'd walked in shadows the entire two miles. Nico came with an escape vehicle and that was where we headed.

"Be careful." I pulled the two-way comm from my ear, since I didn't need to hear him in stereo. The devices helped inside, when I needed details from him or to relay when I had the pieces ready to go. Now comms were superfluous and added a risk of being tracked by their radio frequency.

Nico nodded and removed a twin tiny device from his ear. He raised his chin, motioning toward the end of the tube. "This is bigger than I'd thought. Is the figurine here too?"

"Yes. I wrapped it in packing and placed it at the top. I fitted a piece of cardboard so neither touches the other in the cylinder."

Nico held up a hand to signal a stop. "Rest a minute. You need to put these on." He pulled a pair of folded rubber boots out of the backpack he carried. "We're going into water."

I plopped down onto a fallen tree. "How far are we wading?" The black footwear came almost to my knees.

"About a mile." He put the tube into the space the boots had taken in the backpack.

"Good thinking."

"It's cold though," he said. "The water, I mean."

"End of January in France—what are the odds?" I grinned.

I stood and shifted the crossbow into a more comfortable position. It would have been easier to refold the weapon and reattach the bulky thing to my thigh in a streamlined state, but the risk/reward ratio favored this version.

We set off again, a bit faster, but side by side so we could talk. Nico asked, "Any snags?"

I thought back to the director's office. The false wall I'd accidentally noticed in my routine visit last week. The serendipitous way I'd been led to these two finds. "I almost tripped the alarm on the figurine case. Missed a second wireless setup at first. The painting was a cinch once I cut it away from the frame. Would have preferred not to. Always better to keep a work whole and on the stretcher, but like so many nowadays they'd safeguarded this one with sensitivity alarms set into the frame. If I'd removed it from the wall to take away the canvas intact, all of security would have been on me in an instant."

"How are you going to get the items back to the original owners?"

"Let Max do the honors," I said. Recovering stolen objects was hard enough in my "reclamation projects," but returning them myself without making people wonder made it doubly difficult to stay under the radar. This wasn't a sanctioned Beacham Foundation job, but the painting was known as stolen, which made the idea viable. My boss would dearly love being in the spotlight for restoring lost treasures to grateful owners. "I'll tell him the items were turned over to me anonymously, asking the foundation to make sure the rightful parties received them. Max'll eat it up like clotted cream."

"Some people in the chateau are going to be *frustrato*," Nico said, brushing leaves from his pant legs. "They can't claim a loss and can't claim the items again when Max brings them back into the public realm."

"If he actually does. I'm going to suggest the handovers be quiet affairs, to better safeguard the artworks' return." I stood and reset the goggles on my face. I thought I heard something the way we'd come. "How far is the creek?"

"Not far." We kept walking.

In the distance, a dog barked. Then another.

We shifted to a jog, then a run.

* * *

A few hours later, now dry and warm from the somewhat decent heater in the Peugeot, we cruised into Paris. While Nico drove, I'd added a beige winter-weight tunic to my ensemble to give me less of a cat-burglar-on-the-run look and to hide the hood. Wet wipes removed the charcoal from my face. We found a short-term parking spot across from the Gare du Nord train station.

Nico tapped the screen on his phone and got out of the car as he said, "Just sent your ticket and itinerary to you. I'll escort you to the Eurostar train platform. We have to hurry, but it will be safer with no waiting."

"You don't need to see me off," I said.

We walked fast since I had no bags, plus the still-dark morning was chilly and neither of us was bundled up warmly. Nico wore a black leather jacket, and I had my hip-length navy wool pea coat. The treasure, the crossbow, and the rest of my heist paraphernalia—like the lovely electronic devices from my wizard in Zürich that opened all manner of digitized doorways—stayed hidden in the locked trunk of the car. Those would arrive in London later with Nico.

"Seeing you to the train is *obbligatorio*," he said, his heavier than normal Italian accent signaling his fatigue. His words, however, told me he was stressed. "If I didn't, I couldn't finish what I need to do because I'd be too busy worrying if you boarded safely."

"Just be careful. Don't drive until you get some sleep." I received a grunt in reply.

We were both on edge, but I'd already calculated the odds as staying in my favor to return to London without picking up an enemy. Getting out of town last night had been the riskiest part. Still, I knew better than to argue with Nico when he landed in one of his darker moods. I switched topics. "So you'll surface in London or New York in the next few days, and you'll let me know if you need anything in the meantime?"

"Yes, and I'll be monitoring you on GPS the whole time. Tell Jack not to worry."

Jack Hawkes was the newest member of the team and started out as a thorn in my side. He'd finagled his way into my boss's good graces to get me assigned to work with him when I thought he was either MI-6 or a conman—I was semi-wrong on both counts because he used the skills of both occupations. He continued trying to run every play his way, especially when my safety was in question.

"Hawkes is going to do whatever he wants to do, and likely whatever will irritate me the most. But I'm going to continue fighting him on the bodyguard idea."

Nico gave a long sigh. We stopped for a break in traffic. When he didn't talk, I said, "You know I'm right. I can't do all the things I have to do with a body-building babysitter on my heels. I may not be able to explain it to Jack, but you shouldn't need an explanation too."

In response, he put a hand at the small of my back and ushered me across the street. Seconds later we were inside the station.

I hadn't asked his plan to get the items in the cylinder out of the country. It was better if I didn't know, and he probably wouldn't have told me anyway. For that matter, neither of us said much as we hurried through the huge open area and found my queue. Too much on both our minds.

The last thing my art-liberator-partner-in-crime said to me before we split up was, "Keep alert, but don't concern yourself with me."

There was no reason to doubt him, but always reason for concern.

"Be careful," I warned. Nico nodded. Both of us knew everything got more serious once we parted company at Paris. We could only count on ourselves. He disappeared to accomplish his sleight-of-hand maneuver necessary to get the treasure out of France. I boarded the train and kept an eye out for anyone who paid me too much attention—or tried to look like they weren't watching.

In truth, I saw the next phase of this endeavor as far riskier to Nico than to me. There were so many ways to drive a car off the side of a road. Whereas, trying anything in a Chunnel train with a relatively full car of passengers heading for a business trip or holiday in England was less likely to result in something I couldn't escape. So many additional would-be witnesses. And we'd been careful. We didn't even purchase our seats in advance. Nico bought last evening's tickets online as we stood waiting in St. Pancras station. For this solo return for me, his phone processed the purchase right after he'd parked the car. It was pure luck and stubbornness I'd made this train in time. We'd cut it almost too close.

Once in my seat and the doors *shushed* closed, I swept my gaze and came back satisfied everyone was as innocent as they appeared. That didn't mean there weren't safeguards I should employ. I didn't carry a purse this trip, but I had a couple of lock picks secreted into the soles of my shoes. When I found my seat, I fiddled with my footwear, hiding a pick in the closed fingers of each hand. They weren't big, but they were mighty—and sharp. I also had a "screamer alarm" in my pocket. Normally, I used the little electronic devices to warn if someone entered a door behind me. When the two pieces separated, they offered a high-pitched alert capable of waking the dead. If anyone grabbed me, I intended to pull those babies apart and let them do all my screaming for me.

The sharp picks, the overachiever alarms, and the matron settling into the next seat helped me relax for the first time in nearly twelve hours. The rocking of the train did the rest, and I couldn't keep myself from napping most of the way back to England.

The sun peeked over the horizon a couple of hours later as our Eurostar cruised into St. Pancras International Station. This was my favorite time to disembark from a train at this station, when the early morning light streamed through the skylights. With the brass trim all around, I could imagine myself in a lovely and luxurious birdcage.

As I exited with the rest of the passengers, the public address system voices were British, rather than the French-accented ones I'd been listening to on the train. I took a moment to step away from the crowd, to give myself a chance to look for signs of danger using a full-body stretch to mask my true intention. Well, I really did need to stretch, to loosen the muscles I'd kept on high alert for too long, so the action served a dual purpose.

Though I'd only been living full-time in London a few months, the accented voices around me suddenly made me feel like I was home. Truly home. I realized this was the only place since college I'd allowed myself to settle down in any significant way. Sure, I still lived in a hotel, but I knew most of the personnel on a first-name basis. Things felt...comfortable. Surprising me as I made the acknowledgement. That homey feeling was one I couldn't say I'd experienced often in the previous decade.

Despite the fact we were still trying to learn if my father would again try to kill me. Yeah, that's right, kill me. I realized most fathers didn't attempt to murder their offspring, but when mine did, it was directly after I learned he was the master criminal I'd been tracking for months. Priorities. Oh, and I'd believed he was dead for the past decade as well. It ruined his plans when I learned otherwise.

Regardless, things felt like they were looking up. In the past few months I'd pulled together a marvelous working team. It was no longer Nico and me against the world, like things had mostly seemed before. Adding Cassie Dean as my assistant was a recent move. Cassie was American, like me. She helped run the office and was a genius at art restoration and forgery spotting. And then...Jack.

Well, Jack Hawkes didn't really work for the foundation. He was considered a kind of adjunct member of our team—though becoming increasingly essential by the day. Evidence pointed to a mole, or moles, operating to hinder us in our current project—

trying to stop an international art heist. Jack joining our group made sense. It allowed a tighter rein on information and less risk of leaking critical info to any traitor operating in his organization or the Beacham Foundation. Stopping art heists wasn't in the mission statement for the nonprofit, but protecting art was—and I'd always treated my job description as a flexible work in progress.

Thankfully, Jack worked the same way. To further complicate things, we'd acknowledged earlier in the month we were interested in seeing where our relationship might go—past the work level—and were still finding our way with that. All the while trying to convince each other we weren't making a stupid mistake to even consider trying to be a couple. Or maybe that was just me.

I moved quickly through the station, carrying only my coat and mentally reviewing the cover story for last night about a quick visit with a friend in Paris if anyone discovered we'd gone. Nico was tasked with the real challenge and risks. I only had to keep cool and balanced.

Pushing through the early morning commuter crowd, my watch said I had enough time to go by my place to shower and change before heading to the office. I'd already texted Leif, my self-defense coach, and begged off from the morning's workout, adding I'd be busy tomorrow morning too. I thought I might still get in some time at the gun range later, but while he'd set that up originally, I didn't need him onsite for instruction. He'd immediately texted back a confirmation and warned me to run five miles in place of training. I clicked off my phone in response.

I'd been good. For weeks. This was the first class I'd missed since Jack set up the self-defense lessons after we returned from Germany around New Year's, and I appreciated the way I felt so alive when leaving each time. Well, alive and bruised, but I was beginning to give as good as I got. Progress.

I stopped at the coffee kiosk, grabbed an apple for breakfast, and waited on my caramel macchiato order. I was less than thrilled when I turned away from the cash register to find a smiling journalist squarely blocking my exit.

"Hallo, Laurel Beacham."

Smile, Beacham, smile, I reminded myself. Lincoln Ferguson stood medium height, lanky build, with light brown hair and dressed in a light-brown suit that carried a hipster flair. One might mistakenly think he was an unimaginative office drone, until noticing the sharp-eyed glance he kept on everything around him. There was absolutely nothing at all unimaginative about this man, and I doubted much got past him. No point in not being civil. "Fancy running into you, Lincoln."

"Not at all. Had a tip you were coming back on the Eurostar this a.m.," he said.

My body heat ratcheted up another ten degrees. No way he could know about the heist Nico and I pulled, but even so...

Lincoln Ferguson had become my latest pest. Unfortunately, and even more dangerous from my perspective, he was an excellent journalist and seemed to have an inside track into where I was much too often. I wanted to ask if he had a hacker or a psychic on his payroll, since my plans had been a secret even to me until late yesterday when I learned the painting would be transported within hours—by noon today, in fact—sent out of France and to auction before it again went underground. The ticking clock meant Nico and I had to move fast. Our specialty, though we didn't usually operate under quite so tight a turnaround. But each reclamation had its own idiosyncrasies, and I tried never to lose a masterwork again without at least attempting a rescue.

My quip about a psychic or hacker on Lincoln's payroll, however, would have likely raised the reporter's antenna higher, and I couldn't risk the scrutiny.

Instead, I offered a fake grin and teased, "Who in the world could have tipped you off about my silly errands? I need to let the CIA know about you, Linc, or at least MI-5. You must be clairvoyant. My friend called me last night for a little girl talk. It was a spur-of-the-moment trip."

"A journalist I know in Paris saw you this morning while he was boarding a train to Brussels. He remembered my mentioning the interview with you that I am continually working to land and texted me. He also wanted to know if you're single."

I recognized the emphasis he put on the word "continually" but didn't rise to the bait. I responded to the last line instead. "You know I'm single, and I'm not currently looking." I was a pro with the smile and flip answer, but my conscious mind worked over the possibilities. How many people saw me during this quick trip—witnesses I couldn't afford? Yes, Ferguson keeping tabs on me was annoying, but there were other people whose interest in me was of the...deadly variety.

"It was to see a friend, you say?" He fell into step with me as I moved away from the coffee kiosk.

"Yes, just a few hours of hand holding." I polished my apple against my jacket sleeve but never slowed my pace. "I always like traveling overnight when I can. Much more convenient. I can nap on the return and stay on schedule the rest of the day."

He got the hint. "So you're on your way to an appointment?"

"Yes, first thing. I'll have my assistant call you when she sees I have an opening in my calendar. But I'm truly not interested in an interview, you know." That was when my gaze rested on the figure in the dark Savile Row suit who leaned against the wall of the station. His posture might have appeared casual, but the way his laser look drilled into me was anything but laidback. I caught my lower lip between my teeth as he pushed away from the wall and sauntered our way.

Linc was still jabbering something about our getting together, but I remained focused on the intruder heading toward us. I was also trying to remember to breathe. My mind needed oxygen to form a plan.

"Good morning, Laurel." Jack Hawkes's teal eyes narrowed slightly as he added, "I thought that was you. Can I help you get a cab?"

"Sure, I..." I turned my head to break the connection short-circuiting my brain. Time to switch gears. "Jack, this is Lincoln Ferguson. Linc, meet Jack Hawkes." Then I squared my shoulders for a second and started walking again toward the exit. "You're right, Jack. I do need a cab. We have an early meeting, after all."

"Earlier than either of us expected," he returned, slipping my right hand into the crook of his elbow and making sure to keep my fingers viced in the grip of his free hand. Louder he said, "Nice to meet you, Lincoln."

I thought we'd gotten away, but in a blink the reporter was again by my side. "Do the two of you work together?"

"The idea of the two of us working *together* is a rather fanciful notion," Jack said. "Laurel always feels she is at her best when she's operating solo."

Oh, boy. Thank you, Mr. Hawkes. Aloud, I said, "So much of my work is based on confidentiality. One of the reasons I'm not sure how interesting an interview I can offer to you."

"I'd be willing to take that chance."

"Knowing Laurel, it would be a total waste of time, mate. Trust me," Jack added.

I used our proximity to elbow him in the side, and I smiled up at Linc. "As I said, I'll have my assistant call you when I have an opening."

We were finally outside in weak January sunshine. I saw Jack's Audi, but he hurried me along the taxi line to the front cab. Lincoln remained doggedly at my side.

"Aren't we going in your car?" I asked, pointing.

"I'll follow."

Wonderful. As he played moving recon, he'd have the time and temper to plan a lecture I didn't want to attend.

"I think you need to know a few things before you jump to conclusions," I whispered, hoping Linc didn't hear.

"Good. We're finally thinking the same way," Jack returned, his voice pitched equally low and frown firmly in place. "Informing others is always an excellent plan."

We both looked back to gauge if the reporter picked up any of our conversation, but he was busy continuing a persuasion tactic. "Just give me a chance to change your mind, Laurel."

The cabbie opened the back door and I slid onto the seat, hoping my pest wouldn't follow me inside. I almost panicked when he leaned in, but it was only to hand me another of his cards. "All my contact numbers are on the back. Your assistant can't miss me." He raised his light brown brows and gave me a boyish grin.

Yeah, neither of us was fooling anyone. Jack was especially not pleased, but his words were somewhat gracious when he said, "Mind, I think the cabbie wants to be on his way." And he slammed the door a split second after Lincoln cleared the opening.

The cab pulled away, and I watched Jack grab a card Linc extended. Then Hawkes hurried to the black Audi. Perfect parking karma. He whipped a quick turn and was behind us in an instant. The man had what it took.

I just wondered what kind of karma was headed my way the next time he caught me alone

TWO

An hour or so later, showered and dressed in a copper DKNY suit for business, I slung the strap of my new winter Prada bag onto my shoulder—purchased on sale since the spring line was already out. I phoned Jack to try to ascertain a barometer reading for the rest of the day.

"As we discussed earlier, Nico's on assignment, and I'm on my way to the office to see how the restoration work is coming along. Then I'll—"

"I've already been by," Jack said. "No one is working on the office. No one looks to be working anytime soon."

His voice sounded gruffer than usual, and I hoped it wasn't because he was still angry about my accidental rendezvous with the reporter—or anything else that happened at St. Pancras a half hour after dawn. I yawned just thinking about it, and reminded myself to add Lincoln Ferguson to my agenda. I couldn't risk running into him again with Jack around, and the reporter seemed determined to pursue me until I gave an interview.

"So what's on for your day? Or is the schedule top secret?" I asked, attempting to deflect. He'd finally given me a few specifics about who he worked for, and I thought teasing might remind him we had our own agendas. He didn't work for MI-6 as I'd previously guessed, but close.

"You're pretty much my itinerary today," he said. "I found a backup office for the foundation and picked up the files from Cassie's place last night. I'm currently en route to your hotel. Have you had breakfast?"

"An apple and coffee, but you already know about that. I'm planning to have brunch with Cassie. Would you like to join us? We'll let you pay."

He laughed. "How could I turn down such a magnanimous offer? See you in a few minutes."

"I'll be in the lobby." Yeah, I didn't believe his good humor was real, but I was willing to go whatever distance he wanted to play it.

This keep-Laurel-protected-at-all-times thing had taken some getting used to. Oh, who was I kidding—I hadn't stopped trying to reconcile myself to the idea. But when your late father rises from the grave and tries to kidnap you at gunpoint, some changes must be implemented, and I understood the reasoning. I didn't like the idea of Jack becoming my personal estate agent, but he knew London better than I did, and the prospect of his coming through on a new HQ took one rather large item off my to-do list. No doubt, the place would be ultra-secure. Possibly even boringly so, but I made myself promise to adapt. It would relieve Cassie's worries considerably.

I'd vetoed the bodyguard idea Jack broached immediately following our last misadventure—repeatedly vetoed it. My duties toward saving art always had to come first, and I didn't need anyone "looking out for my wellbeing" and throwing roadblocks in my way. But most important was the fact there were too many things in my life I couldn't risk many people knowing about. Even Nico didn't know about all of them. Leaving me with an incentive to play along with what made my team at least marginally satisfied.

I was getting better at not striking off on my own without a chaperone. Well, again, except for last night, but Nico was beside me for most of the outing and had an electronic eye and ear on me when a physical one wasn't possible. Not that Jack or Cassie would be pleased if they knew I'd gone rogue in a high-stakes operation with Nico aiding and abetting me. A conversation for another day...Or one to avoid entirely.

When I crossed the lobby, I waved to the desk clerk, an attractive young Serb with flawless English and a perfect morning disposition. I waved as he greeted me by name. On one of the sofas, an older dark-haired man sat reading a Spanish-language paper, someone I hadn't seen before. I smiled at the bifocaled eyes I could see over the top of the newspaper, but received no response.

Jack's black Audi S5 glided up to the curb. I exited the revolving door. My favorite doorman smiled and opened the car's passenger-side door for me. As I slipped into the soft leather seat, the aroma of rich ground roast coffee mixed with the new car smell I usually associated with the Audi. Two lidded cups stood in the middle console with a white paper bag alongside. My stomach rumbled.

"I knew coffee and an apple wouldn't hold you 'til brunch," Jack said, grinning as he tossed the bag my way. "Mostly warm orange scone." He pointed to the console. "And the cup in front is the mocha caramel concoction you like so well."

"Thank you." I flashed a smile, then dove into the bag. "There's only one."

"I ate mine already." He shifted gears as we moved forward. "Don't worry, you don't have to offer to share."

I patted his hand on the stick shift. "You're a good man sometimes, Jack Hawkes."

"Not really. I just know your appetite." He downshifted again, then asked, "What were you doing in France last night?"

Damn. I decided to take the offense.

"What the hell, Hawkes? You flagging my passport?"

"Of course your passport is flagged," he responded, his tone irritatingly nonchalant. "If you get kidnapped, I want to be able to put up every available roadblock."

New tactic. "Nico was with me. We did everything last minute. Nothing to worry about."

"Nico wasn't with you on the return. And I didn't even need the CCTV feed to see you waylaid by that reporter."

This was not going according to plan. I took a moment to breathe, pulling the scone from the bag to briefly stall before I said, "I'm sorry if I worried you. Nico traveled with me to Paris and made sure I was safely boarded on the return train this morning. We had some unexpected foundation business to take care of, and he'll be back in a day or two."

"Why didn't he return with you?"

I wanted to sigh, but knew it would be a mistake. Instead, I raised my chin and kept my voice decisive. "There were some loose ends he could handle alone, so I came back on an early train." I took a bite of the warm scone.

"What kind of loose ends? And why didn't you phone and tell me last night?"

I took an extra second or two to finish chewing, then swallowed and said, "Jack, it was confidential foundation business." I again placed my hand over his, feeling the tension under his skin as he gripped the stick shift. The laughing voice on the phone was definitely a ruse, and I felt kind of guilty for worrying him. But not enough to be contrite. He had his job; I had mine. Even if my overnight venture had to stay off the books. "If I'd had any other choice I would have done things differently. I couldn't tell you last night, and I simply cannot tell you now." That's what confidential means, I thought, but I didn't dare say it aloud. I could see the muscles in his jaw relax, and I wanted to continue making headway. "Everything worked out. I can't promise it won't happen again, but if it does I will take every safeguard possible."

"And you'll call me."

"If I can," I said, using the firm but soothing tones I would on a child I was trying to placate. Inside, however, I was seething from frustration. I knew he had resources, but I hadn't thought about him flagging my passport or having me monitored on CCTV. Again. I thought I'd fully explained why it irritated me anytime he played video tag without asking first. Not that I would ever agree.

I needed to cook up some alternative means of addressing this problem when I had the luxury of time. Make a few phone calls. Likely, Nico would have to work some of his magic too.

I sipped my coffee and asked, "What is the new Beacham

address? Did the queen have a palace for let so you could keep the guards around?"

He smirked. "I'm not even going to touch that one."

"So?"

"Nothing palatial. Definitely quieter."

"No guards?"

"No guards."

Sure, I was teasing, but I kind of felt let down when he gave up so quickly. I finished my scone and felt better. Food had a soothing effect on me. "Is the address prestigious or back alley?"

"It's not like you can have a spot in 10 Downing Street."

"Just checking."

"But it's not back alley." Then he gave a shrug. "Not out in the open either. That's what I liked best about the location."

Why did *that* not surprise me. I sipped my coffee and kept quiet, waiting for more information which apparently wasn't forthcoming. Finally, I said, "Well, where are we going?"

Jack pointed through the windscreen. "There." He pulled into a parking space close to a takeaway window in a red brick building.

It was a Chinese restaurant with several floors above. I had a strong suspicion the restaurant owner and family lived on the floor directly over the business, which meant the London Beacham office had likely gone from six steps below the pavement to three flights up.

"Top floor?" I asked.

He nodded.

"Elevator?"

He gave me a crooked smile of condolence.

"Great." Probably the thing I liked least about London. Too many buildings and too few elevators. I looked at the lovely Jimmy Choos I'd slipped on earlier.

May need to start wearing Nikes and carrying my stilettos, I thought. Aloud, I said, "Let's go. Give me the grand tour."

We walked around the front of the restaurant and entered an alley with a flower shop along the other side.

"There's another entrance through the restaurant, but this way is less public," Jack said, pulling open an alley door. We entered a small back foyer with a deep stainless steel sink taking up one wall. An open doorway to the kitchen showed controlled chaos as everyone scurried to get ready for lunch patrons. I scanned the kitchen help as we moved to a nearby staircase. Everyone was Asian, most about my age, fifty-fifty male to female ratio, with lithe athletic bodies. I had a feeling this was Jack's way of working around my "no bodyguard" mandate. When we climbed the back stairs and I saw the steel door at the third-floor landing, I was certain. When he keyed a complex code into the security box on the wall to the side of the door hinges, I was positive.

"What, no retinal readers?" I quipped.

He chuckled and opened the door, waving a hand to signal me to go first.

"Hi, welcome," Cassie greeted us. Her hair was back to all blonde except for an indigo streak running down the right side. She had a handful of files, and a large manila stack on one of the heavy wooden conference tables took up about half the space. An identical equally imposing table sat at a right angle, making for one continuous work area. She continued, "I've started setting up. Feel free to jump in or change anything you like." Nodding toward the aroma that emanated from the coffeemaker, she added, "But what you probably need is in the corner there."

I smiled. "Jack picked me up a cup on the way, but thanks."

On the far wall, the only one without a door or window, her personal whiteboard was already in play and she had attached copies of most of our objectives: people on the left and prints of art objects on the right. In the floor, near the middle space, she'd dropped an aerial view of the palazzo in Florence that Moran used for a forgery factory. Every expert in their field has a veteran master nemesis, and until last fall I always thought Moran was mine. My track record for retrieving art was impressive, but any loss I'd ever had could be tracked directly back to Moran and his unending talent for spiriting away art. That reason and his staggering ego was why Jack and I originally pegged him as public art enemy number one on our hit list for the international heist.

We now had additional bad guys to choose from, but Moran planting a forgery factory in a Renaissance-era palazzo in the shadow of the Florence Duomo proved he still held the record on egocentric one-upmanship.

About a month after we left Florence in the fall, we managed to secure the aerial shot of the deserted palazzo. Cassie clipped the picture to the top of the stack of printouts that Nico produced when he searched the history of the building's owners. I picked up the papers comprising our limited chain of evidence.

"What's this? Why are we revisiting the palazzo information? Something new develop?"

Cassie shook her head. "I had them in my hand and wasn't sure where they needed to go. I was thinking about adding the aerial shot to the board but didn't know where it fit in the present setup. So I left the pages on the floor. I'll stick them in a file drawer when we get one."

"I think we're good with the two tables. We can make do with boxes," I said, eyeing the space. It was large and open, probably thirty feet by forty. A widescreen television was mounted between two of the windows, with a blue multi-headed adapter cable hanging from the bottom. Shutters and curtains on the large windows afforded us total privacy. While this setup might have sounded like overkill three floors above the street, we'd all learned not to take anything for granted. "A couple of chairs would be nice." I looked out the windows. "And a fire escape."

Jack spoke up. "Chairs are coming. I figure we don't want this place to look too public and occupied, but it can be functional. And the fire escape is on the other side of the building. I'll get us a rope ladder to keep here in the space, but I didn't want to make it easy for someone to bypass the keypad and get in through other means."

Made sense. I nodded in agreement.

I walked to the middle of the room and did a full slow pivot. The walls were ecru, the shutters and curtains an even brown, and the floor was covered in a variegated sand toned, level loop. "The carpet's clean. Functional. Yeah, I like this idea. Kind of 'war room primitive.'"

He grinned and took off his suit jacket to hang it on the doorknob, then ran his hand down the teal silk tie that matched his eyes. "We might need a coat rack, too. Or at least a couple of hooks for the walls."

"Hooks. Keeps with the primitive decorating plan," I said.

"Oh my god, you two." Cassie shook her head. "Let's do some work and stop with the interior design talk, okay?"

Her tablet sat atop one of the boxes. I picked it up, surprised. "We have wi-fi already?"

"Jack has a guy," Cassie said. "He was leaving with his tool belt as I got here this morning."

I looked at Hawkes. He raised his right eyebrow and gave me his "it's nothing" shrug. There was no point in asking if the connection was secure.

I looked up at the cameras near the ceiling. "Are those live?"

"They are now. Once secure wi-fi was available." He pulled a key from his pocket. "Here is your key, and the security key code for this week is written on the ring tab." I opened my hand and he dropped the key onto my palm, closing my fingers around it. His hand was warm, and he held my gaze a second longer than necessary.

I smiled, but turned away to keep myself from being sidetracked, dropping the key onto the tabletop next to my Prada. "Who paid for all of this? Cassie, did you—"

"I called in some favors," Jack said over my shoulder. "We need a place to work and the stuff out of Cassie's flat. For its safety and hers."

"Have there been any attempts—"

Cassie shook her head and Jack said, "No, but the risk was always there. A whole new group of people know us now and will be looking at who we're each connected to."

I knew a great security system protected my assistant's flat.

The building's owner took its historical status seriously. Which was why she'd taken possession of the files in the first place. But Jack was right. As we investigated the bad guys and their connections, the bad guys were likely investigating ours too. Any additional risk to Cassie was unacceptable in my book.

"So what's new on the agenda?" I asked. "I assume the office tour wasn't the only reason you cleared your schedule."

Jack walked back to the door and removed a smartphone from his inside jacket pocket. "Since you came up with your brainstorm in Cologne suggesting we focus on incoming shipments with multiple copies of artwork entering through various customs posts, I began inquiries. A number of interesting developments came to light." He moved to the flat screen and synced his phone to it. Soon, his recently received email attachments on art copies and forgeries were readily viewable to the three of us.

As Jack's thumb brushed the face of his phone, crates appeared on the widescreen with different agents pulling out sample pieces of art from each. He explained, "I expanded on the ideas you and I spoke about on the return flight from Cologne, Laurel, to follow artwork coming in labeled as copies and then see where it goes and whether it changes classification later. I've been in touch with the customs departments of all the European countries, but because I have better opportunity for faster information about pieces going in and out of the U.K., I convinced the various offices to trail bona fide copied art labeled with anywhere in Great Britain on the bill of lading."

He carouselled through the pictures of the shipments separated by countries of origin. Each country's initial photo showed confiscated crates in groups of three or four.

"How many in all?" I asked.

"Copies, or numbers of works in all?"

"Both."

He sighed. "Dozens of different pieces, and at least five copies of each."

There were several shots of the single pieces, both crated with its mates and shown close up for detail. I was mesmerized by the varied objects, from religious icons to reproduction tiaras, ancient statuary to Chippendale chairs. But as Jack changed the screen with a swipe of his thumb, I saw the majority of the shipments were paintings.

"And this is all within...?"

"The last six months," Jack said. He quickly flipped a few screens and added, "This is the latest. Came in last week to Calais with a shipping label to London. Spanish shipping papers, but they look to be forged like the others. Different this time, as there are just two copies, but both have forgers' marks matching one we've flagged. I don't have a theory on the anomaly of just the pair. The thieves may be shipping the rest of the copies separately, but it's another trail to follow."

All the air left my body. I heard Jack talking, but my concentration remained locked on the painting's sharp contrast between the dark and light images, a knife showing its use with dark scarlet, the way the clothing realistically draped on the bodies, and—like a spotlight—the image of the artist's face at the top of the crowd of five. An excellent forgery of the same Caravaggio masterpiece I'd liberated a few hours ago.

I leaned against a table and gripped the edges. Jack and Cassie remained focused on the screen and didn't notice I was trying to stay vertical. Then he said, "Isn't this a copy of the same painting we saw in France last week?"

Words wouldn't come from my mouth. When I didn't answer right away, he turned and looked at me. I took a deep breath, then cleared my throat and waved a hand. "Frog in...throat. Caramel...coffee."

He raised an eyebrow.

I tried again. "Yes, I think...it's the same composition."

"It was supposed to be some kind of special printing, right? That's what I remember the director saying." Jack kept his damned questioning eyebrow lifted, and I knew his puzzlement had nothing to do with the image on the wall.

I nodded. "Digital. New process." There was no point in trying to say anything else. My vocal cords felt paralyzed.

Throughout the exchange, Cassie's gaze flipped back and forth between us like a spectator at a tennis match. I didn't want her trying to connect dots. I coughed. "Jack, why don't you fill Cassie in on the painting we saw while I head down to the kitchen for a glass of water."

"I can go—"

"No, I'll be fine." I felt in my pocket to make sure my phone was there, then I removed the jacket from the doorknob and laid it carefully across the end of the closest table. "Just down the stairs and right back. Maybe I'll introduce myself to a few of our neighbors. You and Cassie stay here and talk."

I shot out the door before he could say anything else, dialing my phone as I walked.

"Nico, where are you?" I was on the next landing, halfway down the first step toward the middle floor so Jack couldn't see me if he looked out the door.

"Nice to talk to you, too," Nico replied. "Why are you whispering?"

"Because I don't want Jack to hear me."

"I should have known."

I blew out a breath. "Don't make this more frustrating. I...Oh my god, Nico. We may have screwed up our best lead yet."

THREE

Standing on the beige vinyl floor of that landing, guilt and regret washed over me. We'd been waiting for a break, and like the rest of this ill-fated case it looked like my midnight venture with Nico destroyed everything. Our spiriting away the painting meant we couldn't follow it to the auction which it was slated to join. My brain whirled with the possibilities. The fact there were only two copies in the confiscated case likely meant our art heist criminals also learned about the auction and had to move faster than normal to substitute a copy for the original.

My flight from the office and the scrutiny of Jack and Cassie was a desperate attempt to reach Nico and see if he had any ideas on how to salvage the situation. In that moment, however, I came to a decision. "Nico, hang on, I'm going back up."

"What?"

"Just a minute." I stared upward, toward the door, but couldn't yet make myself move.

No. At some point I had to be a grown up and realize I couldn't withhold information my whole team needed. It was time to 'fess up. Another look up the steps, knowing what was behind that steel door, and I nearly changed my mind. Down the next half-flight, in the hall of the floor below ours, a man poked his head out of a doorway. I stared at him. His eyes grew wide. He hurriedly ducked back inside his office and clicked the lock.

Great. I knew the kind of expression I wore at times like these, with eyes like blue lasers. I might as well introduce myself as the weirdo new neighbor.

Nico asked what was happening, and I told him to wait. I clattered up the stairs and grabbed the doorknob when I reached the top floor, then slammed into the dark red immovable object. "Dammit." I looked at the keypad and realized my key with the code was where I'd left it on the table. Before I could knock, Jack threw open the door.

"Forget something?" He grinned, then frowned. "What's the matter?"

I held up my phone and hit the speaker option, then I set it onto the table closest to our group as the door latched behind us. "Nico, this is now officially a conference call. We need to fill Cassie and Jack in on what little we know, and we need to get you back here to London. Copies of the painting we…rescued…last night hit an email to Jack as incoming through customs."

"Rescued?" Jack growled.

"Last night?" Cassie's blue eyes widened.

Nico cursed in Italian over the speaker. I looked at Jack and nodded.

"I know you think I lied to you," I began. "But the painting has been on the foundation's 'lookout' list for decades. We truly were recovering it for foundation business. Just not exactly the way I'd implied." I looked down to momentarily escape his angry glare. "We were going to have Max return it to the true owner and maintain our anonymity."

"Jack, I can send you the file with the list Laurel is talking about," Nico said. "She's telling the truth."

"Oh, I'll bet you can send me all manner of data to shore up Laurel's story." Jack turned away from me and put his hands on his hips. Then he whirled back around and demanded, "That doesn't explain why you have to hare off by yourselves. Nor why it had to be a super-secret middle-of-the-night escapade."

I leaned against the tabletop, crowding him. "Because we found out late yesterday the painting was going to be sold at auction. The pickup was scheduled by noon today. Since the forgers worked off-script by sending only two copies for your pals to confiscate, it sounds like the criminals were caught off-guard by this maneuver as well."

"An auction? A legitimate one requiring provenance? Or the shady kind?" Jack asked.

"I didn't have time to check. Just like we didn't have time to canvass document forgers to see if anyone at the France facility had ever had papers forged to show ownership of the painting. My guess was no, since the director lied about it being a copy," I said, crossing my arms tightly across my chest. "I'd already put some plans in place to get the painting back through proper channels once we had some breathing space in our schedule. But my quiet inquiries brought surprising results instead, and I learned from one of my personal connections about the sale. If we didn't want to lose the painting again, we had to...re-appropriate it last night."

"You mean steal," Jack said.

"I'm not sure it's stealing when it's already stolen, and we're going to return it to the actual owner."

"Pretty it up all you want. But if the timetable was as tight as you say, the two of you took a huge risk without an adequate window to prepare."

Okay, that made me mad. "I'm standing here, aren't I?" I turned toward the phone. "You're not in handcuffs or jail, right, Nico?" The only answer I received was a chuckle. Yeah, I thought, laugh while you're a safe distance away from Jack's scowl. "Where are you anyway?"

"Heathrow," Nico replied. "My plane landed a half hour ago, and I'm almost to the Tube entrance."

Jack spoke up, "I have everyone in a new location. The address is—"

"No. I won't have the items until later," Nico said. "I'll pick them up and go to Laurel's hotel. It will be after six."

"In my room or the lobby?" I asked.

"Whichever you prefer."

"We'll meet you in her room," Jack said. "And what do you mean by items? You stole something other than the painting?"

"A figurine," I said. "Small." I held my hands a few inches apart.

He shook his head.

I felt like shaking Nico. That he was in London and the items in question weren't with him had me on edge. "Why did you separate from the...you know...stuff?"

My techno wingman chuckled again. "You make it sound like I'm moving drugs."

"This isn't funny, Nico."

"*Dio Mio*, don't worry. Clive is taking care of everything. He said to tell you hello, by the way."

"Clive with Whyte Noyse?"

"*Sì.*"

I'd flown with the heavy metal band recently to Florence, and they brought Jack back home when he'd been wounded in a rescue attempt. Clive was the band's amazing roadie. Nico and their publicist, Patricia, had some kind of relationship. I asked, "You arranged everything with Patricia, right? Are you with her now?"

"We're meeting for a late dinner. But I'll see Clive before. Our package is coming with the instruments."

It all made sense again. Clive would get our items through with the band's gear. "We'll try not to keep you too long tonight. Patricia probably doesn't like to be kept waiting."

Again, we heard a chuckle.

But Jack didn't see anything humorous. "In the meantime, come on into the office and you and Laurel can fill Cassie and me in on all the unilateral decisions the two of you made last night and why."

"No," Nico replied. "I'll meet you both tonight and hand over the package. I have something to do before I come in."

"What is too important—"

Nico interrupted. "I'm getting into the train, and I'm turning off my cellphone. *Ciao.*"

And that was it. Nico was gone.

Jack gave me a blank look, his mouth opening and closing, but no words came. I looked at Cassie, and the two of us broke into peals of laughter.

"What the bloody hell?"

I held up a hand of acknowledgment, but there was no way either of us could stop laughing and explain to him how many times we'd seen Nico do exactly the same kind of thing to Max. Jack had heard the stories, but a person's first experience was always the funniest—for everyone else.

We stopped when Cassie looked at her watch and gasped. "You'll have to fill me in later. We have a conference call with Max in fifteen minutes."

"Max? Our boss Max?"

She nodded.

A glance at my phone screen said it wasn't even eight a.m. in New York. "He's not in the office yet."

"He's in Paris, meeting with a funder. He wants our input."

Paris! Where was my early warning signal for when Max entered my time zone? I shoved my phone into my Prada and tossed Jack his blazer. "You handle Max, Cassie. Give him the virtual tour of the new space, but don't you dare give him the entry code to get in the door."

"Where are you going?"

"Jack's taking me to brunch. Or early lunch." I opened the door and waved for him to follow. "Anywhere but here."

She started to follow. "But Max—"

"You scheduled the appointment, Cass. This is your chance to make management points."

"The funder—"

"Can be handled by Max," I assured her, standing back so Jack could move into the hall ahead of me. "He just wants a pretty face for the funder to look at. I guarantee your smile during a web call this morning will look infinitely more natural than the forced one I'd muster. Good luck!"

Jack was already on the next landing and checking his phone messages when I sailed down the stairs. He looked up. "Isn't video conferencing with the head of the foundation part of being manager of the London division of the Beacham Foundation?"

"Fifteen minutes is not enough time for me to prepare to meet with Max under any circumstances," I said, continuing down to the next floor. He stayed close on my heels. "He'll go easy on Cassie. And we really do have other critical things to discuss."

"So where do we go?"

I sighed and slowed down. "I don't care. Anywhere quiet and private is fine. But I don't want to go too far in case Cass does need me for some reason. I may have acted like I'm throwing her to the wolves, but I don't want to do it literally."

"You simply don't want to be there for moral support." He grinned.

I hitched my purse strap higher on my shoulder and faced him. "Do you want to know what you said you wanted to know? Or do you want to wait three hours while I double team with Cassie to satisfy Max?"

"Point taken."

"Thank you." We resumed our trek down the stairs, and I asked, "Are we driving somewhere? Or what?"

We reached the ground floor, and he turned me into the short hallway to the left. "They should be setting up for lunch," he said. "But I'll bet we can find some privacy in the restaurant. Maybe even a cup of tea if you'd like."

"Anything more substantial?"

"You truly are always hungry, aren't you?"

I grinned at him.

"If you already know the answer to the question, why bother asking?"

Minutes later, Jack charmed the hostess, Lea, and introduced us. She settled us into a corner booth on the edge of the empty sea of tables. I slid into the half circle of black pleather and surveyed the crimson, ebony, and gold décor. I peeked through the lattice separating the dining area from reception and saw a huge lit fish tank for good luck. Hopefully all that feng shui good fortune funneled in an upward direction toward the top floor and didn't homestead on ground level.

"Tea in just a few minutes," Lea promised and started to turn away.

"Could we have something else too?" I asked quickly. She faced us again and tilted her head to the side. My mind ran through Asian menu items. "Maybe some crab rangoons? Or anything fast and easy?"

"Soup?" she asked.

The lovely chicken broth with fried onions floating in the bowl. "Absolutely. Thank you." I smiled. She nodded and turned away.

"Happy now?" Jack asked as she moved at an elegant quick step toward the kitchen.

"We'll see. But probably," I pulled out my phone to text Cassie where we were and to warn her not to tell Max I could readily make a command appearance. She texted back that I'd better bring her some rangoons too.

Minutes later we had our soup, a teapot and cups decorated with Chinese scenes, and a matching plate covered in warm crab rangoons resembling edible lotus blossoms. Yes, I was definitely happy with the selection. As Lea moved away, Jack said, "I guess we start with what you know."

My spoon was halfway to my mouth, and I finished the motion before I said, "Look, I'm sorry, but cut me some slack about this, okay?" I picked up the pot and filled each of our cups with warm green tea. "I had no idea the sale we were trying to short circuit had anything to do with what our group's been working on. I realize it looks like I acted rashly—"

"You got that, huh?"

I set down the pot before speaking, afraid I might otherwise pour tea in Jack's lap. "You're unattractive when you're an ass, Hawkes." Actually, he'd looked really good the entire morning with that whole anger vibe going, but I wouldn't admit it out loud.

"Why didn't you tell me?"

"So you could try to talk me out of it?"

"You know I probably wouldn't have."

I lifted my cup and stared at the liquid to keep from meeting his gaze. "The fact you said 'probably' gives the answer better than any argument I could make."

"It was dangerous."

"I've done dangerous before. And Nico was my wingman."

He spoke softly. "You could have had extra help."

"Are you mad at me for messing up the potential break in the case, or because I didn't let you tag along?"

"I never 'tag along.'"

My cup hit the table too hard, making for a louder than average sound in the nearly empty space. I took a breath before speaking. "Don't do this, Jack. Don't make me change everything I do just because...just because. Damn." My jaw clenched, and I knew the smart thing was to quit talking. Instead, I bumbled on. "I haven't had anyone who loved me and worked to keep me out of trouble since Grandfather died, and I'm not looking for that aspect in our relationship."

He jerked back like I'd slapped him. Something told me a slap would have been less painful. I was trying to figure out a response to anything he might say, but he surprised me by changing strategies.

"Let's contact your source. See what else we can learn to tie to the copies."

I shook my head. "We can't. He was leaving for Barcelona. He runs a thriving pickpocket trade down there after the new year."

Jack nodded. "Okay, then why did he even know about the painting? And why did he give the information to you?"

"I told you." My rangoons were getting cold and that would never do. I picked two from the plate and handed one to Jack. "The painting has been on the foundation's list for a long time." I bit into one succulent lotus petal and almost swooned. Exactly what I needed. "At some point in the past I'd mentioned it to this source. I don't remember when, but it's something I do anytime I talk to grifters and pickpockets who work a large area. Especially if they work multiple countries. They're extremely observant about things beyond just their mark. He recently heard about the painting from one of his stringers and learned it was heading for the auction. He contacted me yesterday and told me I had to move fast. Since I already knew the location of the Caravaggio, and had an idea how to successfully retrieve the piece, Nico and I went to France."

"You don't think that could in any way tie in with the reason Max is in Paris?"

"God, I hope not."

"Could your avenues of inquiry since we saw the painting be a reason they decided to get rid of it?"

I shook my head. "My guess is no. I'm not saying that to be defensive either. All the inquiries I'd made were on the facility and the personnel, especially the director. I did seek out architectural information on the place in case I needed it later, and I received rudimentary plans from a British source on historic European homes and landmarks a few days ago. Getting those plans felt serendipitous once the auction information came in."

"You never mentioned seeing the painting to anyone?"

"Of course not. I didn't mention it in any of my inquiries. My standard procedure in this type of situation is to first get data on the players holding the piece."

Lea and another girl who could have been her younger sister, and probably was, had been placing soy sauce and salt and pepper at the other tables. As they neared ours, she asked, "Is everything okay?"

"Yes, thank you," Jack said, letting his expression relax to a quick smile.

I brightened my tone. "Perfect. Thanks so much."

She smiled and motioned for the other girl to follow her to the kitchen. I resumed using the deep plastic spoon to eat my soup, and Jack did the same. When we were once again alone in the space, he asked, "And this auction is?"

I grabbed another rangoon. "Sometime within the week. The only information I received pointed to the painting being moved in less than twenty-four hours from when the source notified me. We had to hustle."

His expression darkened again, but he continued eating his soup and didn't lecture me. Finally, he set his empty soup bowl aside and mused, "So we have no way to contact this source. You don't know when the auction is being held, or—"

"And we don't even know if the auction is connected to the copies flagged by customs," I interrupted. Then I put my left hand over his right. "I know in the office I jumped to the conclusion Nico and I had messed up an opportunity with this job, but it could be a leap of logic for us to continue that path. I'm not saying this to make excuses. Since the panic passed, I've been reasoning things out, and it seems likely these could be two separate heist opportunities. One, an auction with items lacking provenance. And two, a play by the thieves in our original heist mission to steal the stolen painting from the French facility and replace it with a copy. With it a coincidence they're both happening at the same time."

We'd first discovered the forgery angle when a stolen art object resurfaced, only to have a mark showing it was made by a master forger—who was dead. That led to finding the Florence palazzo, and we soon learned as many as five copies were made of any masterwork we presumed was part of the heist. This was the first time we'd only seen two copies of a work.

Jack stayed silent. I waited as long as my patience lasted, which wasn't long, then I said, "Well? Any ideas?"

"It still bothers me there are only two copies confiscated. An anomaly."

"Good point."

He stretched, but didn't put an arm across the back of the booth behind me. I wondered which transgression of the morning had him still ticked.

"We could go to Barcelona, find your pickpocket and question him," he said finally. "See if he knows anything else he didn't tell you or has learned additional details since you talked."

"Which you know as well as I do would be a waste of time and lead to frustration on both our parts." I grabbed another rangoon. There were only three left, and I wanted to make sure I got my share. Jack took another. And then there was one.

"So we blow off the auction?" he asked, pulling a petal from his flower.

I let out a long breath. "I can't tell you how much I hate time/space dilemmas like this. If we could clone ourselves, I'd say, yeah, go after both. But..." I popped the second half of my rangoon in my mouth. "My moral compass doesn't allow me to possibly give up on grabbing the other stolen works we'd find if we pressured the auction angle." I licked crab and cream cheese from my finger and noticed Jack watching me. "On the other hand," I continued, "while we can't prove a connection between the auction and our current assignment, I say we need to give it up as the maneuver would stretch our resources too thin."

"You wouldn't want to send Cassie and Nico down to Spain to ask around?"

"Nico maybe, but not Cassie. She'd be out of her element in Barcelona but helpful to us here. Though I don't want to send Nico alone to ask questions either. He needs backup that knows the city and the players if he's going to have any success finding my source in Barcelona."

Jack nodded, but frowned. I thought for a moment. There was an idea hovering on the edges of my subconscious—

I snapped my fingers. "I've got an idea. Let me see if I can reach her."

"Her?"

"Clara Ochoa. You saw her at Christmas when you and I met on Oxford Street before we flew to Ireland."

His eyes widened, and his dark brows shot toward his hairline. "You don't mean the waif."

"I positively do." Clara was a young new recruit in my list of—hopefully—reformed petty thieves who could provide information. She was also originally from Barcelona. I said, "I don't know that I'll send her with Nico, because I don't want to mess up anything the shelter has done to make her an honest London resident. But I do want to see if she'll tell me anything to help him once he gets there."

"Then?"

I did not relish what his reaction would be to what I was going to say next, but I plowed forward like a trouper. "If we do feel a need to pursue the auction angle, it would be a good idea for me to head down there with Nico. Then you and Cassie can follow up on the copies here."

"Cassie and me? Why not Cassie and Nico?"

"Because Nico can't talk to law enforcement and customs with the same authority you can. However, he's a pro at talking to pickpockets and assorted thieves."

The silence again, but I expected it and waited. My argument was sound and he knew it.

"Speaking of law enforcement," he said, changing the subject, "I may have an interview date firming up with the retired detective on your mother's case. The file info on her accident investigation was as good as I expected, but I'm hoping a face-to-face interview will help jog the detective's memory. Want to come along?"

Like I needed to be hit with further surprises today. I hedged. "To New York?"

"Yes."

No. Yes. I don't know. I wanted to say all those things aloud but didn't. Because I did know, really. I wanted answers, but I didn't want to have to think about what those answers might tell me. About how the story of my mother's death might change to talk of murder. And I definitely didn't want to sit near a retired cop whose words might open emotional wounds I'd worked to keep closed and buried since I was four years old. "I...uh...maybe. Let's see how busy we are when the time comes."

The look he gave me was kind. I didn't want kind—it felt too much like sympathy. Tears pricked my eyes.

"I need to use the restroom," I said, scooting out of the booth. "I saw it in the hallway as we came in."

"Okay, I'll pay and we can sneak back upstairs and see how the meeting is going."

I slung the strap of my Prada onto my shoulder. "Get Cassie some rangoons. I'll be right back."

FOUR

As I entered the small one-person bathroom and locked the door, my phone trilled. I took a couple of deep breaths to control the tears and dug through the Prada. Caller ID said *Marci*. Ah, the breath of fresh air I needed. She was one of my favorite friends from a decadent summer abroad during college. The one directly after my father supposedly skied to his death. I knew Marci from a few finishing school adventures years earlier, and we met up in London that summer and partied everywhere her credit card would take us. She probably got me into as much trouble as we each got the other out of, but she saved my life. Definitely. Let's just say I hadn't handled the new grief and disappointment well.

In the years since, we'd met for dinner and parties and filled out guest rosters in similar circles, but they were just quick connections. A reunion was long overdue.

"Girl, how are you?" I smiled into the mirror as I answered the call, using my free hand to run a corner of a paper towel under my lower lashes and catch any moisture. Just seeing the name on the screen was enough to help stop the tears.

"I'm fine," she said. "Are you still a badass?"

"The baddest." We both laughed at the inside joke and favorite greeting that tied back to a rather obnoxious—turned frightening—admirer of Marci's, who learned what a girlfriend's wing-woman could do. The guy probably still walked funny.

"What's going on?" I asked and tossed the paper towel. "Last I heard you were in the Far East."

"Macau, yeah. I did my stint for the family investment holdings, but tour of duty is over and I'm back. I'm getting married!" Her voice rose on the last two words and we squealed a little when she added, "He's an Italian prince."

She added, "And I won't even make you bow before me. Well, maybe one curtsy."

"All your dreams are coming true," I said, with just a hint of sarcasm. I really liked her, but Marci had always had a princess-diva complex.

"Anyway, I'm having a fabulous engagement tea for all my girlfriends at Mummy's and Daddy's this weekend," she continued. "Just a bunch of my besties on Saturday. When I heard you're back in London, I had to call—"

I chewed my lower lip. "Look, I'll try, but—"

"Don't say no, Laurel. I'll send a car to fetch you. You can bring a friend if you like, and you don't even need to pack. I just returned from Paris and I'll let you pick favorites to wear. Please come. We'll have fun, I promise. Try telling me you don't need some fun."

No, I couldn't tell her I didn't need some fun in my life. But it was Thursday, and I had no idea where I'd be in a couple of days. "I'll see what I can do. Can I reach you later at this number? Maybe tomorrow?"

"Of course. But I only want to hear a yes when you call back. Please, please, please."

I laughed. "I'll do what I can. I promise."

We said goodbye. I tossed the phone back into my purse, washed my hands, and took a good look at my eyes. If I smiled a lot I could hide everything, but I needed to dive back into work or those tears would make a return visit in the first quiet moment.

As I exited the restroom, Jack stood in the hallway outside the door. He was reading the screen of his own phone, and his cell hand also held a white bag with grease spots showing through. I could smell the warm rangoons inside.

"Something interesting?" I asked, motioning toward the phone.

"Huh?" He looked up, then back down as he shoved his cell into a pocket. He almost acted guilty. "Work. I need to go talk to someone."

"Should I go too?"

He put a hand at the small of my back and steered me toward the stairs. "No, sorry. It's not *foundation work*."

Ah, another dig at our early-morning rendezvous. I wanted to say "smart-ass," but instead I replied, "Oh, I get it. Q and C duties."

"Q and C?"

I stopped on the step above him and leaned close to whisper, "My personal code for Queen and country."

He chuckled. "Precisely."

As we resumed our climb, he asked, "Who were you talking to in the bathroom?"

"Old friend. Called to ask me to come to some girls' weekend tea at her family's place in the English countryside. What is it you Brits always call big old houses? A pile?"

"Usually an old pile. Unless it's Windsor Castle—then it's a noble pile."

"Well, it's not Windsor, but house is kind of a misnomer for something so impressive. I've only seen pictures..." This was getting to be too much information, so I cut to, "I tried to let her down easy, but she made it practically impossible. I'll call back tomorrow and tell her no again."

"A problem?"

"Not really...Some misgivings on my part. It's hard to sound like I'm anything but wistful as I'm turning down the invite since it would be great to see her. She also said she'd send a car, and I could bring a friend."

"I don't think I—"

"Don't worry. If I took anyone it would be Cassie. You aren't equipped for a girls' weekend."

"Thank god. You do realize you're nearly thirty. I think you and your little friend are a tad old to be known as girls."

"I have a couple of years as yet, thank you." I grinned and gave his cheek a sharp pat. He flashed a half grin. "She's already past thirty. You get a bunch of us together in a room, however, and the girl tag fits like no other. You would definitely be uncomfortable and want to flee."

"No argument."

"But kind of a rite of passage thing," I added. "And it's so much fun to find out what everyone else is doing."

On the first landing, he pulled me to one of the corners and spoke in a quiet voice. "I do have another bit of news you need to know. Something you probably want to hear without an audience."

Cassie. He's talking about not wanting Cassie to know, I thought. This had to be about my family. I looked up when he paused.

"The man in the photos with your mother..." His voice trailed off. Moran had recently sent me items that belonged to my mother. Items the old thief apparently had in his possession for nearly twenty-five years, since she died when I was four. Each time I'd received one of the "gifts," a photo was included—different scenes, different decades on the calendar, but both photos featured my mother and a man who resembled Moran's grandson.

I was almost afraid to hear anything else, but I did want to know. "Go ahead. Say it."

"I have confirmation his name was Paul-Henri Aubertine. A man we now believe was Moran's much younger brother."

"Was?"

"He died later the same year as your mother. In a car crash in France. A few miles down the road from his home. Single-vehicle accident."

"In a car crash. Near his home. Just like my mother's death." I spoke mechanically but couldn't stop myself. "Aubertine was the name used for the architectural firm I learned designed Moran's chateau in Le Puy-en-Velay."

"Yes, from what I've confirmed, the brother started PA Designs as a legitimate business, then Moran kept it in operation after his death. Likely for ulterior motives, but quite possibly to honor his brother too. The extensive measures used to distance Moran's criminal activities from the architectural firm are telling."

"So Aubertine is Moran's real name?"

"No way yet to be positive, but it's a good supposition."

I looked away. "And my mother had what was likely a decade-long affair with Moran's brother. Who may have been a good guy in a family of criminals, or...not. But my mother chose to have a long-term affair with him."

Jack took hold of my shoulders and made me look at him. "Again, too much is conjecture at this point. We have two photographs taken years apart. They could have just met up again when the second snap was taken."

My mind cast back to the look shared between my mother and Aubertine in the later picture. "You don't believe that any more than I do. Don't candy coat the story, Jack. I need to be able to trust you on this. Besides, Moran had her jewelry and jewelry case. How could he have gotten that kind of personal property unless my mother left it with her lover, his brother? And the compact I was given first. It was the kind of keepsake treasured by someone who wanted a sensory reminder until the loved one returned. A means to catch the scent of my mother's powder while she was away from him."

Pressure built behind my eyes, and I couldn't keep my voice from cracking. I needed a moment to process and pushed away from the wall to resume climbing the stairs. Jack followed silently.

We hit the next landing and started up the last flight. I figured if I was going to ask what truly needed to be brought up, I should do so. Given this new information, if we wanted to get a jumpstart on my mother's case, and how it might in some way relate to our current tasks, the time had come for me to talk to the one person most likely able to tell me about her and the liaison with this particular member of Moran's family. "Let's switch to a somewhat related subject and talk about getting me an opportunity to connect with Margarite. Maybe sometime next week if possible?"

Margarite was someone I'd met through Jack and this case.

From evidence in the first photograph I'd received, she was also someone who knew my mother in the years related to at least one time my mother was with Paul-Henri. I explained my reasoning, "I think she could fill in holes about what kind of relationship my mother had with Paul-Henri, and whether she was...affiliated with...Moran's family in the intervening years. As well as give me possible ideas about...uh..."

"Ermo Colle," Jack finished.

He knew I hated to make any reference to my father. The pseudonym was more palatable. "Right. So, can you give me a way to get in touch with Margarite?"

"No."

I stopped and turned. "Why not? She could have key information. Don't you trust me?"

"Of course I trust you to talk with her." His eyes were soft, and I wanted to fall in. "Unfortunately, I can't find her at present. I've made several attempts, but all my normal avenues to communicate with her are dead ends."

"Could she be in danger?"

"I'm not getting worried yet. She has a habit of running off a couple of times a year, often when she has a new lover." He shrugged. "I left a voicemail for Dylan, but he's in a series of banking conferences in Milan. If I don't hear from him soon I'll find out which hotel he's staying in and try that route.

"Dylan?" Now I was confused. I'd first met Dylan when he and a friend's proximity helped me escape from two of Moran's men, and he'd called Cassie a couple of times recently. But he'd been nowhere around when I'd met Margarite on the yacht in Miami with Jack. "Why call him to find her?"

"Because Margarite is his mother."

Finally, it made sense why Dylan's eyes reminded me of someone else when I saw him on New Year's Day. That was the first time I'd seen him since meeting Margarite a few months earlier. But there was no time for musing. "Something else occurred to me while I was huddled in my coat this morning on the train."

"Um-hmm?"

I didn't know what that meant, but I figured it was best not to find out in case he revisited his irritation about my going AWOL. I plowed ahead. "When my father faked his death, there was a body found. A body with a dental history close enough to his to fool authorities and the insurance company. The payout money went to settle debts, but he could be pursued for fraud...or...I could be."

Jack squeezed my arm. "You can't be charged with fraud if you weren't part of the deception. But you bring up a good point. I'll make some calls. See who could have been involved in the fake identification, if the evidence was compromised, or if the dead guy's teeth were made to match before he was buried in the snow. Following the money usually helps too."

"If we can follow the insurance money at all," I said. "I was a sophomore in college then. Running as much on anger as intellect. The money went out as fast as it came in to get people to stop hounding me. But how do we know part of those wolves snapping at my hands weren't agents of..."

"Good point. I get it, and I'll follow up to see if any incarnation of Ermo Colle was around then to receive insurance proceeds from his own demise. To law enforcement, the man in the snow was your father. Still is. I'll call Swiss authorities and get people working on the very cold case of who was actually buried in that avalanche."

I didn't want to risk my voice cracking again from emotion. I simply nodded.

We'd reached the landing for our floor. As we neared the dark red steel door Jack's hand left my back to punch in the code, but he stopped when I asked, "Is anyone else on this floor with us?"

"We have the floor. If you think we need extra space—"

"Sorry, no." I shook my head. "But before we go in there are a couple of things I want to discuss."

He raised a questioning eyebrow.

"Originally, we assumed PA Designs was Philippe Aubertine, but your new information implies the name stood for Paul-Henri instead."

"Exactly."

"So should we operate under the premise Moran's true birth name is Philippe Aubertine?"

"That's my theory," Jack said. "The history tied to the name has been around long enough to correlate to what we believe is Moran's age. It doesn't give us much intel to use, but there are some current references, especially with the wine industry. Enough to make it appear he may be planning to resume his original name when he retires to that vineyard Rollie told you about."

The first time we met, Rollie—before I learned he was Moran's grandson and heir apparent to the art crime empire—told me his grandfather wanted to retire and turn over the criminal enterprise to him. This was also before I knew I'd actually run into his grandfather in his rustic vineyard owner disguise earlier that same day. We hadn't yet located the vineyard in particular, but I had no doubt there was one somewhere around Puy de Dôme, France, and probably completely on the level. Somewhere near where I was shot at by a phantom motorcyclist, just before the man I now knew was Moran burst onto the scene and made the gunman roar off in escape. I met Rollie in Le Puy-en-Velay that afternoon, supposedly by accident, but I later realized no one in the Moran organization left anything to chance. At first, I'd thought Rollie was a friend, just a nice guy. Now, I knew first impressions could be terribly wrong, and I'd glimpsed the darker sides to his character.

"Given that Moran has never let himself be tagged back to that name before, why did he use it when he rescued me in the French countryside from the motorcyclist with the gun?" I asked. "If he'd used any other name, we would never have connected those points of evidence."

"Again, this is only a guess, but it's likely the way people in that area around Puy de Dôme know him. His way of disappearing in plain sight, despite the fact the mansion in nearby Le Puy was listed as a holding by the Moran persona. Maybe also his attempt at seeing if you'd recognize the family name? A test perhaps?"

"To see if my mother mentioned the name of her lover to her

four-year-old daughter before dying in a car crash that is looking more and more like it was caused by her husband?" I took a second to compose myself before continuing. "Yeah, I guess he could have wondered. But everything we found on PA Designs said they were legit, and you repeated that again a few minutes ago. Obviously, nothing new has cropped up in this arena. Except for the fact Rollie used the firm as a blind for his employment when I met him."

"My theory is Paul-Henri was never a part of Moran's criminal enterprise, and when he died Moran kept the business operating as a clean entity."

"In case he needed its legitimacy?"

Jack shrugged. But it was really an "I'm sorry" look, as if to say he wasn't sure. When he spoke, I understood. "Or to turn it over to someone he wanted to keep safe and out of the eyes of the law and criminals."

I gave him a side-eyed look. "He was turning it over to Rollie. He wants to turn everything over to Rollie. Moran confirmed it when he and I talked in Germany a few weeks ago."

"Does he? Only Rollie said he was gaining the design business. Just like Rollie said his grandfather didn't want him away from the country so much while there was work to be done at the architectural firm. At least, that's what you told me last fall. In reviewing your conversation with Moran at Baden-Baden, I also find it interesting he never directly told you that he wanted to turn the organization over to his grandson—just mentioned he wanted to retire."

"You don't mean—"

"Yes, I'm thinking Moran considers turning everything over to you. At least the design firm in its entirety. Every executive's name on the firm's masthead is clean and respectable. Has been since the firm's inception. And the CEO is still listed as Paul-Henri, despite his being dead nearly a quarter century."

"Wow." I leaned against the wall for support. "You believe I'm really the result of my mother's and Paul-Henri Aubertine's affair?"

He reached out and took my hand. "I don't know. Though,

considering the possibility would not only explain Moran's actions regarding you and your safety, but it—"

"Explains why Rollie can smile at me, but have a look in his eyes saying my safety isn't his biggest concern."

"Yeah." Jack pulled me into a hug and stoked my hair with his free hand. "You okay? This has been a lot to digest in one big chunk."

"It's better to know than to keep guessing at everything." But even the scent of him and the musky sandalwood cologne he wore didn't calm me like usual.

"Do you ever remember someone in your family doing anything that seemed like it was for a paternity test? Drawing blood or swabbing—"

"No." I closed my eyes. "I had my tonsils out when I was ten. It could have been done then, but I don't remember any other time. Grandmamma was with me the entire time I was awake before and after the surgery. My father was in Florida, as I recall. The way my father treated me didn't change afterward. If he did get a test done then, the outcome didn't please him."

I pushed away, but he kept hold of my hand.

"I'm okay, Jack," I said. "You have people waiting. You need to go."

He handed me the bag of crab rangoons and keyed in the long code to open the door.

"Be sure and put your key and code in your purse," he reminded. "It's still on the table where you left it."

"Thank you, Mr. Observant." I smiled.

"Anytime."

He leaned down and brushed lips over mine, then wrapped his arms around me and kissed me like he meant it. I felt things were finally right again between us, after the rocky way our day started. Maybe this big revelation he'd been waiting to tell me contributed to his crossness at our early morning encounter.

I stepped away and he reached out and grasped the doorknob. But before the door opened, Jack stopped.

"Will you be here all day?"

"Probably," I whispered. We were still in close proximity. I took another small step back. "Until it's time to meet Nico at my hotel."

"I'll come back and drive you." He ran a hand down my arm, then clasped my hand, giving it a squeeze.

"Or Cass and I can share a cab. I'll be fine. Don't fret." My fingers returned the squeeze.

He laughed quietly and shook his head. "You don't make it easy."

"I'll try. I promise." Standing on tiptoes, I tried to steal another quick kiss, but he caught me around the waist and held on. As we broke for air, I asked, "Can you do another favor for me before you go?"

He raised a dark brow.

"Open the door and take a quick look. Check if I can get inside without Max seeing me via the Skype connection."

"Sure." He held a finger to his lips and turned the knob, pushing the door just enough to look in. A quick nod to Cassie and he let it almost close again, holding the knob to keep the latch from engaging. He leaned close and spoke low. "She's talking on the tablet, but she moved so he won't see if you stay along the wall."

"Thanks."

"Stay alert. And remember, I'll pick you up tonight."

Another kiss to my forehead, and he ushered me through the doorway.

FIVE

I kept to the left, hugging the wall as Jack suggested. Cassie didn't look at me, but flashed an OK sign with her fingers behind the tablet so Max wouldn't realize I was anywhere nearby.

Working in silence was difficult, but I was committed to the subterfuge. I pulled my phone from the Prada and put it to silent so the device wouldn't rat me out if someone called. Then I texted Nico to see what he was really up to. No response. That was annoying, but it wasn't remarkable. I'd hoped he'd disconnected earlier because Jack was in on the conference call, but apparently I was persona non grata at the moment as well.

My mind strayed from the task at hand to what I could send as an engagement gift to Marci. I forgot to ask the name of her fiancé and couldn't look at anything personalized. No way I'd be able to get away this weekend no matter how fun it sounded, so I needed to send a present that came off as special. I didn't just like Marci; I needed to stay in her circle of friends. In our line of business, one could never tell when a social contact was the difference between getting out of a tight mess...or not.

At the same time, we had too much to do if we wanted to narrow this thing down, and no present ability to find my source—who was likely picking pockets in the Gothic Quarter of Barcelona. Which made me remember I needed to contact Clara Ochoa, "the waif" as Jack called her, to see if she could help us at all with information. I doubted the last name she gave was her real one, but Clara was probably true enough.

I looked at the time, almost noon, and ran my finger along my phone screen to flip through the directory until I reached the number for Maybelle, the administrator of the homeless shelter where I'd sent the girl. I couldn't risk calling and have Max hear, and Maybelle was usually too busy during this time of day to take a call anyway. My thumbs dashed around the small keyboard, asking if Clara still lived at the shelter. I received a quick message back: *Later.* I hoped it meant Maybelle was busy, not that Clara was in jail somewhere. Given I'd met the girl on Oxford Street at Christmastime when she picked the pocket of a Member of Parliament, my fears were well founded. I'd kept her out of trouble then by picking her pocket and returning the cash-laden wallet to the MP, without either of them knowing anything had happened. Until I confronted her. I'd been working to build a rapport with her since then as a means of gaining a possible new source for street intel.

Leaving me with another stalemate in a day filled with them. Patience, Beacham, patience.

I kept one ear tuned to the conversation going between Cassie and her tablet, but I got bored quickly at the kind of funder talk I always turned over to Max. My boss was speaking at an almost tolerable level. I usually got either the loud voice or the louder one. I presumed the concession was due to the funder, whose French accent was easily recognized and made me doubly glad I'd cut and run earlier with Jack. The Gallic money man was uncomfortably attracted to me, and I didn't relish the thought of having to tactfully thwart his verbal advances while my boss was on the same call.

My mind wandered back to Marci's engagement party, and I had a sudden epiphany. I pulled up a website of an up-and-coming artist I knew and paged through her current inventory. What I wanted was already sold. Damn.

Xanda, I texted, *do you have any signature-designed champagne flutes that aren't on your website right now?*

A second later, she responded, *I'm working on a pair of wedding toast flutes with a gold peacock feather design. Would that be appropriate? They'll be done this evening.*

Thank goodness. One task I could cross from my list. *Perfect*, I texted back. Then she quoted the price and I nearly swallowed my tongue. Still, this was Marci, and anything from Xanda would be exquisite. I told her to consider them sold and deliver them to my hotel. I would get a shipping address sometime tomorrow from Marci and send them by courier.

In the next instant, my ears pricked at the conversation I overheard.

"I'll talk to Laurel about your request, Max," Cassie said. She kept her gaze firmly directed toward the tablet. "But we have a lot going on. Several open commitments. And it takes both of us to get the foundation work done and supervise the construction schedule for making our regular office space habitable again."

"What open commitments?" Max's voice rose in volume. I chewed my lower lip.

We purposely left our boss out of the loop on most of the heist information. He knew, of course, about forgeries getting swapped out for originals. An age-old truth that came firmly home to the foundation earlier this month when a priceless tapestry was exchanged during a restoration job spearheaded by yours truly. It was only after the artist was murdered we learned she was somehow tied to the art heist players we were working to stop and apprehend. Her death was ordered by Simon Babbage, traitor and former head of the London Beacham office, who was killed on Rollie's orders after it was proved he was a triple agent and working for Ermo Colle in addition to Moran.

"Different little things—including the reason I came to New York," Cassie replied.

We'd had a lead based on art books that Cassie continued to pursue from this side of the Atlantic. She found a link over Christmas, then she and Nico followed the informational thread and interviewed one of the photographers whose work was published in the coffee table edition utilizing forged copies no one was yet aware of—until Jack and I visited Florence in October. I held my breath, waiting to see how this conversation played out.

"I would prefer to see *Mademoiselle* Laurel," the funder whined.

I'll just bet you would, I thought, forcing my lips tighter together.

"Cassie would be even better. Trust me on this, François," Max said. "I have great plans for Miss Dean."

My assistant shot a quick and worried look my direction. I raised an eyebrow. Yes, this was getting interesting. I knew letting her go to New York was a risk, no matter how logical the plan.

"Max, I really don't see how either of us can leave at the present time," she explained. "We're just a two-person shop here. Let me discuss all of this with Laurel, and I'm sure she'll get back to you sooner rather than later."

I knew that last bit was directed at me. The slight shake in Cassie's hand said she was getting close to her breaking point. I glanced at the door and considered walking over and slamming it, pretending I'd just walked into the room. But before I could go from thought to action, Cassie gave a quick goodbye to Max and a respectful one to the funder, then tapped the screen. The *whoosh* from the tablet's external speakers said the connection ended.

"Oh, my nerves are shot." She slid up to sit on the table. "We are walking such a fine line here telling Max as little as we have."

"Like there's a choice? Max already compromised the mission when he told Tony B my schedule, which led to me getting kidnapped. Remember? That's just one recent instance where he should have kept his mouth shut but didn't." I walked around the table, sat, and put an arm around her shoulder. I had longtime experience with Max. Decades more. I was still in elementary school and coming with Grandfather to the foundation office when Max was learning the ropes. I knew his weaknesses and he knew mine. "If he learns anything about the heist, it will be told to other people for dinner party fodder and as a means of making connections. This would be too sexy a secret for him to keep. Trust me on this. And we're still not sure there isn't a mole in our or Jack's ranks."

"But Simon is no longer a threat," she said.

"Simon was a rat and the conduit for the bad guys in this scenario, sure. However, we don't have the luxury to believe he's the only one. Jack was the first to notice the bad guys had too much information, even before he and I joined forces. He thought the mole was internal to his organization, but I continue to believe it's in Beacham. Or, at least, we have an active one."

"Isn't there anyone you trust?"

"You and Nico. No one else." I reached around her and scooped up the tablet, then opened the list of Beacham personnel and board members. I highlighted about sixty percent. "These are all of the people who were with the foundation when Daddy Dearest was still alive. Well, when we really knew he was alive and before he faked his death." I stopped and took a couple of breaths.

"We know Simon was working for him while pretending to also work for Moran—working against all of us in aid to my fath..." I nearly gagged, and corrected, "Ermo Colle. Any of these people could be sleeper cells ready to feed new information to the Colle organization. Their loyalties may have always been to him instead of the foundation. After what happened in Baden-Baden, I have no doubt the stakes have risen higher. If there still is a Beacham onsite mole, we have to work very carefully when it comes to Max."

"Makes sense," Cassie said. She jumped down from the table and walked to the coffee station. "Hazelnut okay?"

"Sounds great." If there was one thing that helped calm my nerves it was coffee. But I had something else to address after inferring what our boss's tone implied during the end of the conversation. "I get that Max wants you to help him with this funder. The rich old letch prefers blondes and Max knows it. But this is more, isn't it? Max tried to poach you while you were in New York, didn't he?"

"Not poach exactly," Cassie said. She added cream to her coffee and brought both cups back to the table. "But he did drop by a lot to check on my progress and tell me some of the ways it was beneficial I was doing the research in New York."

"You mean besides the fact the photographs and publishing house were located there?" I said wryly. "Level with me. What perks did he offer you?"

"He suggested I might be better utilized in management than in research."

"Son of a—" I stopped and took a deep breath, then exhaled slowly. "I will string him up, I surely will." Then I stopped again and looked at Cassie. "On the other hand, I can't ethically do anything until I know what you want. It's your call. Would you prefer a different career track in the foundation? I'm sorry, Cass. I should have asked before I blew my top."

She was already shaking her head and trying to shush me. "If I wanted a position in New York, I would have never pursued the Victoria and Albert Museum internship that brought me to London originally. I didn't want to leave the U.K. when the V and A let me go. If I hadn't wanted the job you offered, I would have turned you down." She looked at her hands, clasped tightly around her cup, then her gaze met mine. "You've given me greater challenges and more scintillating assignments than I could possibly dream of. I can't say I won't ever go to Max and say 'please transfer me to management,' but just now I wouldn't take another position if he tripled my salary. My expertise is needed, and I feel a part of the team. Max can't offer me any equivalent in New York."

I said quietly, "He can offer safety."

"No one can do that." She reached out to touch my arm. "I'm safer on this team, and I'm part of keeping each fellow member safe. We all know the risks. And who's to say leaving wouldn't increase my vulnerability? New York has no idea what we know. Who and what we've uncovered. Max and company aren't really qualified to deal with any of our personal safety issues. You said it yourself when you pointed out how easily a mole could have been hiding in the foundation as a sleeper for a decade or longer."

"We truly have no choice," I said. "If I tell Max who Ermo Colle is, we open a Pandora's box." I took a sip of coffee, my stomach knotting up at my indecision.

"But you did tell him."

I shook my head. "Not who Colle actually is. Just that Simon had double agented Moran and Beacham by pledging an alliance with Ermo Colle. I had to tell the name. Even if I can't give the full range of ramifications associated with the bastard. Otherwise, Max would have no way of knowing he should be on his guard against any affiliation with Colle and the organization."

"Is that enough?"

"Good question." I set the cup on the table beside me and clasped my hands in my lap. "I've wrestled with what to do. One part of me worries Colle will surface with a new face and a new name. Moran warned me that would happen."

"If Colle's alive."

"Right." If I hadn't killed him. I'd spent practically the whole month, every day since we'd returned from Germany, wondering if I'd killed my father. I didn't feel guilty. Oh, no. I was past that by the evening after the event. No, I wanted confirmation he was truly out of my life for good.

Something deep inside me said he wasn't dead though. I hoped the tiny, quietly worried voice was wrong, but instinct said differently.

"Jack said to let him handle it," I said finally. "He can check out things we couldn't possibly gain access to. Even with Nico's hacking superpower." I rubbed my hands up and down my jacket sleeves. But I wasn't cold, just anxious. "If we need to tell Max anything...we should wait until Jack says to do so. At least run the idea by him first."

She laughed. "We've come a long way in a few months. The first time I met Jack you were running from him. Now we're putting the foundation's fate in his hands."

I picked up my coffee and looked at the cloudy dark surface, wishing I could see the future in its depths. "Yeah," I said. "Funny how circumstances change." Then I shivered.

SIX

We worked in mostly silence for the next hour or so. I went back over every step I'd used to gain information on the painting we took from France, looking for any possibility I'd overlooked to keep my request quiet or let details slip. Since I didn't use criminal elements to gain intel—had only heard from my pickpocket source because of conversations we'd had about the painting in the past—I could only assume if the forgery thieves heard about my plan it was through respected links, not criminal ones. I listed everyone I'd asked for data and added names I knew of peripheral people who may have learned too. Nothing set off any alarm bells.

This was all necessary, of course, but more importantly it kept me from dwelling on the new bombshell Jack offered about my mother's case. And who might truly be my father.

After finishing my lists, checking and rechecking each point, I refamiliarized myself with the files and notes compiled from what Cassie and Nico discovered in New York. Then I reviewed the digital prints.

My team went to the Big Apple looking for leads on paintings photographed for a coffee table art book Cassie saw over the Christmas holidays. They returned with new prints of the paintings featured in the publication, furnished by the photographer to show the full image out to the edges. Edges that revealed the forger's mark we were following. I'd been mentally reviewing the data ever since.

Though the photographer could help with enhanced prints, he

couldn't offer much supplementary aid. The actual paintings arrived in the publisher's office via delivery service, and the courier came back after the photo session and retrieved the paintings for return to the owner. Next, my dynamic duo set out to interview the courier who handled the masterpieces, but despite best efforts, they found no trace of the named delivery service recorded in the file, nor could they locate the courier who made the two trips into the building and signed in each time with security personnel.

While interviewing the photographer, the editor, and the managing director, Cassie and Nico uncovered a couple of other unsettling facts. The photo session occurred three years ago, long before the four of us became involved in the job to unravel the rumored heist. This was also a good year and a half before forgers started getting killed who were likely connected with Moran's and Ermo Colle's separate criminal groups. From what could be ascertained or assumed, Moran's organization thought Simon was still a double agent for them at this point, working against the interests of the Beacham Foundation. But since I now knew my father was the public head of Ermo Colle during this time, and Simon was aligned with my father and just picking up an extra paycheck from Moran, the scope of the deception grew substantially. And none of this even counted the crates of forgeries and guns Jack and I stumbled onto when we checked out a rooftop in Florence.

I studied the sheet on Cassie's interview with the legitimate owner of both paintings in question. "You said the owner, Mrs. Conner, vowed she'd never sent the art via delivery service for any photo session."

"Right," Cassie confirmed, turning away from the whiteboard and walking over. "She said the paintings never left her eastside penthouse. Neither have been in for work or cleaning in the last decade either. Just dusted by her maid."

"She showed you the paintings as they hung on the wall?"

"Yes, and no forger's mark appeared on either of them in the place they appeared in the photographs."

I brushed the photo and the image of a gilt frame. "What about the frames? Did they look like the ones in the pictures?"

"Yes. I had a copy of the photo with me when we met with Conner, and even she mentioned the similarity."

"And the publisher said they'd communicated solely with Mrs. Conner's personal assistant?"

"Affirmative. They showed me copies of the emails in the files. Conner confirmed the email address was one she used for business, but she uses no secretary or assistant for anything related to her art collection. And she never sent or received any communication with the publisher." Cassie put her hands on her hips. "Any ideas what it means?"

Pulling out both prints of the forgeries again, I studied the almost infamous marks in the corners of the paintings. "She was hacked by someone who used her email as a means of getting those pictures into the published book. But why? How does this con get them the paintings? Unless..." I was getting a brainstorm.

"Unless what?"

I held up a finger for silence. A minute to think. How would this have worked? "One of the things that hit me with the forgery factory in Florence was the audacity of setting up the elaborate scheme in a historic palazzo so close to the tourist area around the Duomo. Almost to prove they were too good to worry about risk. If they used the news of the book as a challenge...To prove they could get the forgeries in anywhere..."

"You said after talking to Rollie you felt strongly the forgery factory was Moran's deal. Are you saying he did this?"

"Maybe." I set the pictures into the folder and closed it again, slipping it back into the box we were using as a temporary filing cabinet. "But my gut instinct says this ploy was Ermo Colle's instead. The audacity of this setup simply made me recall what I felt about the other one."

"What makes this tip the scales for you that it's Colle?"

"If I went to Mrs. Conner's penthouse, I'd bet you anything she knew my grandfather and likely my father too," I said, crossing my arms and leaning against the table. "Dear old Daddy with his larcenous mind quite possibly knows every piece of art sitting anywhere in the state of New York."

"You think he's going to steal from people your family knew?"

I shook my head. "I think it's more than that. Learning about the book could have given him an opening for beta testing his plan, because he knew of the two paintings Mrs. Conner owned. He could use the knowledge for a trial run."

"What did it accomplish?"

"I don't know yet. But I will. Maybe his original idea was to get the true Conner paintings in a swap somehow, but the plan fell through. Or perhaps it was as simple as getting two forgeries into a published book and have everyone believe the works were authentic."

"Would Simon have known about Mrs. Conner's collection too?" Cassie asked.

"Doubtful, but not impossible. He always worked this side of the Atlantic. When he did go to New York, he stayed focused on gala events, rather than meeting old money art collectors. But to be honest, I don't know what circles he worked before he took on the London office. He was enough older than me that he was over thirty before he hit my personal radar."

Cassie polished off the bag of rangoons after the conference call, and we each settled down to work our own to-do lists. But by one o'clock, I was ready for a meal. I scooped up my Prada and the key from the table. "Feel like exploring the neighborhood and hunting down some lunch?"

She hugged her torso. "I'll bet Jack would prefer we ate downstairs."

I put on my coat and then grabbed hers. "You don't work for Jack and neither do I." I tossed her coat and she caught it. "I want a salad, and not one with peanut dressing. A salad with lots of bacon and cheese and goodies atop the lettuce. I say we find someplace close that offers great lunch options. Preferably one with breadsticks too."

"Breadsticks sound good."

Less than ten minutes later, we were seated at a picture-perfect French-themed corner café, our coats across the back of the spare chair and our menus in hand. Although it was already past noon, a handful of people remained seated in pairs and singles at the round wooden tables. Our waitress returned with baguettes and a bread knife in lieu of breadsticks, took our salad orders, and said she'd return momentarily. Cassie toyed with the small vase in the middle of the table that held silk flowers made to look like lavender. I gazed at the Provence-imaged wallpaper and smiled. It was time to go back to France for a while—a legitimate trip. A few days of R and R at a spa with lavender oils and massages and I'd be ready to face anything.

My phone rang. It was Jack.

"Hello, we're waiting on salads," I greeted him. "Want to come and join us? But we won't share our bread."

"Believe it or not, I'd jump at the chance," he returned. "But I can't. I'm getting sent out of town. I couldn't talk my way out of the assignment."

"Is there a problem?"

"No, just bad timing. I need to be someone I was once before. With luck, it will just be for the night, but either way I'll be back in London by Saturday."

"Okay..." I let my word hang. When he didn't respond, I asked, "Are you meeting with Nico and me tonight? Or am I doing the debrief?"

"That's why I called. I'm being deployed immediately."

"What? You're not on some military mission."

He chuckled through the phone. "It just means I'm getting sent on an assignment. I can't tell you much about it. I'm going to be undercover."

"That's what you meant by being someone you were before?"

"Yes, I'll definitely not be me," he said and laughed. His voice went quieter when he added, "It will just be forty-eight hours at the most, but I'll be out of touch throughout. I don't like it, but—"

"Stop. You need your brain in the right place to do something like this. Quit thinking about my well-being and keep yourself safe." Inside, I didn't like it. At all. Every time we'd been separated lately something went sideways and people got hurt. But so far it hadn't been me, and he needed to remember that fact. "We have safeguards in place. And I can call Superintendent Whatley if Cassie and I need protection from Scotland Yard."

"I can send a b—"

An epiphany hit me. My self-defense coach. "I'll call Leif if I think I'm in any danger. I can pay him extra to cancel his classes until you get back."

Jack didn't answer at first, and I was afraid we were cut off. "Hello? Are you there?"

"Yeah, I'm thinking," he replied. "Okay, with Cassie, Nico, and Leif, I guess you're covered."

"I should hope so." To distract him from his concerns, I said, "Cassie and I have some new theories to pursue about the New York lead, and Maybelle is going to get with me later about Clara. We'll have good new intel to run by the time you return, so come back ready to work."

"Sounds like an order."

"You bet it is."

He sighed. "They're calling me. I have to go."

Things suddenly felt very heavy. "Be careful."

"That's my line," he said, his voice low, almost a whisper.

"See you soon."

"Yeah."

I hurried and tapped the screen to end the call so he wouldn't think I was one of those moony girls who waited for the guy to hang up.

The waitress came around with our salads a second later, but I'd lost my appetite. After doing little more than picking at the bacon bits and bleu cheese crumbles for five minutes, Cassie said, "He'll be fine."

"What?" I looked at her. "Of course he will."

"Then would you please eat that salad like the real Laurel eats?"

Before I could humor her, my phone alerted me to a text from Maybelle.

"Well, it looks like Clara has a job. Good for her." I memorized the address of the commercial laundry service employing the girl and her schedule before texting back my thanks. "Maybelle doesn't want us contacting her at work unless it's necessary. But Clara has a new cell phone and Maybelle gave me that number too. Since we're at a standstill with Jack gone, I'll call later and see if I can set up a time for the three of us to meet."

I'd barely set my phone onto the tabletop when it began ringing again. "Oh, hell, it's Max."

Cassie put down her fork. "Want me to talk to him?"

"No, remember, I'm trying to be a grown up today. Even if just periodically." I tapped the screen. "Hello, Max, Cassie said your meeting went well."

"Did she also tell you I need her here in Paris?"

He was in bluster mode—and loud, as usual. I stood and motioned I was going outside to talk. Not that it offered any further privacy, but at least I wouldn't annoy the few patrons still left in the café.

"Yes, Max, she did." Traffic noises provided new background sounds. I pulled my coat around me as the late-January wind raced down the street. "Unfortunately, there are only the two of us—"

"Only for a couple of days. You had no problem with her absence when she was in New York."

"She was in New York working under my instruction, Max. To get information I needed. Remember?"

"And you work under my instruction, Laurel. If Cassie is too valuable an employee to send here to assist me, then I need you to come as the funder originally requested."

"You and I both know he simply wants to flirt with a blonde American before he commits to his newest pledge amount. You should have thought of that ahead of time."

"I need an assistant."

"Then call Doris to book herself a flight across the pond." I almost chuckled when I thought of Max's middle-aged schoolmarm-like assistant wining and dining the French funder.

"Laurel, I'm telling you—"

"Stop." In that instant everything felt way...too much. "Max, I can't take your yelling at me anymore. Give me five minutes to talk to Cassie and I'll call you back."

"But I want—"

"I know what you want, Max, but the Rolling Stones got rich telling us you can't always get what you want." I tapped the screen to end the call with him in mid-splutter.

Cassie had pushed her empty salad bowl aside and was again working on the bread when I returned to the table.

"He hasn't given up, huh?" she asked.

"No. Unless I want to tell him everything that's going on, which I don't, one of us has to go to Paris." I stabbed at the salad with my fork.

"Or we could both go and have a great long weekend on Max."

"Ha! You could get by with it, but he'd grab me by the hand and pull me on the plane when he leaves. Probably make them open the hatch and drop me out over London as he continues on to New York."

"Stop exaggerating." Cassie laughed. "He simply wants some support."

"He wants a pretty blonde to flirt with his funder and make the money guy happy." I set my fork down and took a sip of water. I sighed. "You wouldn't think I was an awful boss if I made you go, would you?"

"You're not an awful boss. And a trip to Paris is such a hardship." She laughed. "But you told Jack you'd have me here while he was gone."

"I forgot about what Max said while you were on the Skype call. Nico will be around. I'll make him play personal assistant to me until you get back."

Cassie laughed again. "He'll only do what he wants to do."

"I can work with those restrictions." I took another sip. "But I need to stress this is short term so Max doesn't get any ideas."

"Would it help if I called my friend Monique and asked if I could stay with her while I'm in Paris?" Cassie asked. "She's been wanting me to come visit."

"Perfect. Max won't be able to argue since you'll be saving him money by skipping the hotel, and you'll be able to duck out when you need to."

My phone rang, and I didn't even have to look to know it was Max.

"I said I'd call you back."

"I thought you forgot," he said.

Did I truly want to make working with this man my life's career? Oh, yeah, I liked saving art. "Well, I think we've figured out a way for Cassie to come and help you for a day—"

"I need her through the weekend at least."

Glancing Cassie's way, I gave a wink.

"No way I can do without her until next week, Max. Unless you want me to hire extra help."

"No, let's play it by ear. Get her over here, and then if you need her back sooner, call and we'll work something out."

"Alright, she has the corporate credit card and can put all her travel and lodging expenses onto it."

He spluttered a moment, then said, "Let me talk to her."

I handed her the phone and finished my salad as she gave monosyllabic responses to the rapid-fire requests and information he passed her way. I could hear him clearly, as could the last two diners on the far wall. Everyone else had left within the last few minutes. The waitress came and collected our empty bowls. Cassie hung up and handed back my cell.

"You didn't mention Monique. You're getting good at this need-to-know stuff," I said.

She grinned. "Thanks, boss. I've learned from the master." Pushing her bread plate aside, she continued, "I'll call Monique en route. If she has no scheduling conflicts and I can stay with her, I'll give Max the news when I arrive in Paris."

"And I'm guessing he wants you to leave like an hour ago."

"Pretty much." She rifled through her small bag and pulled out her own phone to check plane schedules. "If I hurry, looks like I can make it home to pack a bag and get a shuttle from Heathrow that will have me in Paris before five."

Half an hour later, I was back in the new office, alone, proud of myself for getting past the code box without any difficulty. Before I dove into files, I sent a text to Nico. No reply—no surprise there. I tried to check his GPS, but no luck. There wasn't any reason I could think of for shrouding himself electronically, but Nico always kept to his own counsel.

I called Clive to thank him for his help in getting Nico home.

"Sure, no trouble," Clive said. "But when is he coming by to pick up his stuff?"

My grip on the phone tightened. "What time did the two of you set?"

"An hour ago. He seemed antsy to get the things. I thought it might take me longer. Said I'd call him otherwise. But got it all through okay, and now the stuff's sitting here looking at me."

I glanced at my watch. "Clive, how about if I come and get it?"

"Perfect. I'm staying at the Ritz. Meet me in the bar."

"It's kind of early..."

"It's five o'clock somewhere," he said.

Yes, it was. But I was worried the clock might be ticking louder for Nico.

SEVEN

I used my taxi app to call a cab, then again tried to reach Nico, phoning as I turned everything off and locked the door. When his voicemail kicked on I left a message. Mentally counting stairs as I went, I hit redial. By the time my feet landed in the back foyer of the building, I'd heard his voicemail message three times. Normally robo-calling irritated him enough to answer. The question was, why go incommunicado and blow off the meeting with Clive too?

Times like this I needed someone to bounce ideas around with, but Jack and Cassie were out of touch. I didn't know yet if I should worry about Nico, or if he was deliberately ignoring my calls. Yes, the meet-up at my hotel was at six, but it wasn't like him to miss the earlier appointment with Clive. One part of me wanted to worry. A lot. But my rational side said I needed to wait until I knew there was a problem. Which meant I would wait until six o'clock to decide if I could panic. I added panic to my mental to-do list.

While I waited for the cab, I ducked into the florist shop next door, thinking I might send a congratulations bouquet to Marci along with the champagne flutes. Opening the door set off chimes.

"Hello." A pleasant-faced woman in a green canvas apron greeted me through the doorway to the back of the store. "Can I help you with anything?"

"I'm trying to get ideas for a friend's engagement event. Thought I might send flowers as part of my gift." As she neared the counter, I held out a hand and added, "Want to introduce myself, too. I'm Laurel Beacham, and my group and I have taken an office on the top floor of the restaurant next door."

"I'm Sandy Duncan." She hesitated a moment before she took my hand, but gave it a good shake in the end. "The owners are nice people. Handy to be able to grab takeaway during working hours too."

"Your accent is American," I said, then guessed, "California?"

She laughed. "Guilty. And days like this I miss the sunshine."

I nodded. "Completely understand." Then I pointed to a large bouquet on one shelf of the cooler. "Does that travel well?"

"Yes, absolutely. We can ship anything across the U.K. without difficulty or harm to flowers." She quoted me a price for the bouquet and asked where it was going to figure shipping.

"That's the problem," I said. "It's up north, but I don't have an address yet. I should have one tomorrow," I said. "I'll come back then." My taxi pulled into the alley. I said goodbye and made my way to the Ritz.

Clive was at the bar as promised, his hand wrapped around a glass holding amber liquid and the now infamous protective tube lying perpendicular to the top of the bar. The small locked case with my electronic gizmos sat nearby. I slid onto the stool next to him and pulled the tube and case closer.

"Hey," he greeted me through the mirror behind the bar. "What'll ya have? The band's buying."

"They're all staying upstairs?" I asked. The band in question was the heavy metal rockers Whyte Noyse. I'd met Clive and the musicians in October when I hitched a ride on their private jet.

He shook his head. "Nah, London's a pit stop on our way to the American tour, so any personal business can be taken care of. Too many interruptions during a tour. Everyone else has a place close by, but I stay here."

"You make such a sacrifice for the team."

He grinned and finished off the rest of his drink. "You don't know the half of it. I need rest before taking those boys on the road."

Those "boys" were in their forties and fifties, but I had little doubt he had a big job ahead of him as the band's chief roadie. I'd seen him in action, watched how effortlessly he made all problems go away. He looked scruffy on the outside, but it wouldn't have surprised me to find a Mensa card in the man's wallet.

"So where's your guy?" Clive asked. "I called Patricia and she couldn't reach Nico either."

This was so not good. "I'm really not sure. Nico has his own way of doing things, but he usually shows up wherever he's promised. I'll do some checking. I'm waiting to see if he shows up at my hotel tonight as planned."

A couple of boisterous businessmen entered the bar, and Clive leaned close to ask, "It's not something like that guy we picked up in Florence for you?"

That guy was Jack, hurt in a rescue mission to help me. "I'll let you know if I learn anything." Then I changed the subject. "But, wow, an American tour. You must have a lot of work ahead of you."

He shrugged. "Learned the ropes already over the years, so it's just become adjusting to new PR people in the same old cities. The fact the boys only play like they party these days, instead of getting wasted and busting up themselves and the rooms like they used to, really helps make my job easier." He leaned back. "Hey, you gonna be over there anytime soon? We're starting in New York and LA, then crisscrossing the States for the next couple of months."

"Sounds great, but my schedule tends to stay in flux."

"Well, let me know if you get to that side of the Atlantic and I'll leave a couple of backstage passes for you to any of the shows. Just ring me up and they're yours."

"Thanks." I tapped the tube. "And thanks for this too. Going to make someone very happy to see it after all these years."

"Figured it was art. Wanted to look but didn't take the chance." He grinned. "I didn't tell Gordon either."

Gordon Silvers was the band's oldest member and bass guitarist extraordinaire. He was also an avid art collector—and as Clive put it, "a bit focused, if you know what I mean." Substitute focused with obsessive about English artists and the true picture emerges.

"Well, this is an Italian painting, so he wouldn't have been interested anyway," I said.

"Natch."

I bussed his bearded cheek and thanked him again, wondering how I was ever going to pay the guy back for all the help he'd given us in the past few months. The small case went into my purse, and one end of the tube followed. I used a small carabiner clip to attach the loop at the end of the tube to the strap of the Prada. I zipped the purse closed until the zip reached the round obstacle. Not a perfect mode of transport, but enough to keep my hands free.

Minutes later I waited as the Ritz doorman signaled a taxi for me and stepped up to open the back door.

Then a dark hood was slipped over my head, and my arms were pinned to my body. The hood was short, but someone tugged a drawstring to tighten the covering under my chin.

I screamed and kicked, and I heard people rushing toward us. But my attacker pressed something cold and sharp to my throat and said, "Back off, or I'll kill her." His accent sounded Cockney.

He started dragging me. No matter how much I fought, my Jimmy Choos couldn't get any traction on him or the ground to make a getaway. I heard running feet, but the sound seemed to be going away from us. Surely someone was calling the cops.

I couldn't risk screaming with the knife at my skin. I'd already felt it prick me during his excitable delivery and didn't want to risk making him antsier. The only thing left to do was wait for a chance to react. My senses heightened, and I counted steps, worked to try to see if I could smell anything of the attacker, felt his clothing to try to spark any memory. Nothing.

When we got to the curb and he started shoving me into the back of a car, I countered his attack. I wasn't going anywhere with him—knife or no knife. He pushed me toward the seat, letting go of my arms long enough for me to brace against the upholstery and kick back like a mule. The stilettos didn't provide the impact I'd wanted. I connected, and the thin heels had to hurt, but it wasn't enough. He roared and pushed hard, bashing me into the other side door. I saw stars under the dark hood. He slammed the door, and I felt blindly for the handle to open the street-side door. Found it, but the lever rocked in my hand, useless. I ripped at the hood and squeezed over the top of the front seat.

Able to see again, I checked the ignition. No keys. And I had no idea how to start a car without them.

I looked back to see where my attacker was and if I recognized him, but had another surprise. A hipster with light brown hair stood on the sidewalk holding the knife and looking at me through the windows. Then he opened the driver side door and offered me a hand out.

This was my attacker?

One leap and I was out of the car. One punch and Lincoln Ferguson's nose was bloody.

It was only then I noticed a much bigger bruiser lying unconscious on the sidewalk and a rusty metal pipe at Lincoln's feet.

Oh, yeah, my attacker had a Cockney accent. Linc's was middle class London.

I shoved the strap of the Prada and its extra cargo onto my shoulder and wondered how much trouble I'd gotten myself into this time.

"I thought I was saving you." Lincoln's voice came out distorted, what with his holding back his head and pinching his nose so it wouldn't continue bleeding all over his white shirt and brown jacket and all.

"Sorry, I just figured that out a second ago."

The doorman and a uniformed police bobby arrived. I gave the officer my side of things and handed him a business card. "I'll be in later to press charges."

"Very good, miss."

He took Lincoln's information as well, but lucky for me the reporter blamed the attempted kidnapper for his bleeding nose.

"Let's go to the hotel bar and get you some ice," I said to Lincoln once the officer hauled the would-be kidnapper away in cuffs. "Or would you like me to take you to a trauma center?"

"Try ice first. Don't want to be a bigger story than I am," he said, following as I led him back toward the Ritz.

Clive had left the bar behind me, but the same bartender was on duty, and he seemed to know his way around helping a guy with a bloody nose. I guessed even upscale hotels had bar fights on occasion. Some ice, a couple of paracetamol, and a ruined white towel later, Lincoln was ready to take his pound of flesh from me.

"I guess you know what this means," he said.

"I definitely owe you an interview," I replied.

"And a dinner too."

"Don't tell me you really want to eat with me tonight after I socked you in the nose," I said, smiling. "I am sorry, by the way, for confusing you with the bad guy."

He nodded, then winced and dabbed a nostril with the towel. "We'll make it sometime next week. I'll call you."

Despite needing to keep all of this on the light side, I wanted to run away and start searching for Nico. I had no idea where to begin, but sitting in this booth with an injured man who saved my life only because he'd been stalking me for an interview was not my idea of a good use of time.

Just then, my phone rang and Cassie's name popped up. Thank god.

"This is my assistant." I held up the cell. "She's out of the country on a work assignment, and I need to talk to her. I'm going to step outside for a better signal, but I promise I'll be brief."

He glared at me. Instead of saying anything, he shifted the ice on his face and waved a hand to kind of shoo me off.

I answered while walking into the lobby.

"Hello, Cass? Are you still at Heathrow?"

"No, we just landed. The plane is still taxiing to the gate."

I saw the gray skies outside the huge windows had turned drizzly. "Oh, damn."

"What?" she asked.

I let my gaze sweep over the elegant space. "I'd planned to go outside to take this call, but I left my coat in the bar, and if I go back in there Lincoln might have recovered enough to get nosy about our conversation."

"You're in a bar with Lincoln Ferguson this time of the day? Are you doing the interview finally?"

"Something like that." I didn't dare tell her what had actually occurred until I had a better handle on the details myself. One peep of danger and she would catch the next plane back. Max would fire both of us. But it did remind me that I needed to call Leif. "It's been crazy this afternoon. Not the least of which is due to my worries about Nico."

"Why? What happened?"

I found a wingback chair near the front windows which offered a modicum of privacy and settled in, keeping a close eye on anyone who might be watching me. "Nico didn't connect with Clive for the package. Our boy wonder also doesn't answer his phone, no matter who calls—"

"Not just you?"

"Clive said Patricia tried earlier."

"On a scale of one to ten, how worried—"

"A nine while I wait for him to knock on my hotel room door at six. The meter shoots up to a fifteen-plus on the worry scale if he's a no show."

"What are you going to do?"

"Talk to Superintendent Whatley," I said. An older, beefy-built guy seemed to be watching me from the entrance to a hallway. Worth trying to get a picture of him once I ended this call and could walk closer. I leaned back in the chair so my face was mostly hidden by the floral upholstered wing. "Scotland Yard can put out alerts and see if Nico's passport has been used to exit the country again."

"Yeah, since he just arrived back, he probably still had it on him."

Which meant if anyone took him, they wouldn't have to use a

phony passport. I didn't like this, but I wasn't ready to send out alarms either. I also didn't like the way the suspicious man here at the Ritz stepped back into the hallway so he was again hidden.

I hadn't realized how long I'd been quiet until Cassie said, "Laurel? Are you still there?"

"Oh, yeah, sorry. I was watching someone."

"Anything else you need me to do?"

"No." I shifted slightly to get a better look at the hallway opening. "You're going to be busy enough."

"Okay, call me when you know something."

Suddenly I felt like such a ditz. "I'm sorry, you called me and I just loaded you up with my worries. Is there something you need?"

Cassie sighed. "While I had the time in flight, I've been trying to think if there is any way I can help while I'm in Paris. Is there something I can do while I'm here? Beyond looking pretty while I sit next to Max, of course."

I laughed. "I know how frustrated you feel, Cass, but just keep your eyes open. Also, familiarize yourself with the background on the Caravaggio painting when you have the chance. Because of its stolen status, there are files on the foundation server that might include info not readily available in public databases. I'm not sure when I'm going to turn the work over to Max, but in case it becomes a way to spring you from this short-term Paris sentence, it could be important for one of us to know the background well."

"Will do."

The man in the hallway and a second man, this one much younger and taller, stepped into the lobby and walked out the front door. My paranoia level reset to zero. I tuned back in to the phone call. "Actually, there's something else I want you to do in the meantime. At least until we hear from our wandering Italian geek. You know those bulletin boards Nico uses to contact his hacker friends when he needs ideas about something?"

"Sure, he showed me a couple, but I doubt I know all of them."

"That's okay." The plan was forming in my mind. "Whenever you have a chance, scan the ones he's shown you. If there is a problem and he wants to contact us and can't do it directly, he might try sending a message through one of those. I'm still holding out on this all being Nico wanting private time for some reason, but I'd like to stay ahead of the game in case he's been abducted like in Rome. He and I have used some code words through the years, and I'm thinking if he's been taken by someone, and they let him use a computer, he might try sneaking something through that way."

"So he's been kidnapped?" Stress made her voice rise in pitch.

I went super calm. "I'm just taking precautionary measures. I have no reason to think kidnapping, but you know as well as I do that precedent was set the day after New Year's, and we still don't know who took him then or why. On the off chance we need to get help and move quickly, I want to stay prepared. I won't lie to you. There's no reason yet for worry, but I can't discount it."

"Tell me what you're really thinking, Laurel."

She was getting as difficult to fool as Jack. "I don't want to set off any alarms. Remember, I tend to think in more of the abstract in these kinds of things and then determine how they might all fit together."

"Talk abstract to me then."

One long breath later, I began, "When he was taken in Rome, he realized the kidnappers didn't want him hurt. That's why he faked having a concussion, so they left him hidden until Jack and I found him. But they came back for him as soon as they could. They wanted Nico for some reason, and when they kidnapped him they took both our favorite geek and his equipment."

The younger man returned to the hotel, glanced at me as he stepped into the lobby, then quickly looked away and hurried back into the haunted hallway. Nothing special about his appearance and no time to get a picture, but he did look to see if I was still there. Alarm bells in my head were clanging louder.

"Laurel? Laurel, are you still there?"

"Yeah, Cassie, sorry. Had someone who seemed too interested." I stood and walked to the corner of the lobby. "I've moved. I'll see what happens now."

"Tell me the rest of what you're thinking."

Remembering Jack's talk in Germany about directional mics, I spoke quieter into the phone. "Whoever Simon truly worked for, he knew how important Nico was to me in completing every assignment."

"You think Simon had one of them kidnap him in Italy, and Moran or Colle has maybe done the same today?"

"It's just something I've been worrying about since I can't reach him. But remember, Nico could be simply acting like his prickly self," I reasoned. "After all, he did hang up on us when Jack started questioning him."

"And you and I laughed."

"Because it was typical Nico. Which is why I'm refusing to get alarmed unless I don't see him tonight at my hotel. Just taking the precaution of having you watch the bulletin boards."

"I'll start looking through them, going back until about noon today," she said. "Then I'll check for current listings throughout the evening."

"Perfect. Call me if you find anything that might be relevant. But don't overthink this. That's my job."

She laughed. "Will do. Anything even remotely connected to him though, and I'll let you know."

"Thank you."

Lincoln Ferguson walked out of the bar and headed for the front door. My champagne-colored leather coat was slung over one arm. He looked like a walking crime scene with the blood down the front of his shirt and jacket.

"Cassie, I have to go. But I'll leave my phone on. Stay alert."

"You, too."

I hung up, then called out, "Lincoln, are you looking for me?"

He nodded and wandered my way. "When I saw you'd left your coat behind, I thought you'd be freezing, so I was bringing it out."

"Thanks. I realized I'd forgotten it and stayed here by the windows for better reception instead." He held my coat to help me put it on. The warmth felt good.

Little lines of pain showed around his eyes.

"You look like you could use some rest," I said.

"Brilliant observation," he replied, offering a weak smile. "I'm grabbing a cab and going home. Can I drop you someplace?"

Slipping my arm through the crook of his elbow, I said, "The cab is on me. I'm betting the doorman will make sure he gets us safely into a vehicle this time."

"But you're okay, right?" he asked. "About almost getting kidnapped, I mean. You aren't scared?"

Unfortunately, I was getting used to things like that happening, but I couldn't tell Linc. I tried a flip answer instead and laughed, but the sound was even brittle to my ears. "Probably someone thinking because I came out of the Ritz my family would pay a ransom. Too bad the fool didn't know my family is broke."

EIGHT

As soon as I entered my hotel room, I called Superintendent Whatley of Scotland Yard. He'd been my first call and chief liaison for a couple of other crimes lately. I wasn't sure how much he knew about the larger ramifications of our mission, as I'd left Jack to decide and disclose information to authorities. But between my attempted abduction today and nothing coming from Nico, initiating a conversation with a branch of law enforcement who already knew me felt like a good next step. I called his mobile number.

"Whatley," he answered.

"Hello, Superintendent, it's Laurel Beacham."

"Hello, Miss Beacham. How are you this evening?"

"It's been a little busy." I briefly outlined the attack in the afternoon outside the luxury hotel, and how the perpetrator was caught and taken away by a Metropolitan policeman. "I gave my statement and a business card to the Met officer, and there was another witness who corroborated what happened."

"Just a minute," he said. I heard computer keys clicking and realized he was still at the Yard. After hearing him "hmm" a couple of times, he spoke up again. "I need to speak to someone on this. Please hold for a moment." He set down the cell phone, but I could hear bits of conversation from Whatley's end while he talked on another phone. When he mentioned the Ritz, I assumed he was talking to the officer in charge of the arrest. He came back on the line with me. "Yes, the man, an Alfred Halborn, has been charged with assault against a newspaper reporter, and with an assault and attempted kidnapping of you. The car was towed in for the crew to work over, and a solicitor already appeared saying he's been retained for Halborn. Despite the fact the perpetrator hadn't been fully processed nor had the opportunity to make a phone call himself."

"Sounds interesting to me."

"To me as well." I heard a chair squeak. He asked, "Was Ferguson with you before the incident?"

Tamping down my irritation about the way the reporter popped up around every corner lately, I kept the story simple. "He recognized me and was luckily coming from a nearby location. When I was grabbed, those at the hotel knew Halborn had a knife to my throat and were afraid to do anything that might risk injury to me. Ferguson witnessed him shove me into the backseat of the car and used a piece of pipe he found nearby to knock out Halborn."

"Lucky he was there at that moment."

You'll never know, I thought. Aloud, I said, "But this leads me to why I called, and your information about the solicitor adds to my concerns. I was told to come in to the Met precinct station to give my official written statement and formally press charges. However, my fear is—"

"Someone might make another kidnapping attempt when you leave."

"Exactly."

His voice turned brisk. "Your fears are well founded. I'll get in touch with the necessary people at the Met to get this taken care of properly. It looks like the reporter has already made an appointment to come in tomorrow morning. His assault should be enough to hold Halborn, but your charge is the stronger of the two. Despite that being so, there is a clear and present danger in letting you come in on your own."

"Could the Met record a Skype interview with me? Would that be enough in the short term?"

"I'll make the suggestion. When they do need you in person I'll escort you myself."

"Thank you so much, Superintendent."

"You're quite welcome. Is there anything else?"

I looked at my face in the full-length mirror hiding the closet. Worry lines traced around my mouth and forehead. Until I knew for sure Nico wasn't showing up, I couldn't risk saying anything. "No, that's all, but I'll be sure to call if anything changes."

"And Hawkes is handling your protection detail?"

Another thing to remember—I had to call Leif. "No, he's presently away on assignment, but he's set me up with someone to handle those duties."

"Very good."

"Thanks so much, Superintendent. You've been most helpful, as expected."

"Anytime."

I hung up the call and immediately dialed Leif. The call rang five times, then went to voicemail. My message was brief. Less than a minute later, he called me back, his Nordic accent strong as he said, "Hello, Laurel. Sorry. I am juggling my luggage and could not reach my phone."

"Are you going somewhere?"

"I am already here. My mother's birthday is this weekend. Since you canceled your classes for the rest of the week, I rearranged my schedule and caught an earlier flight. There is no problem, is there?"

Great. Another option down the tubes. "No, Leif, just making sure you got my message this morning since it was so early and voicemail and all. Meant to connect with you sooner, but the day's gotten away from me. Have a great time. Give your mother my best wishes on her birthday."

He laughed. "I will do that. And I will see you on Tuesday morning. I have a couple of new moves to teach you."

I caught myself a second before I said the old moves had worked quite nicely already. Any conversation along those lines might alert him to the real reason I'd phoned. "Terrific. Can't wait. Enjoy your weekend."

"You as well, Laurel."

I hung up the phone feeling itchy with anxiety. All alternative plans had been exhausted.

By six o'clock I was endlessly pacing my hotel room. By six fifteen I'd moved to the small front lobby, where I paced the carpeted area with the chairs and fireplace. The dark-haired man on the sofa was now reading an evening edition of *The Guardian* and gave me a series of puzzled looks. I'd already made the desk clerk swear he'd call immediately if someone tried to reach me through the hotel switchboard. My cell phone may as well have been glued to my left hand.

At 6:23, Cassie called.

"Are you in your hotel room?" she asked.

"I'm in the lobby staring out the front windows."

"Go to your room and call me back, so we can talk in privacy."

"Right." I ran for the elevator, then paced that small area as I waited for a car. Nothing about her statement made me feel the least optimistic.

On my floor, the key opened the door and I hit redial simultaneously, letting the door *thunk* behind me as the lock reengaged.

"You can talk?" she greeted me.

"Did you find something?" My patience level sat at zero.

"On one of the bulletin boards, yes. It's kind of a goofy board where people post really whimsical stuff as they're also asking for information. I think they try to outdo each other sometimes on the nerd-comedy end. Anyway, I just saw the username GorgeousGeek—all one word. It's one I've seen Nico use before."

The nickname I gave him. Of course.

Cassie continued, "The message said, 'Floating the river with my amigos. Comfortably working on my base tan.' Then it says he's looking for a bunch of coding stuff that I don't understand, but I figure it's the way he got someone to let him use the bulletin board. And why did he write the Spanish word for friend instead of the Italian *amico*?"

"Because he's tipping us off that he is not with friends. Floating the river signifies the Rhine River."

"He's not going to be sunbathing this time of year."

"No, he's not literally on the river. He's telling us how to find him." I scooped my tablet off the desk and used one hand to pull up a map of the region around the Rhine. "He's trying to tell us his location. It must be a place that starts like either the words base or tan. Just a minute." I traced the river with my finger. "Okay, my guess is he's in Basel, or he knows they're taking him there since he'd still be en route unless they flew. It fits the best. And 'comfortably' tells me he isn't feeling like he's in immediate danger."

"You don't think he's switched sides?" Cassie asked.

"No. Bite your tongue. He's saying he's being treated well enough. Not harmed."

"Wow. You guys have this whole secret code thing, huh?"

I smiled. We'd employed the method off and on through the years. Not just when we needed to alert the other about danger, but when we were trying to keep our communications confidential from Max and others. Simon was someone who knew we used it but didn't have the key, so never knew what anything meant. Or even when we were talking in code.

"Yeah, we've used this before as needed. It's pretty simple, so we won't forget. But effective. Are there any symbols coming after the coding stuff he's asking about? Especially symbols that are duplicated?"

"Three plus signs are separated from the rest of the message by several spaces, followed by three pound signs. But the repeated pound signs just denote it's the end of the message, right?"

"No, the hashtags say to hold back. He might already have an idea for escape. At least I hope that's what he means. The three plus signs are good because it tells me he thinks he can keep in communication with us this way."

"So I should keep an eye on this bulletin board?"

"Yes. Send me the link and I'll watch it too. I don't think we'll get regular messages from him, but maybe he can let us know for sure how many people are holding him and give a specific location."

A sigh filtered over the line. "I wish you could talk to Jack."

Like I hadn't already wished the same thing. Aloud, I said, "I'll contact Whatley again if any message sounds stressed, but otherwise, I think we're left with Nico calling the shots."

"What do you mean call Whatley *again*?"

Oops. "Nothing. Just call him. Like I have before."

"And you've talked to Leif?"

"Yeah, I'll see him soon." Like Tuesday.

Cassie sighed again. "Okay, if you think Nico has things under control, I guess I'll just keep an eye on this board."

"I know you're concerned. I am too. But there's no way Nico would have shared that code with anyone, so the message must be valid. As hard as it is, we need to trust him to know what he's doing. We could mess things up by acting rashly."

"But what *is* he doing?"

God only knows, I thought. "I imagine he's trying to get intel on Ermo Colle's organization. This kidnapping has to be Colle's work."

"Why not Rollie or Moran?"

Because I had another person try to kidnap me today, and because I think two others watched me in the hotel lobby soon after, I thought. It was the kind of tag-team approach Ermo Colle employed when Jack and I were in Rome and Germany. And when Moran's watchers paid attention to who was watching us along the same route, they reported how many different people followed us at each juncture. Obsession overkill.

However, I couldn't have her thinking I was going to disappear any second, and one hint of what transpired in the afternoon would send her spiraling. She was new to the job. Until last fall I'd run solo most of the time, so I didn't take near misses as seriously as I probably should have, but I didn't have the luxury of changing tactics. "Remember, I know who Ermo Colle really is. I know his manias and his need to know everything about everyone. Someone like Nico is a trophy for that kind of personality. I don't like the idea, but my instincts are telling me it's likely Colle."

"Would he hurt Nico?"

"Not while Colle gets what he wants." I heard a gasp and quickly added, "Nico can read paranoid people as well as I can, Cass. He'll figure out what to do. We can't help but worry until we see him again, but at this point our only option is trust Nico."

Time to change the subject.

"How are you getting time away from Max?" I asked.

"I'm in the bathroom," she said. "He probably thinks I'm having some phase of kidney failure by this point. I should go."

I reminded her to get some sleep and not to sit up all night hoping for another message. Then we promised to talk again in the morning and hung up.

Before I got more worried and forgot to follow through on anything else, I phoned Clive and asked him to call Patricia.

"Nico's been delayed," I said. "Something came up and he couldn't call himself. But please tell Patricia he'll make it up to her soon." Closing my eyes, I sent up a mental prayer for my last statement to come true.

I told him I needed to run so he wouldn't ask anything uncomfortable, but I could tell he didn't completely believe my assurances when he said, "Okay, keep me apprised if I can do anything. I'll be here until the first of the week. Cheers."

With that task completed, I was left to face the question of what I should do myself. Did I run everything lone wolf and maybe make things worse? Or simply hole up in my room and order food in until Jack or Leif returned?

The house phone rang and for a moment I had the irrational thought that Nico was finally in the lobby.

"Hello," I answered.

"I have a package for you at the desk, miss. It's marked fragile."

The painted flutes, of course. "Did the person dropping them off look like an artist?"

"Electric blue and magenta streaks in her hair," he replied. "Rather unconventional dress."

Yes, that was my artist. "I'll be down in a minute."

Before I could hang up, he said, "Another thing. There was someone else here just before her asking for you. He left, and I was about to call you when the second person showed up. At first I thought the young man was whomever you said earlier to let you know about, but there was something off about him. He didn't have your correct name either. He kept saying Laura. I told him we didn't have anyone here by the name Laura Beacham, but he was welcome to leave his card or a contact number. He became agitated then and hurried out the door."

"Was he very tall, thin, blond? Maybe wore a suit?"

"That describes him."

My second watcher in the lobby of the Ritz. The one who came back after leaving with the stocky guy from the hallway. "Thanks so much. You handled it exactly right."

"But you do know him?"

"No. I've only seen him once. If he comes around here again, whether he asks for me or not, please text or email me."

"Absolutely. I'll also ask security to pull a print of his face from tonight's surveillance video."

"Awesome idea. Thank you."

"I can have the package sent up to you," he offered.

And that's when I had my third epiphany of the day. I was on a roll. "I'll come down. I may be going out in a short while, and if so I'll need the package."

I replaced the receiver, then hit the number Marci used to call my cell phone earlier.

"Laurel!" Marci greeted me. "You're coming, right? I won't take no for an answer."

"Then you'll get the answer you want," I said, smiling at how well this was going. "One question. Would it be an inconvenience if I came a little early?"

"Like tomorrow?"

"More like tonight." I held my breath.

"No inconvenience at all. I'll have our London driver ready the Bentley and come fetch you. It's a bit of a journey up here to Yorkshire, but you can sleep on the drive back. How soon should I send him?"

Oh, Marci, I may never sleep again, I thought. Aloud, I said, "Wouldn't the train be easier on everyone? We'll be arriving awfully late by car."

Marci brushed the idea aside. "Piffle. Dalton loves to drive. It's his job. Cook will put a basket together, too, in case you feel like a snack along the way."

"Alright, I guess. If he can give me at least an hour to get what I need together, that would be terrific. I'll be packed and ready when he gets here. Give him my number to call when he's close and I'll be downstairs in the lobby so he won't have to come up."

While the party in the country took care of my hiding out and security concerns, I had several things to do before I could leave London. First, and most important, I needed to figure out what to do with the treasures Clive produced in the Ritz bar. The figurine was small enough to fit into the safe in my room but not the tube, and I wasn't comfortable removing the painting from its stiff leather cocoon. I also wasn't crazy about leaving something worth so much money in a hotel room safe that likely had an override code known by too many of the hotel personnel.

I trusted the people who worked there to a point, but I didn't know how far Colle might go to get the pieces. Or Moran and Rollie for that matter. There were all kinds of people in my life I couldn't trust not to bribe the hotel employees. I pulled a large shopping bag from my closet shelf and set the tube inside. With it leaning at an angle, nothing appeared above the top edge when I pulled the handles together in one hand. Good. This might work.

When I stepped off the elevator at the lobby, I was glad to see the clerk alone at the desk. "Hi, I've come down for my package."

"Yes, Miss Beacham." He pulled a square, brown paper-wrapped parcel from below. "Here it is."

I pulled it with my left arm to wedge next to my body. I held up the shopping bag in my right. "Also, I have an item too big to fit in my room safe. I'd like to put it into one of your boxes in the large safe room."

"Of course." He pulled the swing gate to invite me behind the desk and waved for another employee to take over for him. We walked through the open door in the back wall and entered a quiet hallway. A few minutes later I gratefully hid the tube behind a steel door with a long key, and the box with the painted flutes now rode comfortably in the shopping bag in place of the art.

I almost forgot. I had one other request. "I wonder if you have any wrapping paper I could use," I asked the clerk. "For a wedding tea."

"Yes, I believe we have some solid colors." He checked inside one of the cabinet. "Here's some white and a nice white bow. Would that work?"

"Perfect, thank you." I slipped the supplies into the bag.

Back in my room, I felt like a weight was off my shoulders. The gift was wrapped in a few minutes. Then I packed without much thought, randomly pulling clothes from the closet. Until I realized the clothes tossed on the bed would take care of me for a two-week Atlantic cruise. It was one thing to plan for every eventuality and quite another to senselessly overpack. Trimming my options down from three bags' worth to only three days' needs, I sorted and packed—and unpacked—until I just had my hanging garment bag and a carryon. I also changed from my work-and-almost-kidnapped outfit to a comfortable pair of lined navy wool slacks and a winter white Merino wool sweater. I'd already kicked off my Jimmy Choos and sat on the bed to pull on my short black travel boots. The driver called my cell as I was in the middle of inventorying my Prada, deciding which gizmos went and which stayed behind.

"No way it's been an hour already," I said as I hung up. But I looked at the clock and learned I was wrong. Glad I'd thought to tell Marci to give me an hour when she said he was at the London residence.

I put on my long leather coat, slung my Prada on my right shoulder, and grabbed the small carryon with the same hand. The garment bag hung down my back, with my left hand holding the hanger side handle at my shoulder.

The drizzle had stopped, and the doorman opened the walk-through glass door for me as the black Bentley idled noiselessly at the curb. The trunk lid, or boot, rose slightly like magic, and the driver exited the vehicle. He took my carryon, and I started to turn and sling the garment bag around.

Suddenly, I was knocked to the ground.

"See here!" someone shouted.

My garment bag was ripped from my hand. I fell semi-forward, with my shoulder taking most of the impact, but my face still managed to graze the rough pavement.

The doorman gave chase, but the thief disappeared in the darkness. The driver helped me up. I was shaking.

"Are you okay, Mi—"

I interrupted him. "No injuries, everything is fine." It wasn't. My left shoulder was bruised from hitting the hard surface, and I was bleeding from the cement scratches at the side of my chin, but at least I succeeded in stopping him from saying my name out loud. Too many ears could be listening from the shadows.

The driver reached into the front seat for a box of tissues, and I took several to dab at the blood. I thanked him.

"If you want to return to your room for clothes to or to clean—" he started.

"Let's go," I interrupted him. "I'll borrow clothes from Marci." I didn't want the thief to have the chance to double back.

The driver was bright enough not to argue, and he opened the rear door of the Bentley. I slid onto the buttery leather seat. He put my carryon bag alone in the back and climbed behind the wheel.

I could forget about sleep. For the miles between London and Marci's place in the York countryside, I'd stay wide-eyed and searching out the back glass to check if anyone took the opportunity to follow us.

NINE

Normally, a Bentley made me feel like I was cocooned in luxury, but my nerves were too far on edge for me to relax into the experience. As we cruised away from the hotel, the driver, Dalton, informed me we would reach Yorkshire in about four hours, then suggested phoning the police about the mugging before we left London.

"Or we can stop and make a report to the police," he said, turning his face slightly so I saw an almost-full profile with an aquiline nose as he spoke. "You'll likely need one for the insurance adjuster."

"No, I'll take care of it later." I took a deep breath before I added, "It's just stuff. I'll borrow something from Marci when necessary."

Yeah, just stuff I couldn't replace with my maxed-out credit cards. Let him think I was one of the airhead rich who couldn't be bothered about the loss. It was better than explaining what was actually going on. I wasn't positive, but it did seem like Dalton took a few unnecessary extra turns before leaving the London environs. Possibly to check for tails. My vigil behind us—and I checked out the back glass a lot—revealed normal traffic. No too-interested headlights seemed to follow the Bentley, but I appreciated any additional evasive maneuvers the driver utilized.

I was doubly glad I'd accepted Marci's offer for the car rather than my suggestion of the train. The latter might have meant a faster trip, but who could guess what might have happened if I'd taken the public late-night option. I certainly didn't want to find out.

Even though she'd already offered when I talked to her around noon, I called Marci once we were on the A1 and heading north to ask if I could borrow some clothes. Even went so far as to make light of the event and joke how some homeless person would be wearing my favorite pink DKNY outfit and emerald green Diane von Furstenberg wrap dress. Though better odds said my clothes would be tossed instead.

She had no problem with the request. "Of course you can borrow whatever you like. I'd planned to put you in the room next to mine anyway so we could catch up, and it will be convenient for you to get into my closet anytime."

After we hung up, I used a penlight to better assess damage. Makeup would mask the chin scrape, but I wanted to sob over the rough scarring the pavement left on my coat when I was knocked to the ground. Hopefully my drycleaner could work a miracle on it when I got back to London. The leather had saved my body from getting further battered, and I was grateful for that. I gently rolled my hurt shoulder to check range of movement. It seemed manageable. Hopefully a hot shower at Marci's would help the shoulder and the tightness I was feeling in my torso over getting tossed into the kidnapper's car earlier. I dabbed the nick under my chin again to make sure blood didn't hit my white sweater.

The long drive gave me time to think about everything that had happened. I texted Clive and asked if anyone had bothered him at the Ritz while the treasure tube was in his possession. He said no, asked if he needed to be worried. I stewed for a minute then responded, *No, I'm only double checking.* He asked, *Heard anything else from Nico?* I was relieved he worded the question that way, and I felt no guilty pangs responding, *Yes, he sent a message. Thanks again for letting Patricia know he'd be a no-show.*

I left it there; I didn't want to tell an out-and-out lie, and anything I said beyond might dislodge the kernel of truth I clung to so fiercely. Yet, this gave me new concerns about using civilians in any phase of our operations. Assuming the man who knocked me down and took my garment bag did so in hopes of gaining the Caravaggio.

I'd made this assumption because the bag was the only thing I carried which was large enough to completely hide the painting. But if he was a follow-up to the guy in the afternoon who got conked on the head by Ferguson, why was I thrown into the car along with the painting? Instead of just having my Prada stolen with the tube sticking out of it? And how did they know I had the Caravaggio?

Maybe I was looking at this all wrong. Or maybe we had two different teams in play again. Just once I'd have liked for something to make sense.

Pulling up my email, I grabbed the link Cassie forwarded so I could find Nico's message. This was a popular board for geeks and nerds, hence what Cass had called the "whimsical stuff" that got posted. As usual, Nico was smart in choosing where to post. Beyond his GorgeousGeek moniker, I recognized another username as a friend of Nico's from emails I received a couple of times a year. The friend asked, *Hey, old man, you losing your coding mind?* Which shored up my belief Nico used this board posting to send messages to us, rather than because he needed info he should already know.

Still, the requested coding data was given. Which meant if Nico had used this fake knowledge gap to kill time before he did something to aid his captors, asking for coding info he already knew, he needed to find another method to stall in the future. Other than a *thx* by Nico, there wasn't anything else, but I continued scanning the board.

After tagging along at one of Nico's gamer conventions and smiling at the sweet techy guys who fawned over me there, I knew many of the usernames they posted under. I also knew the email addresses of several of these nice nerds, since they liked to keep in touch on the off chance I'd come to another such event, and they regularly asked if I would attend as their arm candy. If Nico sent anything to them, I hoped they would think to forward it along to me. I couldn't count on it, but I didn't want to risk emailing the individuals directly with the request either. One of them might think he could play James Bond and send something back to Nico that would blow up the whole thing.

I needed to be patient until Nico set whatever plan in play. But patience had never been one of my virtues.

About halfway to Yorkshire, the driver made a courtesy stop for me, and when we got on the road again I opened the container the cook sent. I could get used to being taken care of. I had missed such attention desperately through the years, but often found myself amazed at how far I'd come in the self-sufficiency range since Daddy's fall from grace and wealth. I wondered again how many of those millions he'd presumably "lost" before his faked death had actually been squirrelled away in a Swiss bank account until he came back to life with a new name and face. The pittance left in the estate went to pay down on the bills and loan sharks. The only way I'd gotten through college was to sell the Jaguar Grandfather left me and live on the small trust Grandmamma bequeathed with a note that it came only to me on my nineteenth birthday so my father couldn't touch it. She might have loved her son, but she obviously had few illusions about him.

There were so many times in college when I'd raged about the fact my grandparents hadn't put up safeguards to stop my father from gutting the family legacy. No one wants to think their offspring might do something so reckless, and Grandfather said a couple of times just before he died that what my father needed was greater responsibility. So maybe he thought the inheritance would make my father grow up. Instead, it made him even more duplicitous. He took away every familiar thing in my life. I'd lost my family, my status in our economic circle of friends, the only home I'd ever known, and, of course, the money. Basically, every shred of security. I was completely on my own.

According to Moran, my father was afraid of me. Thinking back to the night in Baden-Baden, when my not-so-late father pulled a gun on me after I recognized him through his new fake name and face, I had to believe Moran was right. Angry as I too often stayed the last decade over what had transpired, my father was probably right to fear me as well. And that wasn't even counting the fact I now knew he was the criminal mastermind I'd been pursuing for months.

Once we exited the A1, the roads were dark and the night truly felt as if the midnight hour was near. Dalton talked the canned tourist bureau speech about the few landmarks we passed along the way. I hadn't been in the area in years, it was such a trek from London, but I recognized the lights of York as we drew close then bypassed to head to the north side of the county. I was barely awake when we finally turned onto the lane that morphed into the drive to Robbsham, the estate Marci's family had lived at for about a dozen generations.

Lights still glowed in several windows of the Jacobean façade, and the butler met the car as Dalton pulled into the front circle. For a moment, I felt like I was living an episode of *Downton Abbey*, except then all the servants would have lined up to greet us. A blond Labrador retriever sat by the front door, the apparent stand-in for the rest of the sleeping house staff. The butler, Barnes, introduced himself and carried my one small carryon and the shopping bag with the flutes inside as he escorted me through the two-story grand entrance. The dog trailed alongside Barnes.

"Nice dog," I said.

"She belongs to his lordship," Barnes replied.

We entered the hall under the upstairs balcony and continued until we came to the media room, where Marci laid curled up on one of the six royal blue settees as the *Sex and the City* movie streamed on the wide screen.

Marci, or Lady Marcella Menton, was the only child of John and Cissy Lambsley, who were also Lord and Lady Menton. We first met when Grandmamma sent me to finishing school in Switzerland the summer between ninth and tenth grades. I learned enough to pass the social tests, via Marci's whispered prompts. But I spent most of my evenings opening windows to sneak the two of us back into the facility long past curfew. Our bond grew stronger when I returned to Europe a few years later, broke this time, to spend that fateful summer trying to forget my troubles after Daddy Dearest skied off the side of the Alp. Allegedly, of course.

I touched her shoulder, and her eyes opened when I said, "Wake up, sleepyhead."

The butler took his leave. The dog walked over to Marci. My friend gave a languid, beautiful stretch, then ruffled the dog's fur affectionately and jumped up to hug me hello. I worried about how thin she felt under my hands.

She pulled back and brushed away the curls that fell in my eyes. "Oh, I'm sorry," she said, stifling a yawn. "I was going to stay awake until you got here, but I zonked out." Marci still looked like a grownup Alice in Wonderland with her straight, naturally white-blonde hair. All she needed was a velvet hair ribbon and a large white rabbit by her side. She had the large nearly white dog instead.

"This is Sugar." She waggled the dog's ears. "She lives for Daddy, and when he's out of town she's a little lost. She won't bite or anything."

"I love big dogs," I said. "No worries."

"I have wine." She waved me toward the back counter. "Fancy some? Did Cook fix you something to eat on the drive? Just ask if you want anything at all."

I couldn't help it, I laughed, and that made Marci laugh along with me. "It's so good to see you, Mars."

"No one calls me that but you." She hugged me again. "God, I've missed hearing you say it. Can you stay all weekend? Please?"

"Let's take this a day at a time, okay? Remember, some of us aren't marrying princes and have to work for a living." I caught up her hands, then raised up her left. "Omigod, how many carats? Fifteen?"

"And a half." She gazed at the rock on her ring finger. "It's decadent, I know, but it's a family heirloom, and I really love him, Laurel. I'd proudly wear a glass chip if he put it on my finger." She smiled and her face lit up as brightly as the diamond. "Prince Giovanni. But I call him Van."

Tears pricked my eyes. "Dammit, Marci, I can't decide if I'm thrilled for you or jealous as hell. Let's just go with thrilled. Deal?"

"Deal."

I yawned and she followed suit.

"Oh, heavens," she said, waving a hand once the yawn ended. "We both need to go to bed. Come on. We'll get you settled for the night. All safe and warm. Amazing to believe you could get mugged in front of your hotel, with the doorman and Dalton standing right there."

You don't know the half of it, I thought. Same kind of riff raff attacked me in front of the posh Ritz. But aloud, I said, "It happens. One bag, a few favorite outfits. I got off lucky."

She put an arm around my shoulders and steered me back the way I'd come with Barnes. "You're sure you're all right?"

"Slightly battered, but I'll soldier on."

"Of course you will," she said. "The man's lucky he got away before you could kick the hell out of him. He did steal your clothes. You should at least report it."

"It was just a crime of opportunity. I'll deal with it later." Besides, I thought, I'm getting used to arriving at destinations without my luggage.

Sugar kept pace with us, and Marci gave me the mini-tour along the route. When we reached a room near the staircase, she switched on the light. The room was decorated for a man's tastes with oak paneling and leather furnishings. She turned to the dog. "Go to bed, girl. Time to go night-night."

The Lab entered the room and settled into a large padded dog bed beside a huge oak desk. Marci turned off the light but left the door open. "Daddy's study. She'll be waiting for us in the morning, trust me."

When we got upstairs, she turned right and led me down the wide hallway. The suite near the end of the hall was hers, and as promised I had the one next door. She turned on the lights to mine and showed me the bathroom and the extra towels and blankets. I tried not to ooh and ahh too much at the lovely white and powder green décor, with a carved mahogany bed and matching furniture. The room glowed in the lamplight, and I knew I'd adore it even more in early sunshine.

On the pale green bedspread lay a delicate silk and lace charmeuse nightgown in light rose, with a matching robe.

"Is this okay?" Marci asked, waving toward the nightclothes. "Or would you prefer pajamas?"

"Perfect choice. Thanks so much."

She yawned again. I mirrored her.

"Oh, I want to talk to you all night, but I'm so tired. And I think we're making each other yawn," she said, squeezing my hands. "I never knew planning a wedding over a year's time took so much out of a person."

"But it's going well?"

She waggled a hand back and forth. "Some days, yes. Others? Eh."

"Will you have it here or in Italy?"

She frowned. "Location is part of what makes it all exhausting—getting Mother to let us have the wedding we want instead of what she mandates."

"It will be beautiful in the end," I said.

"I keep telling myself that." She grinned. "On the positive side, it gives me so many excuses for parties. Now that I know you're working in London, I'll be able to invite you to all the festivities."

Oh, what had I gotten myself into? I smiled anyway.

TEN

After Marci left my room I took another look at the online bulletin board and found nothing resembling a new coded message from Nico. I even checked some of the other boards I knew he used periodically to see if he'd posted on any of them with a different username. My eyes were gritty and my body was starting to feel the effects of fighting off both a kidnapper and a mugger in the same day. I shut down my electronics and grabbed the quick shower my aching body needed, letting the hot jets pound on every muscle group. My shoulder was already showing hints of all the colors it would wear by morning, but the heat from the water did its magic and the fabulous silk gown did the rest. I crawled between the pair of heavenly Egyptian cotton sheets, snuggled under the covers, and my over-stressed brain shut down from utter exhaustion.

I slept about five hours before I woke up in a cold sweat and hearing the little voice in my head chant, *Nico is gone and there's nothing you can do.*

For about the fifteenth time, I reread the cryptic lines on my tablet that Cassie had relayed to me over the phone the previous evening. Still nothing there I hadn't known the first time. I pulled up information on Basel and went into a couple of real estate databases I knew about, looking for any ideas about where he could be held. I even went as far as to check flights to Switzerland. Then common sense took over and I wanted to hit something. As much as I hated to admit it, going to Basel alone without any information was stupid and dangerous. For all the good I'd do, I might as well sit at a sidewalk café and drink hot chocolate, watching who walked by. I'd be just as close to finding Nico that way.

A one-cup coffeemaker and a china cup sat on a side table with a selection of individual coffee flavors. No way I was going back to sleep, even if the sun hadn't yet broken the horizon. I found a pod with a strong blend, made a cup, and then dressed in the same outfit I'd arrived in. The windows in my suite faced east. I pulled back both sets of drapes to open the French doors and watched the morning settle over the York countryside.

I stood on the small balcony in the semi-darkness and wondered what my next move should be. It wasn't like I hadn't run operations alone before, but at that moment I wasn't completely sure what the operation was. I had a missing tech wizard, a forgery ring—or two—a painting I was afraid to get rid of and afraid to keep, and I was hiding out in rural north England without any backup. A part of me wanted to call Max and say I was bringing the painting to Paris for him to take back to New York. But the part of me that was terrified for Nico's well-being reminded me I might have to produce it to set him free.

And really, what would set him free was the biggest question to solve: was Nico taken because he played a part in the theft, or because he was the right hand I couldn't work without? The art heist might be bigger in worldview, but I had to consider what I could personally impact short-term. Instinct continued making me think he was taken for his talents, but yesterday's thwarted kidnapping attempt and mugging left me undecided.

At least Halborn was behind bars, but two additional thugs—that I knew of—were still loose. I assumed last night's mugging was by the young man from the Ritz who tried, unsuccessfully, to get information from my hotel's desk clerk. The clerk had promised to get security to print me a photo of the man. While they were checking that security camera feed, they might as well check the one outside for about a half-hour later. I texted my hotel's front desk while I was thinking about it, asking for security to see if the outside cameras captured a clear shot of my assailant and to print me a copy. As much as I hated to admit it even to myself, I was starting to agree with Jack about the bodyguard, for the extra set of eyes if nothing else.

"Maybe I need a dog. A purse-sized yappy one I can keep around who'll go into barking fits if someone comes near me," I mused, finishing off the last of my coffee as the first rays of light spread across the landscape.

But that wouldn't work either. I'd get attached to the little thing, and if someone attacking me hurt the dog... My memories of Bruno surfaced, the German shepherd Grandfather brought in to protect me soon after my mother's death. Knowing what duplicity my father was capable of now, something I didn't know then, I had to wonder who Bruno was actually protecting me from—kidnappers or someone much closer to me. It wasn't just the dog either. I had a new nanny then, Kelly...Kelly Hobbs. Kelly didn't just help me dress and teach me games, she had a black belt as well. Something I found out accidentally when she subdued a paparazzo who was too keen on getting my photograph. Once I started kindergarten she always took me to school and stood waiting at the door when I got out each day. I often caught glimpses of her in the halls, though when I brought the instances up she told me she volunteered her help whenever someone needed it. Again, with all I'd learned the last few months, I wondered about the complete veracity of her statement.

Yet, my father couldn't have been a threat then, or they would have built better safeguards for the family fortune in the will. Wouldn't they?

"Grandmamma did." I spoke my thoughts aloud. "She tied up the trust she left to me so my father could never touch it."

She passed away two years ahead of Grandfather. He was the one who didn't tighten the conditions and left easy access to his son.

I carried the cup back to the side table, just as my phone signaled a text. It was from Cassie.

When you're awake look at this link.

She'd been luckier than me or had better timing. When the link went live, I immediately knew it came from Nico, because the feed was security footage of me slipping away with the painting. I'd had the bottom of the hood pulled up to cover my mouth and nose. Only my eyes and part of one brow showed around the black material. Was this the kidnappers' way of saying they'd swap him for the painting? Or Nico's attempt to warn me? I checked my email and didn't see an entry. One should appear if the kidnappers made a demand. No, I decided, the video wasn't a demand. Nico sent me a warning. Took a chance. I just hoped it wasn't a last chance.

Cassie answered on the first ring, "You saw it, right?"

"Right." I paced the length of the room. "Where did you find it?"

"On the bulletin board. I woke up about five minutes ago and checked. The link was in the coding part this time, but the message was addressed to *BraccioDestro*. He's used that when he's written me notes. I think it's loosely—"

"Right-hand man in Italian," I said. "Good, Cass. Did he just put up the link?"

"No, he buried it in the coding part of the message, after he said some cobwebs needed to be swept away."

"So you figured out the extraneous—"

"It wasn't hard," she hurriedly assured me. "But it wasn't something anyone looking over his shoulder would know. I bug him when I use mnemonics to remember things. He split up the link with a couple of my favorites. I removed them and *voila!*"

And to anyone else, Cassie's trick letters just looked like extra coding. I shook my head, amazed at my team. I scraped my bangs back with my free hand, pulling my hair for a second to get the blood flowing to my brain to think. What did this mean for sure? I was back to my original either/or conundrum.

"Anything else in the message?" I asked. "Or do we just go with our gut reaction about the video."

"What does your infamous gut say?" she asked.

I sighed. I did not want to say it out loud. "Ermo Colle or Moran has him. Or anyway, some part of either of those organizations. I'm thinking this for the reasons I said last night about Simon knowing Nico's importance and his likely giving that intel to Colle and even Moran. And whichever organization does have him is the same one who planned on swapping out the painting we stole with one of the two copies confiscated by customs in Calais earlier this week. That's my theory."

"The security feed must have been accessible from the computer they're letting Nico use," Cassie said.

"Everything is accessible to Nico if he has a computer," I reminded.

"Right. But why would the forgery swappers have the security feed for a stolen painting? They would only be interested in the painting if they could replace it with the copy. Missing does them no good."

"Yeah, good point."

Cassie sighed over the phone. "Does the fact he sent this footage mean he's been taken by the people you stole the painting from? Or if it's Colle or Moran, are they hanging onto the footage because they want to find the thief and the painting? Or do they already know it was you and want to keep this as leverage?"

"All really scary options."

"You can't pin it down to the most likely one?"

"No. But Nico's clue said he either was in Basel or heading there, so we can probably discount your first option." I sat on the unmade bed, then fell back to the mattress. Indecision like this always made me feel whipped. "It could be either Moran or Colle. My money is still on the latter. But seeing this surveillance video means you absolutely cannot tell Max about the painting until we resolve this. Or at least until I run it by Jack to see what he thinks. Last night I almost wished I'd sent it with you to Paris so the mugger wouldn't have—"

"What mugger?"

Oops. I took a minute to tell her what happened outside the

hotel and to assure her the painting and the figurine were both in the hotel safe-deposit box. "Which means if we need to swap Nico for the art, we're good to go."

"Was Leif beside you when this happened?"

If I didn't stop talking Cassie would be on the next plane back. "Don't worry. I'm safe. I'm tucked away in a country estate."

"Your friend's party?"

"Exactly. The tea is tomorrow, and then she'll send me back home in the same car I arrived in. The driver is a big guy. Total bruiser. Don't worry."

Okay, another lie added to the rest. I mentally apologized to Dalton, who fit the profile of elegant rather than lethal.

But despite my false words, Cassie sounded relieved when she said, "Good. But text me the address just in case of any emergency."

"It's the Robbsham estate in north Yorkshire. Generations' old home of every Lord and Lady Menton. That should be enough if you need to find me. Out the window it looks like Marci's family owns half the county."

"Great. That's sounding even better," she said. "Enough land and activity around that anyone trying to sneak in would stand out right away."

I didn't have the heart to remind her a large tea party was set for tomorrow, so there would likely be decorators finishing up today and extra unfamiliar wait staff hired on for the event. Instead, I said, "I'm covered. Just make sure you stay safe. Does Monique's place have security?"

"I'm at the hotel." Cassie blew out a long breath. "Max wouldn't budge on me staying somewhere else, so she's coming here after work. We were going to hit some clubs, but now...I'm not sure."

"I don't know what to tell you." I hated hearing the disappointment in her voice. "Is there a club in the hotel? Or a place with dancing close by?"

"Yes, we could do something like that. We'd be safe enough, you think?"

"Make sure to keep your drink in your hand at all times," I warned. "Do you still have the stuff I gave you to put on your nails to check? The nail-polish-looking stuff Jack gave me?"

"It's in my purse. I forgot about it. Thanks."

"Be careful, Cass, just...be careful."

"Okay," she said. "I need to go now and get ready. I'm supposed to meet Max downstairs for breakfast."

"Good luck."

"You, too," she said.

She hung up before me, and as the call dropped, I suddenly felt utterly alone.

I moved back to the window to calm my mind. The grounds were waking up, and gardeners moved out from the house with shovels and other tools in wheelbarrows. They wore blue and brown canvas coats, and I suddenly realized I was cold. It was almost February, after all. No reason for the chill to surprise me.

Another cup of coffee would help, then maybe I could head downstairs.

Someone knocked on the door.

"Come in."

A maid poked her head around. "I beg your pardon, miss, but I saw your light was on. Do you need any help with anything?"

"Can you tell me when I should go down for breakfast?" I asked.

"I can take you if you're ready." She pushed the door fully open. The girl looked around twenty, and the light blue dress she wore made her appear tiny.

"Should I leave a note for Marci?"

"I'll tell her when I go in with her tea, miss."

She led the way back downstairs and minutes later I was in the dining room, alone at the long table. The sideboard was already partially loaded, and as Marci's maid left to go back upstairs, a short chubby woman came in with eggs under a silver domed serving tray.

"Can I get you anything, miss?" the second woman asked.

"I'll serve myself. Thank you," I replied.

The eggs were fluffy, the toast perfectly toasted, and the fruit preserves out of this world. I added a few sausage links and potatoes, and I was good to go. I noticed Sugar had silently entered the room as I'd dished up my breakfast, and I slipped her a couple of sausages while no one was around to catch me. She laid down by my chair, strategically placed to catch any food that might escape my plate.

I was on my third cup of coffee of the morning and Sugar had just finished the last of my cheesy scrambled eggs when Marci fluttered into the room.

"Oh, good, you're all taken care of." She turned to the sideboard and placed two triangles of lightly buttered toast on a plate, then poured a glass of juice. "Here, Sugar baby, catch." Two sausage links flew in the air, gone before they could hit the floor.

As Marci daintily nibbled her bread, I was glad she hadn't come down sooner. I would have looked like a pig wallowing through my full plate while she pretended to eat.

"Fancy taking the horses out for a ride?" Marci asked, bringing me out of my reverie.

I contemplated the muscles already not happy with me and my previous day's adventures. "Normally I'd say yes in a heartbeat, but I'm still achy from yesterday—"

"Oh, how thoughtless of me!" She reached over and covered my left hand with her right. "I forgot all about that. You don't need a doctor, do you? I can call one."

I shook my head. "Nothing time and rest won't cure, but riding a horse today would be too much."

"Absolutely." She resumed nibbling her toast. "I was only thinking how best to show you around."

Just then we heard a loud commotion outside. Sugar started barking and raced out of the dining room, her nails clicking madly on the parquet floor. I looked at Marci. "That sounds like a helicopter."

She nodded. "We have a helipad on the other side of the house.

Likely Daddy's assistant coming in from London to pick up some papers. Happens all the time."

"Everything seems so quiet and restful here. The sound of a helicopter doesn't fit the scene."

"I don't even notice it anymore." She took a sip of juice then said, "You need to choose what you want to wear tomorrow. We'll go up and try on clothes. That will be fun."

I looked at her lean arms. Marci had always been slightly smaller than me, but now she was model thin. Probably dieting for the wedding and all the pre-wedding pictures. I began to worry she might not have any clothes to fit me. "I assumed you'd have last-minute tasks before the party. Please don't worry about me, Mars. I don't want to be in the way."

"Nothing of the kind." Marci smiled. "The event planner and I went over details earlier in the week. She's handling everything." She leaned close and whispered, "Including the handling of Mummy."

"I've never met your mother. She's American, right?"

Marci nodded, continuing to whisper. "And since Daddy's in Hong Kong right now on business, she spends all her time trying to boss me around instead of him. I told the planner I'd pay double if she'd run interference with Mummy. I can have the party as much my way as possible, but with minimum arguments about the preparations. My morning is free to spend with you."

I was beginning to imagine Marci's mother as the Red Queen. Maybe a long nap in my room all afternoon would keep me out of the fray. We talked about her wedding plans and laughed over some of the strange places people suggested for the ceremony.

"When I heard cemetery by candlelight, I decided that *friend* might need to be accidently dropped from the guest list," she said about the final story.

"Absolutely agree with those instincts," I said.

My gaze swept the extra-high ceilings and prismatic window wall. The Jacobean influences ran through every part of the house I'd seen so far, with arched openings, lots of columns, and the walls replicating that columnar choice with pilasters ornamenting the corners of many of the rooms, including this one. I turned back to Marci and said, "I can see the Northern Renaissance influence in the house, especially in the carved work."

Marci nodded. "The men who did all the work were German and Flemish."

"Hey, instead of horseback riding, could you show me the house? I'd love a full tour."

"Are you finished? Let's go." Marci dropped the last bit of toast and scooted back her chair.

I pointed to her plate. "Finish eating. I can wait a few minutes."

"I already had tea in my room," she said, waving a hand. "That's usually all I have until noon."

No wonder she stayed so skinny. But I didn't say anything, as much as I wanted to. I kept discussing the house.

"Too many British estates have become national historic trust sites," I said. "With the families living out the final generation in one small wing. It's nice to see a home like this still a living breathing residence."

"Yes. Thank god Daddy's good with money and makes a bundle with stocks and his business assets. Otherwise we would already be moved out too," Marci said. "Mummy came with money, but this place costs a mint for regular upkeep. Luckily, Daddy acquired the Midas touch when he took over the family holdings and moved us into Asian investments that have paid off well. But while I understand business, I don't have his almost alchemist talents myself, and I dreadfully fear I'll be the final generational hurrah for the lovely place. A crushing responsibility."

"What do other estates do to get by?"

She feathered her fingers in the air. "Fortunate ones rent the places out to big BBC blockbuster programs. But that's of course far from the norm. Most, if they want to stay solvent, become places for events or conferences, or rent summer suites out to tourists like an upscale bed and breakfast."

"Might be an idea—"

"Are you out of your mind?" Marci planted a hand on her hip and laughed. "Can you really see me as the innkeeper type? Really, Laurel."

As we moved out of the dining room, Marci said, "You entered through the main formal reception area last night. There are four other formal reception rooms. One can never have too many formal reception rooms, naturally." She grinned. "My favorite is over at Mummy and Daddy's wing. That's also where the master bedroom suite and sitting room is. Then there are six other bedroom suites, the two we were in last night, plus another on our side of the hall, with the rest at the other end."

We were back in the front gathering area adjacent to the foyer. Marci continued, "There are five other bedrooms scattered around for guests, but they don't have an en suite. The family wing is where we have the gallery of famous family portraits. I'll show you all of that after Mummy gets up and is busy with her work."

She stopped. I didn't realize and had to double back when I noticed.

"I just had a thought," she said, grabbing my arm. "You can teach me how to play snooker. We have a marvelous table, but I don't have a clue how to play. Van and Daddy have tried to teach me, but you'd be so much better at instructing me on the principles of the game."

Meaning, I was so much better at snooker than her father and her fiancé. "Tell the truth. You really want me to teach you how to beat them."

She laughed. "I knew you'd be a great teacher for me. You're so insightful."

"Okay, which direction?" I asked.

Marci started to speak, then stopped, looked at something over my shoulder, and a huge smile spread across her face. "Oh, good, you can meet my brother," she said, waving a hand toward the staircase. She called out, "When did you arrive?"

"About fifteen minutes ago. I came to see Father."

My ears were playing tricks on me. I turned slowly and was surprised to see a tall, heavily tattooed, punk-dressed man with a thick white shock of hair above his black brows. I wanted to tell the guy that Billy Idol wanted his hair back, but no words came out of my mouth. Sarcastic or otherwise. Sugar stood at the bottom of the stairs, tail wagging and grinning up at him.

"I know he doesn't fit the family image with this hooligan look, but my dear brother usually cleans up much better than this," Marci said, directing her next comments at her sibling. "Mummy hasn't come down yet, but when she does I guarantee her first words will be 'this isn't Halloween and the new look must go.' I'll call my hairdresser to beg for him to get you worked in as quickly as possible."

I walked toward the strange-looking man, shaking my head at the sight of all the ink on his exposed skin. He remained stock still. I circled around the dog to slowly climb each step, going a couple of risers higher than him so my baby blues could stare right into his bright teal eyes. I said, "I do hope it's not too painful when they remove all the art on your skin, Jack. Because it really cannot stay."

"I'll grit my teeth and do it for Q and C." He grinned.

I couldn't help but return the grin. "So it's temporary?"

"Wouldn't have it any other way."

I took an earlobe between my finger and thumb. "Looks like you had some piercings, too."

He caught my wrist and held it. "The holes won't show in a month."

"Was all of this necessary?"

"I said I was going to be someone else. Couldn't get out of the assignment because I needed to play a repeat performance."

Marci called up, "I take it you two already know one another."

I pivoted her way. "I've never seen this man before in my life."

Jack laced his fingers with mine and pulled me along with him down the staircase. "Let's remedy that then, shall we? Marci, we'll be in the garden getting better acquainted."

As he hurried me toward the French doors along the east side of the house, I spoke over my shoulder. "Tell your hairdresser there's a big tip involved if Jack can be worked in soon. I'd hate for his hair to think it needs to stay this way."

Jack responded by calling out, "Laurel already believes it's her personal duty to give me white hair before my time. She doesn't want the competition."

It was too cold for any blooms, but the chilled landscape gave off the earthy scent of well-tended sod. As we hit the stone pathway, a gardener was at the far end. No one else was close, but I wasn't taking any chances. I pulled Jack behind some tall evergreen bushes, ready to tell him everything that had happened since he'd gone, grateful to finally share the load.

I looked up at him with the goofy hair and...slammed him against the stone wall and kissed him within an inch of his life.

"Wow," he said, as we broke free. "Maybe I need to change my hair color more often."

"Don't you dare."

"So it's the tats that turn you on."

"Dammit, Jack." I rubbed my hands up the rough cloth of his shirt. "I have really missed you."

He pulled me into his arms. "Then let's make up for th—"

"No." I pulled free. "I mean it. I need you." I launched into every incident and harrowing event that occurred while he was incommunicado. I finished by pulling my phone from my pocket and keying up the video link.

"Nico didn't send anything else?" Jack asked as the video finished the second time, and he handed back the cell phone.

"No, just the cryptic message and then this link," I said. "Can you get some whiz-techy guy at MI-6 to see if there's any kind of hidden digital fingerprint to track Nico internationally with this?"

Jack shrugged. "I could, but then my *whiz-techy guy* would probably want to know who the gorgeous blonde is who's ripping off the painting in France."

"My hair doesn't show under the hood."

"The guy I know is like Nico. He'd find a way to figure out

what's under the hood too." Jack rubbed the back of his neck. "Look, don't hate me for what I'm about to ask, but you're sure Nico was taken and not turned?"

"Dammit, you're just like Cassie. She asked the same thing last night when she first reported he'd put the *GorgeousGeek* message on the board. What is it with the two of you? If he'd turned, why would he send messages?"

"Still, you have to admit people and events have not acted in a completely linear order these past few months. From Simon to Rollie to Moran to your father, everyone seems to playing to their own right of center."

"Not Nico. Not every man in my life is playing a dual role, though you certainly acted like you were in the beginning as well, and I..." I stopped talking and looked away, so he wouldn't see the tears welling in my eyes.

"The question had to be asked."

I took a deep breath, keeping my gaze on a rosebush that had been covered to protect it in the January temperatures. I swiped at my eyes. When I could talk without crying, I said, "And I gave you the answer. I know you've had some concerns about Nico's loyalty in the past and voiced them in Rome, but—"

"I just want to know who and what I'm working with. That's why I asked what I did in Rome."

"I trust Nico. I'm not saying he doesn't moonlight on other jobs if he wants to, and I don't ask. But he's always there when I need him, and he currently needs us. And he needs us to trust him." I finally felt ready to turn back and meet his gaze. I stood with my hands fisted on my hips. "So I'll ask again. Do you know anyone who might be able to use these messages to try to nail down a location? His phone GPS isn't tracking, so it's not turned on, and he's using the kidnappers' equipment to contact us with these messages. If we can get some kind of digital fingerprint on the device..." I shrugged. I'd reached the end of my virtual vocabulary.

Jack frowned, pulling his dark brows close together. The white hair made his expression frightening. "I'm not sure what to do.

According to your interpretation, Nico said he was safe enough in the first coded message. If I raise an alarm anywhere we could cock up anything he has planned. But if we can track him at all, I see your point that we should try."

"I know, I came to the same conclusion after weighing the risks all night. I'm so out of my skillset here, Jack." I crossed my arms and looked at the browning groundcover under our feet. "I feel like all of this is my fault. If I wasn't a part of this, Ermo Colle wouldn't have taken Nico. Or Moran. Or Rollie. Or whoever had him kidnapped and tried to kidnap me."

"No, if you weren't a part of this Simon would still be playing all sides without any check whatsoever, and would likely have kidnapped Nico if he's important to their plan—or if they want him out of our plans."

I looked up at him. "I have three smart-ass remarks I could say to you right now."

He threw his hands in the air. "I said that to make you feel better."

"I don't want to feel better. I want to know we'll find a way to get him back." I took a deep breath. "See if your techy guy can find something to help us. If he wants to know who's stealing the painting, tell him. Tell him anything he needs to know to make him interested enough to work this thing. Throw me under the bus. If necessary, take out a pair of cuffs and arrest me yourself. It's a small price to pay."

His smile was wicked, his voice quiet. "I was kind of saving the cuffs for a different kind of activity with you."

"Dammit, Jack." I backhanded his upper arm. "I'm serious."

"I know. However, it won't do any good until we get additional intel from Nico." He took hold of my shoulders, and I shook him loose.

"So it's okay for you to feel guilty," he said, fuming. "But it's not okay for me to give the reasons why you shouldn't."

"Exactly."

"That makes no sense."

"Too bad."

We stared at each other. I finally decided to be the first to blink. "How about we change the subject? I need some time to deal with what's fogging up my brain."

He nodded.

"So why are you here?" I asked.

"I was going to ask you the same thing."

I lowered my voice. "I mean, are you working? Are you still undercover?"

He shook his head and leaned back against the stone wall. "Everything went smoothly. We planned for extenuating circumstances but lucked out instead. I'm working through the debriefing and informational phase of the mission."

"I'm glad." I hugged my body in the chill morning. He stepped closer and opened his arms. I walked into the embrace.

He chuckled. "I never dreamed Marci was the friend who called you."

"I don't think I mentioned her name."

"No, but what you did say about her fits now that I know."

I rubbed my hand along his back. "So her father..."

"And my mother," he finished. He rested his head on top of mine.

I remembered Jack said his mother fell for a married man after she left the artist Sebastian, who was also married while they were together. Obviously, she had a type.

"Marci never mentioned a brother. At least I don't remember her talking about one. But in finishing school we had too many rules to break. And when we weren't partying that college summer we practically lived together, we were usually passed out somewhere. As much from exhaustion as alcohol," I said. "I was working through grief and anger in a quite efficient self-destructive way. Your sister kept me from ending up in the hospital. And she found parties to keep me focused on anything but reality. Siblings didn't really come up in the few quiet and sober conversations we had."

"Given the circumstances, I'm not usually trotted out for company viewing."

I leaned back to see his face. "That's awful."

He shook his head.

"No need to be offended on my behalf. Marci and my father are supportive. But my presence tends to make the dragon lady breathe fire."

"Marci's mother. Lady Menton."

"She paid a lot for that title and intends to get full benefit," he said. Quieter, he added, "Not that I blame her."

I was starting to get a full picture of the outline Marci'd hinted at earlier. "He stayed with his wife."

"My mother wouldn't marry him. She was like that." He took a deep breath. "And Marci's conception was part of the equation. If Lady Menton hadn't realized she was pregnant around the time my birth became news, the outcome may have been different."

"From what Mars told me, the party planner is charged with keeping her mother busy today," I said. "I think the greater the number of changes she asks for, the higher the fee the planner receives."

"Whatever the planner is getting paid, it isn't enough." He chuckled. "So you're the one who calls her Mars."

"Always have." I leaned close and relaxed against his chest. "She said her father's in Hong Kong. Are you staying—?"

"No." I felt his chin on the top of my head, and he just held me. I'd needed this. The last thirty-six hours zapped me physically and mentally. He continued, "I came here because I'm required to report to a member of Parliament, so Father was my first choice. I knew he'd believe what I said without question."

"Guns?"

"Yeah."

I knew he wouldn't elaborate, but I wondered if there was any tie to our heist project. Crates of illegal guns shared space on a Florence rooftop with forged masterpieces when Jack and I tiptoed through there in October. If he believed there was a connection, he would tell me when he could. My patience was getting a workout lately.

"But I can't give this kind of information over an unsecured line to the Far East," he said. "I'll go into London and make some phone calls. See who I can get in to see today. You're going with me."

"Your sister isn't going to like it."

"This isn't the first time I've disappointed her, and I doubt it will be the last. Let's go and get your things."

As I stepped back so he could join me again on the path, I waved a finger in a circle in front of him. "Your fashion faux pas may get you kicked out of any of the offices in Parliament."

"The tattoos will be removed once I get home. And I'll put on a suit and tie." He slipped an arm around my waist. "Satisfied?"

"And the hair?"

"By this evening I'll be my normal hot self."

I rolled my eyes. "Just checking." Then I asked, "Does your sister know...you know...what you do?"

"I've told her less than I've revealed to you," he said. "Not that she really cares what department I'm with, but she wants me to be safe, and this job doesn't promise that. So she doesn't ask. But as an MP's daughter she's grown up with secrets in the house. This is simply another one."

As we reentered the house, I glanced out the front windows. "Where's your car?" Then it hit me. "You don't mean..."

He gave a slow grin and said in what I called his Southern Charmer accent, "We'll be taking to the skies, darlin'. Just think of it as your personal flying carpet."

ELEVEN

Marci's reaction to my leaving with Jack was exactly as I predicted. The way her face darkened when he told her the plan—I chickened out—also made me wonder if she might take after her mother much more than she admitted. However, after he pulled her aside and whispered something in her ear, her face brightened and a few seconds later she smiled. When she joined me to go upstairs to pack, I asked what Jack told her.

She remained cagey, simply saying, "Just that I'll see you soon. We'll have dinner or something. You'll see."

Which made me wonder what "or something" could be.

I didn't push it, however. There was already too much on my mind. The white wrapped gift still sat in the shopping bag, and I pulled it out and handed it to Marci. "This is for you and Giovanni. A celebration gift. And best wishes for tomorrow at the tea."

Her smile broadened as she accepted the box. She started to tug on the bow. "I'll open it now."

"Open it later with Van," I stopped her. "Have a bottle of champagne chilling nearby."

She laughed and set the box on the dresser. "Brilliant. I'll leave it here so I'm not tempted."

When we returned downstairs, Jack was working on his phone, but put it away as we drew near.

"I wish you could at least stay for lunch. Mummy will hate that she's missed you, Big Brother." Marci winked.

"I'm sure she will." He flashed a sardonic grin that looked more mocking than normal given his temporary punk disguise.

A car pulled up at the front of the house, and Barnes passed us to open the door.

"Oh, bother, there's the event planner," Marci said. "I need to make sure she's ready to take on my mother."

"We'll see ourselves out, sis," Jack said, kissing her forehead. "Good luck."

"Bye, Mars," I said, pulling her into a hug. "Appreciate...everything."

She whispered in my ear, "Someday I will get the whole story. About why you showed up early and...everything else."

Pulling away, I smiled and said, "You will," hoping I could keep that promise.

Jack led me back through a part of the house I hadn't seen yet but was equally taken with. Despite the modern touches, it was easy to imagine stepping back into the reign of King James I. We exited the house through a door to the back garden, leaving us within sight of the helicopter. I took a last sweeping glance at the amazing house and grounds.

As he did his preflight checks, Jack said, "I sent Nico's photo to a mate of mine who has access to yesterday's CCTV. He'll do what he can, then report back if he gets any hits or spots any activity to tell us who waylaid Nico."

"Thank you. I assume he'll do it between other duties, right? I mean, if Nico thinks he has a plan—"

"Exactly." Jack nodded. "I stressed this had to stay quiet. If the situation changes, I'm ready to go official. But I don't want to compromise anything Nico is doing himself. Do you have a code for 'send in the cavalry'?"

"Three asterisks." I sent up a silent prayer that things would stay in "trio plus sign" status.

Once the rotors engaged and the helicopter rose from the pad, we could talk with the headsets but still had to kind of shout. Jack gave me a quick aerial tour of Robbsham, nearly three hundred acres of cleared and semi-wild parkland.

"There used to be another couple of hundred acres," he

shouted into the mic. "But all the farmland was broken up and sold. Now Father keeps it open for riding and hunting to unwind when he's tired of London. They hold a kite flying weekend here every spring too. People come from all over. We'll have to attend the next one. You'll like it."

I smiled, but my stomach fluttered. Planning events in the future. Family events. I wasn't completely sure how I felt about the idea, despite my longtime friendship with Marci. He got my attention again by pointing out a couple of other local spots that sat adjacent to the property. One was an ancient pub and inn still catering to the same generations of families who had come through the doors for three and four hundred years.

"They serve a great Sunday roast and ale," he said.

"Sounds like a lovely place to while away a lazy afternoon."

He nodded. "Dogs are respected the same as their owners. Sit on the floor under the booths and chairs."

Easy to imagine Sugar in a place like that and feeling completely at home, waiting for a slice of beef to fall her way.

Too little sleep and way too much stress meant I had a headache coming on. Jack seemed happy to stay less than communicative as we flew the rest of the distance, but I assumed it had to do with the serious information he'd come to deliver and still had to carry with him to London. His conversation was kept to pointing out landmarks and saying we'd discuss things after we landed.

I was more interested in watching him pilot the chopper anyway. I had no idea why I was surprised to learn he could fly. He'd been in the Royal Navy, after all, and helicopters were an obvious tool for that branch of the military. He was just so matter of fact about all of it.

I think his *of course* attitude was what threw me. I'd listened to enough of his half-truths and cocky talk when we'd started working the same clues, I was continually startled when I learned another example to prove how well-trained he was for his job. Though, once I thought about it, I realized most of his bragging usually carried only a conservative measure of the man's true talents. Whatever the job entailed.

I sat in the copilot's chair and watched the English landscape slip past us. This wasn't my first helicopter ride, but I felt as if I viewed everything with fresh eyes. I thought about the aborted tour of Marci's home and wished we had the opportunity to visit the family portrait gallery she'd mentioned. A theory floated in my head about the Debrett's comment Tina Schroeder made when she met us in Miami. Tina social climbed for sport, so I'd dismissed her comment during her introduction to Jack as a side effect of a ditzy personality. Although with what I knew now, I had a strong suspicion if Marci had walked me by the formal portrait of her father, it would have immediately been apparent why Tina thought of the big book of peers and baronages when she saw Jack's face that day. The next time I had a little privacy and a solid wi-fi connection I'd google images of Lord Menton.

While we 'coptered most of the length of the country, I spent my copiloting time making lists on my phone's notes app. We were flying low, but not low enough to have a steady connection. I refreshed my email inbox whenever I could, hoping one of Nico's nerdy friends had sent a message or forwarded an email. All to no avail.

"You're going to drive yourself bonkers," Jack almost-yelled over the comms. "Though you do get top points for loyalty."

"I keep thinking—"

"Overthinking."

I nodded and turned back to my phone.

Much sooner than I'd imagined, we hovered above London's City Airport. As soon as we'd touched down and Jack finished the various paperwork, he called and gave the helicopter's location to someone at the other end of the line, then turned to me.

"Now to grab the first Tube connection."

Jack wasn't the strangest-looking guy on the train, but he was easily the scariest. No one crowded us.

"Where first?" I asked quietly.

He put his arm around my shoulders and pulled me close. "The new office. Get you locked in before I head to Westminster."

"When are you going to...clean up?"

"I'll go by to shower and change on my way."

"I could help."

"Have a thing for bad boys?" He waggled his eyebrows.

"Would I let you stick around otherwise?"

He laughed and the lady across the car moved closer to her shopping bags. Jack's phone signaled a text.

"Bollocks," he grumbled. "Looks like we get you settled at the office and I head straight to Westminster. Cecil secured me an appointment with my first choice of members, but the MP is leaving shortly." He thumbed a return message. "Need to give the heads up about my appearance, since I know Cecil didn't bother because I didn't warn him I still looked like this."

"Seriously, you don't need to walk me to the office. I can—"

"No, you cannot. We're already one man missing, and I'm not thrilled about Cassie being under Max's less than adequate protection. I will get you behind the steel door before I take off for Parliament." He held out a hand. "Give me your mobile, please."

I frowned, opening the Prada to grab my cell from its side pocket.

He worked without talking, pulling a page up onto the screen and setting a bookmark so it could be easily found again. "This app wasn't live yesterday, but it is now." He passed the phone back to me, and I saw what looked like an image of the small foyer off the stairs outside the office door.

"Is this camera in the keypad?" I asked.

"Right. If someone knocks, this makes it handy to look out before unlocking the door."

"Good precaution."

He took the phone back and tabbed through a couple of other screens. "These cameras are set up under the building's eaves, so we have an overhead view of anyone walking near the building or entering through either door on the ground floor. We'll also be able to view the files remotely if we want to see anything going on when the office should be unoccupied."

"And the four cams in the ceiling corners I noticed yesterday morning?"

"Were already live, but now we have the exterior ones around the office too. As well as the ones monitoring the stairway from the floor below." He tabbed a couple times and I could see the squared-off three-sixty-degree view of our war room. The train's mechanical voice came on, and Jack said, "This is us."

We exited near the end of the crowd, then fast-walked up to the street level. The office was three long London blocks away. I caught Jack doing his full-out recon sweep as we hurried, dodging in and out of the sidewalk traffic, and I suddenly felt very afraid. No time for this, I thought. Stop it. I took a deep breath and charged faster to override emotions. In minutes, we were at the rear door of the restaurant and hustling up the stairs.

Jack keyed the code, and I used the phone app to scan the office again. My subconscious was telling me this was silly, but my instincts kept saying "better to check." All clear, and the lock tumbled to allow us entry.

"Go," I said, standing half in the door. "You don't want to miss your guy."

"Yeah, you're right."

He gave me a preoccupied kiss, poked his head in to give the space a quick once-over, then closed the door. The lock engaged. I was safe.

Several files still lay where we'd dropped them on the closest table. I felt the headache growing and headed for the window, hoping to gain a little winter sunlight. Curtains hung to each side, but the wooden shutters completely blocked the glass and view. I opened one shutter and looked out, spotting Jack as he headed back toward the Tube station. I smiled, watching him walk with his confident stride in biker boots and jeans. He finally disappeared in the crowd, and I couldn't help thinking he'd better keep his promise about the hair. I chuckled over the shallowness of my thoughts.

I sent a text to Cass, asking her to contact me whenever Max let her take a break from the meetings. A second later, my phone rang. I expected it to be my assistant, overachieving as usual since I'd just asked her to call, but it was Whatley instead.

"Hello, Superintendent," I said, walking over to sit on the table in case I needed to write notes. "Is this about my interview regarding Halborn? Alfred, was it?"

"The kidnapper, right," Whatley said. "We still have him, though it's taken some work. Had a right pesky solicitor. Your reporter is making his statement as we speak. The crown prosecutor will work on things from there."

My reporter. Well, at least I didn't have to worry about my inept kidnapper being on the loose, though I still had the mugger from last night that the superintendent didn't even know about yet. I started to tell him, but I hadn't the energy. Not like it would have made any difference anyway. I couldn't give a description other than "I think he's a thin young man who took an interest in me at the Ritz after the kidnapping attempt yesterday."

"His statement should be enough to hold Halborn for a while," Whatley said. "Between evidence of your kidnapping attempt, which is backed up by Mr. Ferguson, plus the graphic pictures of his injuries, it will make a good statement for first appearances in court."

"Thank you."

We had just rung off when my phone trilled again. This time, Cassie's name appeared on the caller ID.

"Anything new you can tell me?" she asked.

I crossed my fingers and answered, "Just waiting on Jack. He has some feelers out about Nico. I'll let you know if we get any new information."

"You're with Jack? I thought you were way up north somewhere."

Oh, yeah, I forgot.

"Funny thing happened. Jack came to talk to Marci's father. When he headed back to London, I came with him. I'm in the office working until he gets back." I'd tell her the whole story later, but the headache made me afraid I'd say too much.

I asked how things were going, and she gave me her projected schedule. Then she said, "But the funder still seems miffed you aren't part of this entourage. Max wanted to call and have you jet over here, but I told him you're doing a little fundraising yourself today and dropped the fact you were staying at the home of Lord and Lady Menton this weekend. That pacified him a smidge. Still, I wouldn't leave my phone on if I were you. You don't want him learning you're back in London."

"Good point. But I hate to be completely unreachable. Call Jack if you need us later for any reason."

"Will do," she said, sounding a little wistful when she added, "Are you in the office sorting through the files?"

"You sound like you miss them, Cass."

She laughed. "I do in a way. I'm so bored here most of the time, I wish I had something challenging to make the time pass faster. Have you found anything?"

My gaze traveled to the pages stacked or hanging in various spots of the office. "Nothing so far, but I'll stay with it."

"Okay. I'll keep an eye on the internet bulletin boards. I wonder…Do you think there's anything to worry about with no new messages?"

"The video this morning—"

"Yeah, but nothing since."

I massaged the back of my neck. "Let's see what Jack finds out before we ratchet up our worrying, okay?"

"You're right. Call me when you have something."

"I will. I promise."

We said goodbye and I sent a quick text to Jack explaining why I was turning off my phone. I figured his was off while he reported mission findings, but at least he wouldn't get concerned if he couldn't reach me afterward.

So many pages around me. I grabbed the closest file and leaned against the window wall, letting the meager winter sun illuminate the pages as I leafed through the stapled stack. I made some notes, double checked a few things, then dropped the file on the table and grabbed the tablet Cassie left there. Soon, I was back leaning on the window wall and thumbing through bulletin boards, looking for any new message from Nico. Obsessively making the rotation, just like I'd told Cassie not to do. Gaining nothing for my trouble but bonus time to think.

Cassie's comment about being bored stuck with me. Despite her agreeing to go yesterday, I still felt guilty about it. Those kinds of meetings were so much nothing, with Max and the funder talking old stories and old friends, then sprinkling in tiny bits of time dedicated to talking art resources and ways to help small museums and such places. Writing quick new mission statements for project ideas that would either be polished later or thrown out when obstacles surfaced.

I remembered my first meeting with this same funder, how I figured out quickly that schmoozing the man was the only reason I was there. I'd had my wish list of projects to talk over, with priority codes marked on each one. He'd finally taken my list and pretended to read it, before he slipped it into an inside jacket pocket and offered me wine.

While it wasn't funny at the time, I almost laughed thinking back to my reaction. All my work and preparation, and the only things that truly mattered were my blonde hair and long legs.

So, I charmed him with my wits and wiles instead. And got Max the largest check he'd ever received from the man. Okay, I may not have laughed, but I did chuckle over the memory.

The humor did nothing for my headache, however. My eyes were starting to hurt too. Not enough sleep, too much stress, and way too many recent body slams took their toll. I folded my coat inside out, exposing the satin lining, and set it at the end of one of the tables. After I dug a couple of paracetamol from the Prada, I grabbed a water bottle from the coffee station and drank about half. Then I climbed up on the table, thankful I'd worn the navy wool slacks, and fell asleep.

*   *   *

Shortly after noon I woke to Jack gently shaking my shoulder. Real Jack—showered, changed, and sporting a shorter but more normally dark hair color. It felt like I'd only slept minutes, but a look at my watch told me why he'd had time to return to his normal persona.

"It's after lunchtime already," I said. "I like this look better, by the way."

He laughed. "Naturally you'd think of food first."

"I may have started speaking about food, but my survival skills made me recognize you before I considered the time. Give me some credit."

He used the reflection of the window against the gray sky to check out his hair. He turned to see his profile out of the side of his eye and frowned. "Shorter than I like, but less problem this way with changing back the color."

"I think you look very businesslike," I said, climbing down from the table and reaching to unfold my coat.

"You don't miss my curls?" He grinned.

Ah, those lovely dark waves on the back of his head. I stood on tiptoe, reaching a hand around his neck to run fingers through the cut. He leaned in and his mouth covered mine. I fell into the moment and he deepened the kiss, running hands up and down my back, pulling me closer. I was never so grateful for privacy. Finally, his kiss softened and I pulled back. He grazed my cheek with his hand, and his teal eyes held me.

"Nothing like change to keep things interesting," I said.

"Are you saying you like my hair better like this?"

"Not exactly. But I can live with it short term."

"Can't ask for much better. Ready to get out of the office?"

He held out my coat. I put it on and grabbed the Prada. "Do we have a plan?"

"I do. Some of us work instead of napping."

"Some of us want to spare others from the bad moods that

come from no rest and muggings." I smirked. "Trust me. I took that nap as much for you as I did for myself, and for my headache."

"I'm very grateful."

"You should be."

Jack grabbed the umbrella Cassie stashed in the corner behind the door. We locked the office up tight and headed downstairs.

Outside, drizzle pattered loudly on the wide pavement. We shared the umbrella, staying close to the sides of the building to gain any additional coverage from canvases and eaves. He said, "Let's leave the car and grab a taxi. No parking problems that way."

"Sounds good. But lunch in the meantime, right?"

"There's a good fish and chips place on the next block." He slipped an arm around my waist and we moved down the street to rendezvous with the favorite British meal.

"Is there space available in your agenda for a side trip? Or are you overbooked?" I asked.

He looked at his watch. "Got a call from my mate who's looking for signs of Nico. He said he could meet in another hour. Aren't you starving?"

"Sure, but I'd also like to drop by the laundry where Clara works."

He nodded, but didn't speak. Just pulled me along as the light changed and rain bounced as it hit the street. When we reached the other side, he asked, "You still think that's a good idea?"

I stopped and put my hands on my hips, feeling rain for a moment as Jack and the umbrella took a half-step without me. "What do you have against her?"

"She's a thief and has no reason to be trustworthy."

"She's also a former pickpocket from Barcelona, and we need information on how to find another pickpocket who is in Barcelona."

The wave of people steadily broke around us and kept moving. Jack took my arm and pulled me out of the flow. He said, "We can talk with her if you like. But I don't want to let her know too much."

"Will you stop acting like I don't know what I'm doing?"

"I'm not."

"You are."

He pinched the bridge of his nose. "Let's eat before we fight. I think we'll snipe less at one another once we've had a bite of food."

I wanted to bite more than a plank of fish, but I knew better than to say so. I'd bide my time. Instead, as we started walking again, I changed the subject back to an earlier one. "This guy you have searching the video feeds for Nico. He's good, right?"

Jack caught my hand and linked our fingers, but looked directly ahead as he spoke. "He looks like he still should be head boy in sixth form at school, but he's the best I've seen."

"Sounds promising."

The fish place was shoulder-to shoulder patrons and equally noisy, making both of us antsy. Our meal was consumed at high speed and with little conversation. The rain increased, sliding down the windows in thick gray trickles. When we left, we grabbed a black cab dropping off a fare on the block, a lucky move on what was becoming a gloomy day.

"Why can't this job take me to Greece when it's cold and dismal in London? Or maybe Sydney?"

Jack laughed. "Don't appreciate our winters?"

"For a while, sure." I shrugged. "But I'd give just about anything to slip into a bikini and slide into a turquoise endless pool set outside my hotel room right now."

"Is that a room for one or a couple?" He softly brushed my cheek and tucked a curl behind my ear.

"I thought you enjoyed London winters," I teased.

"I'm a man who appreciates changes in scenery," he said, his voice huskier. "And a change of apparel. What color bikini?"

"A teeny white one. I have a black one, too."

His teal eyes darkened. "Yeah, we should see if we can expand the boundaries of this investigation."

A fast ride later, and we found ourselves in a boring utilitarian building and looking through a doorway into a darkened room manned by an intense-looking young man with glasses. Beyond trying to guess his age, he didn't look like he carried an ounce of fat. One leg kept frantic time against the chair base, thumping to an imaginary beat. Video monitors filled the space around him. Snacks and soft drink containers littered all horizontal surfaces.

When Jack knocked, the guy looked over his shoulder and said, "Hey, Hawkes." After he realized I was there too, he scrambled to his feet, nearly overturning the chair in the process. "Oh, sorry, didn't know you brought someone with you." He held out a hand.

As the guys shook, Jack nodded toward me. "Laurel, this is Williams. Williams, this is Laurel. She's...a friend of my sister's," he finished.

I raised an eyebrow at him. Interesting. He gave a small shrug. I saw Williams's eyes narrow for a second and realized he caught everything that passed between us. Jack was right. He was good.

But an instant later, he acted like he'd seen nothing. "Nice to meet you," Williams said to me. Then turned toward his desk and waved us backhanded into the room. "You have a sister? What's she like?"

"Engaged," Jack replied.

"Figures. Probably marrying a duke," Williams said.

I crossed my arms and stood so the kid was between us. "Actually, he's a prince."

Jack frowned and got things back on track. "What do you have?"

"Oh, yeah, right." Williams spun the back of the chair away so he could sit again and pulled closer to one of the monitors. He spent a few seconds at the keyboard. A black and white image filled the screen.

The shot showed Nico entering Heathrow, bracketed by two men and followed by a third. The man trailing behind was Rollie, Moran's grandson. I wondered if Williams recognized Rollie as a criminal. Decided to wait and see.

My mind raced around the idea of how far off my instincts had been. My father hadn't taken Nico. Something else was going sideways.

Williams kept the group's image on the screen, hitting keystroke combinations when another camera view needed accessing. We watched them pass the checked baggage counters and go up the escalator. I searched for any sign of an escape attempt, but none was made.

Seeing Moran's heir apparent was scary enough, since we were supposed to be notified if Rollie stepped back on British soil and this wasn't the first time he'd slipped the dragnet. But worse, Nico didn't seem to be restrained at all. Just walking between the other pair as they entered the gate marked for a flight to Switzerland. We could see him pull his Italian passport from his pocket and hand it to the flight attendant checking documents before passengers boarded the plane.

I didn't know whether to feel relieved...or ill.

TWELVE

I mumbled a quick thank you to Williams then dashed out of the office and caught an elevator just closing. Jack caught up with me before I'd made it to the building's front exit. As he took hold of my arm, I jerked free and hurried into the revolving door. No plan formed in my head, other than I wasn't ready to talk about this.

Halfway down the block, nearly jogging by this time, he raced ahead and got in front of me. I held up a hand. "Don't say a word, Jack. Now is neither the time nor the place, and I'm not discussing anything yet. You're ready to cast him over to the dark side, I know. But I'm not there yet, and I don't want to argue."

My body felt as physically drained as my brain was mentally spent, and I moved out of the pedestrian traffic to lean against the stone and glass building, the window at my back cold and damp. He stood next to me, glanced around at the people passing by, crossed his arms, and asked, "What do you make of it?"

There was no point in repeating myself. He wasn't listening. Pushing off from the wall, I hurried to the curb, rain be damned, intending to flag down a taxi coming from the east. I even had the irrational thought of standing in the street if I needed to make it stop. Instead, Jack pulled me back under a nearby awning and used the taxi app on his phone. Within minutes, a cabbie curbed a black car a couple of strides away.

"The office?" Jack asked, holding open the door so I could enter the backseat. "We need to try to conference with Cassie. See if she's learned anything and bring her up to speed."

I nodded, annoyed he knew what I was thinking. Despite the

video evidence, I did not believe it. My plan had been to go there, gain some necessary privacy, and pick my assistant's brain. Then think all of this through quietly by myself. Well, I'd get the first half of the chore completed.

He gave the address to the driver, and we sat at opposite ends of the seat. I shook my wet hair so any water fell onto the floorboard, then finger combed it to get the damp curls out of my eyes and off my neck. Leaning back in the seat, I turned my face to the window and watched the drizzly city go by.

The silence got to him first.

"Laurel, you must understand—"

"Hush, please. I need time to process..." I looked at him and waved a hand in the air. "...all of this."

"Williams is putting in a request for flight manifests. Anything he finds, he'll send it to me via email."

"Good. Now please quit talking."

Too many voices roared in my head, but I worked to sort out what was absolutely known versus what we'd seen and heard. In the past few months, the only two people I thought hadn't transformed from good to bad, or bad to good, were Nico and Cassie. My confidence was shaken. Substantially. Rocked but not broken.

The cab pulled up along the mouth of the alley next to the restaurant. I jumped out, leaving Jack to pay the fare. I was halfway up the stairs before I heard him enter the building. The number for the keypad was in my hand, and I was inside the office and turning on my phone to call Cassie when Jack arrived.

At precisely that moment, each of our phones rang simultaneously. I was grateful for the reprieve.

I expected mine to be Cassie, but it was Clara Ochoa instead. "Maybelle said you wanted to talk to me." Her sullen voice still carried a strong Catalan accent.

"I did. I mean, I do." I could hear Jack speaking to Cecil, his director. He'd dropped his voice to a whisper, so I knew the call was probably mission related. I moved to the far corner to give each of us some privacy. "I need to locate someone in Barcelona. Someone who trades in your former profession."

A quiet snort came through the line. I pressed on. "His name is Miguel. I know that is a very common—"

"Miguel with the scar, Miguel with the hat, or Miguel with the monkey?" she asked. "Oh, or Miguel with the limp. There is also an old Miguel."

"Ah, well..." I supposed several of those nicknames fit. Except Miguel with the monkey. I'd never seen him working with an animal. He wasn't particularly old either, but was likely in his forties, and I didn't know how Clara quantified age. "He just went back to Barcelona in the last week. He's been here in London—"

"Oh, you mean Sweet Miguel."

"Maybe—"

"Brown hair, middle aged, wears a cap to cover his bald spot?"

"Sounds right," I said. "Why do you call him Sweet Miguel?"

"He's a soft touch. Tries to help everyone, even when he gets nothing out of it."

Something told me that her use of "sweet" wasn't a compliment.

"Any idea how I can find him when I get to the city?" I asked.

"I could go with you and find him."

"You have a new job, Clara. You don't want to risk that."

She whispered several Catalan words I didn't know, but her inflection told me they were swear related. "I may be ready for a change soon."

"If you help by giving me information on how to find Miguel," I said, "I'll see what I can do for you when I get back."

A long breath came through the phone, then she said, "I need to make some calls. Wait for me to call you back. I will try to do so by tomorrow."

Since I had no choice, I replied, "Thank you, Clara. I truly appreciate any information."

"And you promise to help me get out of the laundry?"

"You know you can trust me."

"I will call back."

And the line went dead.

While Jack finished up his call, I paged through my messages and pulled up the internet boards, but there was no word from Cassie, and I also didn't see anything that remotely seemed to come from Nico.

All the facts swirled around in my brain. But several things stood out clearly, and whether I liked it or not, the facts needed to be thoroughly discussed with Jack and Cassie.

Jack finished his call with Cecil and turned, saying, "I wa—"

And my phone rang again. This time, it was Cassie. I ignored him and answered. "Your timing couldn't have been better, Cass," I said. "Are you someplace you can talk freely?"

"Yes, I'm in my hotel room."

"And you're alone?" I hopped up to sit on the table.

"Yes, why?"

I switched the call to speaker and set the phone on the wooden tabletop, equal distance between us. "Because Jack and I saw something earlier we all need to discuss. Jack, why don't you take it from here?"

"Okay," he said, but frowned. He probably thought I was laying a trap for him, and he could have been correct. I wasn't totally sure by this point. Mostly, I wanted to hear his take on things. See what impressions he had that warred with my own. Discover what I might have subconsciously picked up that he hadn't and vice versa.

But his delivery was almost with military precision, focused on fact and devoid of opinion. As he laid everything out, Cassie gasped several times, the loudest at Rollie's name. When Jack mentioned the lack of restraints, she asked, "Are you sure one of them didn't have a weapon hidden?"

"If he did, he got it through airport security," Jack replied.

"Oh, yeah, right," Cassie said.

"But we can't discount threats of violence," I said.

Jack frowned. "Nico moved freely—"

"We don't know what was said before they entered the area with the surveillance cameras," I argued.

When we finished, she asked, "So are you saying—or trying not to say—that Nico has gone over to the other side?"

"I'm simply explaining what was presented on the video file," he said.

"What we believe we saw on the video file," I clarified.

He frowned at me. "What? You're not saying you think the films were switched or something?"

"No. I'm just not ready to conclude everything was exactly as it appeared."

He didn't respond. Instead, he leaned against the nearby wall and crossed his arms.

But Cassie asked, "What are you saying, Laurel?"

Mentally, I tried to herd the wild thoughts in my head, going for some logical list. "I guess I'll jump to my chief concern. We can hit the minor points when we need to. If Nico switched sides, and is working for Rollie, why did he send the video of me stealing the painting? Sending it the way he did implied the people holding him were either the people we took the painting from or the kidnappers were the thieves who wanted to switch out a forgery for the original. Or, as we initially believed, he was warning me there was a video that showed me in my disguise. Regardless of the possible meaning, the one thing coming clearly in any scenario is he was warning me that I was recorded stealing the masterpiece."

"Okay," Cassie said. Jack remained silent.

"So, if he works for them, why didn't he grab the painting from Clive before he left for Switzerland? Give it to the other side?"

"He didn't have time?" she suggested.

"If he wanted to grab a painting worth millions, he would have done so."

"He doesn't know we know what we do, and he left the painting so we wouldn't suspect he's a double agent?" Jack said.

I shook my head. "If he's conning us, he could have retrieved the painting, then left with Rollie and the others. Or if he's truly going along of his own free will, but his errand would disrupt their schedule, wouldn't they let him catch a later flight so he could retrieve a priceless work of art? After all, if they moved up their forgery operation so much they could only provide two copies instead of the regular four or five, the Caravaggio painting is important to the thieves."

"Oh, yeah, very good point," Cassie said over the phone line.

Jack moved away from the wall and closer to me and the cell. "You're saying instinct tells you he remains above all scrutiny?"

"I'll entertain any idea you want to present, once you explain away the point I just made," I said.

He reached up and scratched the back of his neck. It could have been because he'd just had a haircut, but my money said it was based on more than a few itchy hairs. "Rollie would know from watching the video the person in the cat suit was you. Well, I would know, so I'm assuming he would recognize your shape and movements too."

My face felt warm, but I didn't speak.

"So the video link could be Nico's way of warning you. But the theory could apply equally if he is working for them," Jack finished. "There are a couple of ways the theory could work."

"But why would he warn me, if he knew they were going to try to kidnap me when I picked up the pieces from Clive?" I asked. "If we assume one thing, we have to assume the other."

"What?" Cassie cried.

Oops. Guess I should have briefed her on my previous afternoon's adventures before I mentioned anything. I took the next few minutes to bring her up to date on the kidnap attempt, the rescue by Lincoln, and the tall young man from the lobby of the Ritz whom I believed was my mugger later the same night.

"Why didn't you tell me about this earlier when you admitted you'd been mugged?" she asked. "And where was Leif when this happened?"

I ignored the first question and focused on answering the follow-up.

"He's somewhere in Norway celebrating his mother's birthday."

"But you said—"

"No, you assumed," I stopped her. "And I let you because you were already in Paris, and I didn't want to deal with the fallout from Max if you tried to come back to London."

We were all silent for several beats. Now I had two people mad at me. Eventually, Cassie asked, "What do we do?"

Good question. I looked at Jack. He shrugged.

"For now," he said, "we'll keep sharing any communication we receive from Nico. Laurel's point was valid, but we don't know all of the facts and need to work carefully. Keep all information between the three of us."

In a way, I wished Nico was with Ermo Colle instead of with Rollie and Moran. I may not have wanted to acknowledge Colle as my father—in fact, I didn't even know for sure if Colle was alive after I hit him in the head and left him for dead. But if Nico was with him, at least I knew he would keep my tech wizard safe as long as doing so suited his own purposes. Or while he at least believed Nico could help his operation.

However, when it came to Rollie, there was an underlying ruthless thread in the man I'd seen too often lately to ignore. Since I wasn't sure why Rollie wanted Nico, I couldn't be sure my friend would be safely released. Something told me Rollie wouldn't trust Nico, even if Nico pledged his allegiance to Moran's side. After all, Simon played double and triple spy for months without Moran's sharp mind catching the duplicity. It was Rollie who had spotted Simon's possible treachery to all and had the cad followed to be sure. It was also Rollie who ordered Simon to be picked up, and who ultimately ordered his execution. I had a feeling Rollie didn't trust too many people at this point, a sentiment I understood too well. However, I wasn't ready to throw away my support of Nico.

Then, of course, there was the new puzzler Jack revealed about who might truly be in line for Moran's empire. If Paul-Henri was actually my father, was Moran thinking about pulling me in because he trusted me to a greater extent than he did Rollie? Or was he planning to gift me the design firm—and whatever strings would be attached to it? Either way, that path led to madness, and I could see how Rollie would resent me even if I swore I didn't want to be over any phase of the empire. The clean operation or the crooked. Maybe taking Nico was a part of that. I'd have to bring it up to Jack later, however, since I wasn't ready to reveal the information to Cassie.

"Humor me a minute," I said, rubbing my hands up and down my arms. I wasn't cold, but I wasn't feeling very comfortable either. Too much to think about. "Pretend you're Nico. Give me any reason you can think of that would mean appearing to leave willingly with Rollie, but not taking the painting with you."

"If Rollie didn't know I had the painting," Cassie replied. "If I wanted to sell it myself."

As she talked, Jack half-circled the table and slipped his blazer on my shoulders. "I'm not really cold," I whispered.

"I know," he whispered back.

And I realized I was probably suffering from the many shocks of the day. My nerves were on overload. He'd noticed. I mouthed, *Thank you,* then called out to Cassie, "You think he'd do it to pull a con on Rollie?"

"A con..." she mused. "Maybe go with them or they would snatch Laurel. They wouldn't even have to be after the painting. That would be enough for anyone on this team to agree to go."

"I can believe that," Jack said, walking around me to lean on the tabletop. "If they gave him no option." His gaze met mine and held it. His voice softened. "It would be enough for me."

A lump formed in my throat, so I was glad when Cassie said, "Ooh, I like this theory. It's exactly what any of us would do. But if he went to keep her from getting taken, why was she attacked twice yesterday evening?"

Jack rubbed his chin. "The theory for Nico works if two factions continue working against us," he said. "Especially if Moran is still trying to protect Laurel. If they saw the robbery video, recognized her, put it all together, and said they'd take Laurel if he didn't come along."

"Except Nico and I aren't replacements for one another. He's more behind the scenes than I am, both digitally and figuratively," I said. "His talents complement mine, but they're quite different."

Jack took my hand in his, then cupped my chin with his other hand, keeping eye contact the entire time. "If Moran's group was the one who kidnapped Nico in Rome," he said. "Whatever they took him for at that time likely hasn't changed. If I were Nico, and they came telling me they could only protect you if I came with them, I'd pull my passport and get onto the plane. No arguments."

I didn't feel the least bit cold anymore. But in the back of my mind I worried Jack was trying to sidetrack me.

"Yes," Cassie said, completely unaware of anything going on but the puzzle. "And your idea would make sense if we still figure Colle is the one trying to steal the painting by swapping it with a forgery."

He raised his eyebrows and mouthed, *Still angry?*

I shrugged and mouthed, *Miffed. But better.*

Your loyalty is showing. He leaned in close as Cassie kept up a monologue.

"Rollie wouldn't even ask about the painting because it wasn't their deal," she said. "Nico left it behind without contacting you because they must have shown up suddenly, and he couldn't call or text without their knowing. And he didn't want to tip off Rollie about the masterpiece. But he—Nico—knew you'd get in touch with Clive when he didn't show up at your hotel room—"

I pushed Jack away. "Wait a minute! Yes, yes, that all makes sense." I jumped off the table to pace. "I had the feeling all along the grabs were Colle instead of Moran because there were too many people onsite. Just like when he had us followed from Italy to Germany." I stopped and faced Jack and the phone. "If Colle's the one who shipped the two copies, then Moran is the one trying to sell the copy at the auction."

"Or vice versa," Jack said, cocking his head to the side.

"Yes, exactly, and if it plays out that the opposite is true then it's just as clear," I said.

"Huh?"

"Yeah," Jack seconded. "Care to have a go about that 'clear' comment?"

Folding my hands in front of my face, I paused for a moment to collect my thoughts. "Okay, here's what we have. If Nico is still on our side—as I continue believing—" I might have sent a glare Jack's way, "—he left to protect someone on the team."

"Likely you," Cassie said. Jack crossed his arms and looked annoyed. I kind of got that annoyed vibe myself.

"Maybe. But it doesn't matter. What does matter is he didn't take the painting, but someone immediately tried to kidnap me after I picked it up. Which points to me being followed. Why would I be followed by anyone but Colle if Nico is working with Rollie to insure my safety?"

"If that's why he's with Rollie," Jack said.

I held up my hands, palms out. "Let's stick with one theory for a moment. Extending the hypothesis points to Colle knowing I was there to pick up the painting. If that's the case, his group sent the two copies, which means he has nothing to do with the illegal auction. But if that assumption is correct, it means—"

Cassie cut in, "Moran's group is running the auction and wants Nico to help him retrieve the painting. Rollie doesn't realize it was Laurel in the video."

"That's another option," Jack said, picking up the phone and walking toward me.

"But you don't believe it," she replied.

"I didn't say that."

"Your tone did," she said.

I put fingers to my right temple. My abated headache was returning.

"Don't start arguing, we don't have the time. And, no, what Cassie said isn't exactly what I was thinking. I had been saying we need to either find out something about the auction, or we need to get to Barcelona and find Miguel and determine if there's a way we can attend the auction ourselves."

"That's completely out of the question. Your picture will be with every member of Colle's security team," Jack said.

"Why would he be there if he planned to swap out the painting before it was sent to the auction? The copies are gone, confiscated, and we took the original. He has no reason to attend. It could be the safest place in the world for me, and it lets us see what other players might be a part of this."

"We were tossing out theories. We can't risk your life on what-ifs."

I stopped pacing again and faced him, resting hands on my hips. Cassie's voice spluttered over the phone, and it was almost comical the way he held out the cell so I could hear.

"Cass, quit trying to find words to convince me," I said, then looked at Jack and smiled. "Moran did not try to kidnap me or send a man to knock me down and steal my luggage. The logical assumption is both assaults were from Colle's group. We don't know why Nico went off with Rollie in what seems to be an agreeable manner, but why did he need a three-man escort if he was a willing participant? And why did he send the messages he did if he switched sides? He could have disappeared much easier than Simon ever did."

"And take the painting and sell it to whoever wanted it," Cassie's voice added.

I nodded. Jack frowned.

"Which brings us back to our only lead on this thing," I said. "We know two copies of the painting were confiscated in Calais. But around the same time, the Caravaggio painting was to be sent to the auction. We need to make sure a Caravaggio gets onto that auction block."

"Give up the painting?" Jack and Cassie said simultaneously.

I shook my head. "I said 'a' Caravaggio. Not 'the' Caravaggio. I want to take one of the copies with us to Barcelona. Can you get one, Jack?"

"Let me make some calls," he said. "I can try. But what about the original?"

"I'm going with the initial plan Nico and I were following, to send the masterpiece back to New York with Max. All our theories point to Nico not being held in trade for the painting, and his messages didn't say anything suggesting it either. For that reason, I don't want the true Caravaggio anywhere near me. All the clues point to it not being the way to get Nico released, but it could be a Colle magnet. The faster it gets out of my proximity, the better."

"But I should stress secrecy, right?" Cassie asked.

"Absolutely," I said. "Standard spin. Risk to the source. That sort of thing."

"Got it," she replied. "There is another thing you do need to check on, Laurel. When I tried to use the corporate credit card to pay for my room last night, the clerk couldn't get it to process. He just tacked my room charges onto Max's. I didn't mention it earlier because I was going to call the bank myself, but this is really the first private moment I've had and I need to get back—"

"Yeah, I'll call our account manager myself. Don't mention it to Max until we know something. His first thought would be I blew the budget again, and it's likely just an accounting error," I said, speaking calmly and decisively. Inside, however, I felt my trust foundations start shaking again. I worried that Nico took something more liquid than a Caravaggio painting.

THIRTEEN

The next hour was comprised of a lot of phone calls and juggled schedules. I speed-dialed the bank and within minutes learned the money allocated to the London Beacham Foundation office for operations and physical repairs to our previous premises now totaled a lovely one-pound-eight. That's right, less than a couple of American dollars. The only saving grace was that the authorization code used for the transfer was Max's instead of mine.

"Okay, great," I said to the helpful bank manager. Then I lied like a dog. "I'm sorry we let the balance get so low. I'll order another deposit be made shortly."

I hung up and dropped my face into my hands.

Jack was still talking to customs. "The copies have already been sent on to London? Yes. Who's the contact at Scotland Yard? Brilliant. Thank you." He hung up and asked, "Bad news?"

I dropped cross-legged to the floor and leaned back against one of the table's thick legs. "The office is broke, and according to the bank, the money was transferred by Max to an account in Italy. Though we both know who really has the cash. Between this transfer and the video, I have to admit it; you and Cassie were right. As hard as it is to say out loud."

"Want to talk about it?"

"God, no! Give me one shred of dignity."

Jack joined me on the floor. "I know this has to be difficult."

My laugh was weak. "Yeah, difficult. That's a good word for it. Next we're going to find out Cassie is my father's longtime girlfriend."

"I thought you had Melody holding that dishonor," Jack said. "Outside the casino at Baden-Baden—"

"I know, I know. Yes." As I'd escaped in a borrowed BMW to run back to our hotel and wait for Rollie's guys to rescue Jack—it all still sounded crazy to me—I saw one of my staunchest enemies, Melody Weeks, director of The Browning, disembarking from the back of a long limousine to enter the casino where Ermo Colle was supposed to be. Except when he pulled a gun on me, I'd knocked him out with a weapon Moran gave me, then ran. Thinking about all of it again didn't make it sound any less crazy. "Have you located a trace of Melody yet?"

"Only that she tendered her resignation via email to The Browning's board the day after we were in Baden-Baden," Jack said. "I've left messages for someone to call me if they hear from her, but my checks through customs connections have her only appearing in Germany. Nowhere else since. The open borders via the European Union can make tracking somewhat difficult, but I thought we'd have better luck with her being American."

"Unless Colle has provided her with a second identity too."

"There's always that," he said. "Are you going to get the records emailed from the bank?"

I sighed. "Not yet. But I have to call the construction firms and try to buy some time. Since today is the end of the month, all the invoices should be hitting here soon. I honestly don't know what I'm going to do. I'm not sure if I'm more devastated by the loss of the money and the stress that will entail, or getting scammed by Nico."

He caught my hand and gave it a squeeze. I was so glad he didn't try to hold me, as I would have probably started crying and that would have only made me angrier about everything. Especially Nico's betrayal. This one hurt worse than Simon. Or my father. And a tiny part of me continued whispering not to give up yet. I was such a putz.

"How much are we talking?" he asked.

"All of the money pegged for the construction repairs, and

you've seen for yourself the destruction Simon left behind when he and his crew blew through. Our February operating funds were deposited a couple of days ago, so the totals include my salary and Cassie's, as well as utility bills, funds for upcoming travel, rent..." I shrugged. "You get the picture."

"Yeah, I do."

"And Max will totally blame me because...well, it was Nico, and Nico never respected authority. Maybe Max will give Cassie my job and I can work for her. He likes Cassie."

"Stop beating yourself up. Let's—"

"Let's talk copies." I took my hand away and pushed up from the floor. "You're right. Beating myself up does no good. Catching a bad guy does." But try as I might, I couldn't force myself to add Nico to that side of the balance sheet. I'd have to work on it, after I wiped the apologetic look off Jack's face. "Don't look at me like that. Tell me what customs said."

"Since this shipment was confiscated in a French port, it's a lucky thing I said copies all along instead of forgeries," he began.

Under French law, if Calais learned the works were created as forgeries, the paintings would have been destroyed.

I said, "True. The ruthlessly quick turnaround of French confiscation and destruction of forgeries might be why the paintings we've found were all listed as copies. So far, the snuffbox that started this chase is the only thing trying to ride in as a legitimate work of art. And the ruse worked until Nico examined it in Miami."

"Our customs officials took possession of the substitute Caravaggio works, and I talked to the agent," he told me. "A letter was sent to the address listed on the manifest requesting the copies be picked up at Scotland Yard. He checked and no one has come to collect the shipment. Yesterday, they sent an officer to the address. The report back listed an empty storefront and a 'for let' sign in the window."

"Leading anyone to presume the person who was meant to pick up the dodgy copies never will."

"Scotland Yard is operating under that presumption and it matches my thinking as well."

"They will let us have at least one copy, right?" I asked.

"I'm working on it. I have a couple of calls in, and the agent was running interference for us as well, but the outlook is good. I may be letting certain people assume it ties to a current case I'm working."

"The gun connection?"

He reiterated, "I'm just saying a current case."

Alrighty then. I recognized an Official Secrets Act warning when I almost heard it.

A minute later my phone dinged with a text. Cassie had returned to her Paris meeting and pulled Max away to speak with him in private. Per our plan, she revealed the "wonderful news" of how I'd been tasked with returning the missing Caravaggio to its true owner. She explained my source wouldn't say where the painting had been but was aware it was on stolen lists and trusted the foundation to deliver it to the rightful family and take full credit for the recovery. My assistant, bless her, knew the drill when I wanted secrets kept. Max, of course, had to call and try to weasel additional details, but I was ready for him.

"I'm sworn to secrecy," I said. "If word gets out how this painting came to me, it would put my source in grave danger."

"Ah, yes," Max said, his voice practically normal volume. Other people's normal volume, that is. "He's undertaken a great risk. Absolutely. But to get the okay to remove it from English soil, I'm going to need Scotland Yard's help, and I may be asked—"

"I understand your dilemma, Max." Inwardly, I laughed at how he assumed the person who returned the work was a man. "But it simply cannot be helped. My source delivered the work to me and gave no additional details other than it should be returned and is known for being on our lookout list. I have no idea who stole the painting originally, and I can't even be sure of all the places it may have been in the interim years. You're going to have to call in some favors if necessary, but I have nothing to offer law enforcement."

Jack smirked and shook his head as I said the last phrase.

Now came the hard part. "This really must stay quiet, Max. If the family decides to make the recovery public, we can't do anything about that. But until the work leaves the hands of foundation personnel, we need to make sure the thieves, or any others who might be interested in the painting, do not find out where it is. Otherwise, we risk losing it again." I added extra insurance. "And that wouldn't look good on your watch."

"Oh, right, right. Agree absolutely," Max said.

After a few minutes of discussion, him talking and me listening, he put Cassie back on the line.

"He sounds like he's forgiven me for being out of pocket when he wanted me there," I said softly.

"Correct, let me get those papers," she said, ad-libbing while Max remained within earshot. I waited for her to get far enough away to speak privately, and she came back on the line. "Are you still there?"

"Yes."

She laughed. "Laurel, the man is positively preening he's so excited. He's raced away to tell the donor about this coup for the foundation."

"He just agreed—"

"Don't worry," Cassie cut in. "He promised not to give specifics. Your line about it being on his watch was inspired, by the way. He's excited, but he understands the risk."

"I hope you're right," I said. I felt a burn in my stomach just the same. "When are you and Max coming to London?"

"Sometime tomorrow. Will you and Jack be around?"

"I don't know, but my first guess would be no. If we get any idea how to proceed, we're going to take it, which at this point looks to mean heading for Barcelona. The painting is currently in a safe, so if I leave I'll try to fill out paperwork to get the hotel to let you—"

"No, I have a better idea," she said. "Remember the *special* wall I showed you that I discovered in my flat?"

Cassie had been renovating her floor in a historic mid-nineteenth century townhouse just off Portobello Road. When it was originally built, the room that became her lounge had a secret hiding space. The cache either was not discovered during previous maintenance and renovations, or had been left abandoned and papered over. Once she'd removed the wallpaper and found the spring to release the locking mechanism, Cassie re-camouflaged the hidey-hole with period faux wallboard instead.

"Yes," I said. "I believe the size will be about perfect. Good thinking." We said our goodbyes, and I recapped everything for Jack. "My hotel is a definite stop anyway, to see if they have photos of the tall thin man who asked for me ahead of the mugging. While we're there, we can go into the safe room and clear out the box. Then I can go upstairs and pack."

"Might be better to get you packed first, so we can leave directly after we pick up the other things," Jack suggested as we put on coats.

"Shouldn't we make plane reservations before we leave here?" I pointed at the ceiling and made a circle with my finger. "This wi-fi is probably more secure than my hotel's."

He nodded. "Undoubtedly. But I don't know for sure if we'll have the Caravaggio copy this evening. My conversation sounded hopeful, but..."

"You're right. We need to do this in the best order."

"Besides," he added, as he checked the outside cameras then opened the door, "I think we're going to do all travel booking in person this trip. If Rollie makes Nico hack into my credit card, he'll be able to see the booking, but if we're already in the air and halfway to Spain it won't give him much time to plan any reception committee."

I swallowed hard when I heard the reference to his credit card. He was trying to make things easier on me, I knew that, but it still felt like another blow to the instincts I'd always counted on.

"We'll take my car and leave it with your hotel's valet parking," he said as we reached ground level. "Be safer that way, and we can use cabs wherever we need to go."

"Okay."

On the way to my hotel, however, Jack suddenly decided on a detour by the Ritz.

"I should have thought of going by there before," he said. "I can get Halborn's mugshot sent to me from the Met Police, but I didn't think about the two men you saw in the lobby."

"Fine with me. But if the desk clerk kept his word, we should have a decent shot of the younger man from my hotel's security footage."

At the Ritz, it didn't take Jack long to get the right person to help with our request. I checked my phone's call log to be sure when the call came from Cassie that had sent me out into the lobby from the bar less than twenty-four hours earlier. A few keystrokes later, we were viewing the men in question on the security monitors, seeing them from several angles. Security printed off copies of the two men leaving and the younger man returning, but all the shots either showed the men's heads turned away from the cameras, hands to their faces as they left the building, or with their heads together talking so it was hard to see all the features of either person.

"Suspicious," the Ritz security guy said.

Jack and I agreed, thanking him for the pictures.

It was another short drive to my hotel. Jack and I left the car with the valet and headed to my room. The call we'd been waiting on came as I packed. After Jack hung up, he said, "The Caravaggio copy will be packaged up for us and waiting at Scotland Yard. We can pick it up while we share our photos with Whatley."

"Have you connected with Superintendent Whatley yet?"

"Just by text. Guess it would be best to ring him."

While Jack called Scotland Yard, I added toiletries to my load. I packed light for a change. Though I did add a little black dress to cover all bases, and a wig and my cat suit. Just in case I needed alternative methods to get in somewhere people already knew me—and wouldn't let me in looking like myself.

Everything else stayed casual, but could be dressed up for

dinner. We weren't planning nights out, but with my personal career track I knew to always be prepared for every eventuality.

The phone conversation ended. Jack pocketed his cell phone and roamed the room. I stepped into my closet and assessed what I needed from my locked gadget bag. Two of the electronic wonders went into the Prada, because they'd always gotten through security without any issues. I slid the other two into a couple of shoe bags protecting a pair of black and silver Louboutins, and I worked the stilettos with their bonus cargo into an interior spot in my bag.

"Why don't you have anything to snack on in your refrigerator?" Jack stood peering into the tiny fridge by the desk.

"Because I eat out all of the time."

"So do I, but I still have snacks. You have iced coffee, a yogurt, and a sad apple."

"The sad apple shows why I don't keep food in my hotel room fridge." I pulled out a sweater I'd changed my mind about taking. "I'm not here enough. It goes bad. What do you have in yours?"

"I don't know. Grapes. Kiwi. Hummus—"

"Hummus?"

"Hummus. It's good for you. Has chickpeas. Chickpeas have melatonin. Helps you sleep," he said.

"You have problems sleeping?"

He laughed. "Yeah, I can always use more sleep."

"What do you do when you can't sleep?" I reset the bags with the stilettos so the clothes fit better in the suitcase.

"I eat hummus and kiwis."

"Weird combo."

"They both help induce sleep in a few hours."

"Good to know." I tried to zip the bag, but one of the corners was still too high.

He continued his refrigerator stare-down. "You don't even have a takeaway carton in here. Everyone has takeaway in the fridge."

"What's your favorite takeout food?"

"Curry."

"That doesn't help you sleep."

"Which is why I keep hummus and kiwi. What's your favorite takeaway?"

"You'll laugh."

"No, I won't," he coaxed, walking over to help hold down the corner of the bag.

"Bet you will."

"Try me."

I shrugged. "McDonald's Happy Meals."

He snorted.

"Stop. You said you wouldn't laugh."

"I'm sorry." But he continued to chortle. "Small hamburger and chips?"

"No, I've gone healthy and take the fruit. Remember the sad apple." The zipper finally made it all the way around the bag.

"You like the prize?"

"Sometimes. Most I give away to children acting nicely on the train."

"Bet you had all the tiny Beanie Babies."

"Of course." I put my hands on my hips and pivoted to take in the room and check if I'd forgotten anything. "I was still in elementary school then—primary school to you, of course—and our chauffeur had a Happy Meal and a different teeny stuffed animal for me every time he picked me up in town."

"Your chauffeur."

"Yes. He's the one who introduced me to *Mad Magazine* too. I loved the back cover with the secret message fold."

"Happy Meal and a prize."

"But that's not what I love about them."

He raised a questioning eyebrow.

"I love the cookies. The tiny chocolate chip cookies. Knowing I always have a dessert." I went back into the closet.

Through the wall I heard, "Those are pretty dry biscuits."

"Ah, so you have eaten Happy Meals."

"No, I used to buy the chocolate chip biscuits."

"That's unbelievably wrong."

"Why?" He'd moved to stand by the door.

Deciding I had everything I needed, I came out again. "I don't know. It just is." I rubbed a hand against his cheek and felt the beginnings of what would become a sexy five o'clock shadow. "Obviously, I have some things to teach you."

A couple of strides took me back to the bed and the roller bag. In a row, I lined up that suitcase and my big purse by the door.

"Is that it?" he asked, a surprised look on his face.

I nodded. "I think so."

"One bag. I'm impressed."

"Me too. But I've already lost my garment bag this week with my favorite outfits of the moment. I want to keep what I take to a minimum and try to not catch any additional bad juju."

"I don't think luck has anything to do with it," he said. "Good, bad, or otherwise. You fell prey to someone else's agenda."

I shrugged. He could say what he wanted, but it was my closet that continually emptied of clothing and accessories which too often didn't return. "Before we leave the room, I want to call Clara."

When I dialed her number I immediately got voicemail. I left a message, but called Maybelle and counted my good fortune when she answered.

"I have a minute. Did you connect with Clara?" she asked. Her Brussels accent came through strong.

"Yes, she called me." I explained the earlier conversation and how the sharp-thinking young hustler wanted me to get her promoted out of the laundry job as payment for any help she managed to provide.

"Oh, these girls, these girls," Maybelle said. "I'll see what I can do to make sure she gets the information you need. But I'm not in favor of letting her coerce people into giving her better job opportunities."

"I understand where you're coming from, but if she's truly miserable—"

"She's as happy or unhappy as she wants to be," Maybelle

stopped me. "But I will talk to her and see if there are any changes that can be made. Can I say the three of us will meet about this when you return?"

"Fabulous way to word it. I don't want her to think I'm taking advantage of her."

She laughed. "Clara should be kissing your feet. If you hadn't sent her here she'd likely be in jail. The girl is smart. She knows. But spending so much of her life picking pockets and operating under her own counsel makes it difficult for her to be happy about schedules and managers."

We promised to meet for lunch soon, though it was simply talk since neither of us ever found the time. We hung up, and I took another second to scan the room and review my mental checklist before we left. Jack grabbed my bag. I turned off the light and we headed for the elevators.

At the front desk the clerk was the same one who helped me the previous evening, so I didn't have to explain why we stopped by.

"Security found a couple of good likenesses," he said, pulling a large envelope from below the counter. "We were going to report it to the police, but the doorman thought you wanted to take care of it yourself."

I thanked him and nodded. "We're heading to Scotland Yard now, and we'll share these prints. I've no doubt my belongings are long gone, but at least they'll have a record of the thief. I never thought about him hanging around to steal my things after he acted like he'd left."

"Oh, no," the clerk said. "The man who knocked you down was much older. Here, take a look."

He opened the envelope and pulled out several photos that not only showed a clear, full-faced shot of the tall, thin young man asking for me at the front desk, but images with a timestamp that showed it was the older beefy man from the hallway at the Ritz who barreled into me and swiped my bag. Jack and I looked at each other and smiled. They might have avoided the Ritz's cameras, but the ones at this hotel captured their faces beautifully.

*   *   *

"Still, it's good to have the Ritz pictures, too," Jack said a short time later, as our cab sped toward Cassie's flat. The tube with the art sat on the seat beside us. "The men's body language in those first camera shots showed they were up to something."

"Definitely," I said. "At this point, every new fact has to help somehow. We're due a break."

"Overdue."

We could have made it to our destination quicker via the Underground, but neither of us was keen on carrying a priceless masterpiece into such a public venue. I'd kept it under my coat as we'd moved from the hotel to the cab, but I felt like a neon sign flashed overhead shouting *Here it is!* London traffic was stop and go and irritating as hell, but we used the time to trade ideas and bring each other up to date on any points we hadn't covered already.

The plan was to head to Jack's flat after we secreted the painting at Cassie's, then go straight to Scotland Yard. Superintendent Whatley promised to stay in his office until we made it by with the photos. After we picked up the Caravaggio copy, the next phase was to head directly to Heathrow.

Jack asked the cabbie to wait when we reached Cassie's flat, and I slid the tube under my long coat before exiting the vehicle. It wasn't late, but the days were shorter and dusk had already fallen. The tall bushes along the side of the property blocked the streetlights in the area directly around the door, but I knew from experience where the lock was positioned, and we weren't having to break in. I had the key ready when we got to the outer door.

The building was unlit, but the automatic light in the stairway came on as we hit the first tread. Too early for most people to be home yet from work. Each flat took an entire floor, and we climbed the stairs to reach Cassie's on the first floor.

The automatic light came on in her short hall when I approached the door with the flat key. When I got inside, however,

I left off the flat lights and stopped Jack before he flipped a switch.

"Let's just be safe, okay?" I punched in the code to turn off the alarm. "I think I can do this with the ambient light in the room."

The curtains were drawn. I moved over to the relative area of the hidden wall. A remote light on the television and the small green light shining from the surge suppressor bar gave off more light than one might expect. After doing so much of my non-foundation work in low light like this, I felt comfortable feeling my way through the exercise. Seconds later, I'd found the spring-loaded mechanism and removed the tube from where my coat had been shielding it from sight. The fit was perfect if I put the tube in diagonally. But to make sure Cassie couldn't accidentally forget to only send the painting, I first withdrew the small statuary and wrapped it in a knitted scarf she'd left across the back of a chair.

"Don't let me forget to text her about this," I said. "She hasn't seen the piece, so she won't recognize it. Plus, I'd hate for her to drop it as she pulls out the scarf."

"Will do."

I placed the wrapped figurine on the floor of the compartment in one corner, then angled the protected painting in the fat leather tube across the space above it. The locking mechanism slipped back easily into place, and we were ready to go.

"One question," Jack whispered. "Does Nico know about this hidden spot?"

"I don't think so. Cassie showed it to me one night when I stopped in for a cup of coffee after we saw a show. Should I ask her? Or are you just trying to anticipate pitfalls?"

"Good choice of word, pitfall," he said. "They seem to come from nowhere."

"Hopefully we're getting the jump on the next two or three," I said, leading the way back through the shadowy flat. I rekeyed the alarm and we left.

But when we got back on the front stoop, our cab was nowhere to be seen.

"Hell. I paid him extra to wait." Jack swore.

I wasn't surprised. This was my curse, of course. My carefully packed bag was tucked away in the boot of the missing cab.

FOURTEEN

I stood on the stoop, staring past the property's tall shrubbery to look as far as I could up and down the street.

"Maybe he had to park down a bit," I said. As I moved to the steps, the sound of footfalls and panting came from around the side of the building. Jack pulled me back and behind him. He leaned out and checked around the corner. "It's our cab driver," he whispered.

The cabbie stayed half-hidden by the corner of the house, but waved us to follow him back through the side alley and signaled to stay close to the building. When I started down the first riser, a bullet zinged past my ear.

Jack picked me up and tossed me over the side of the railing, then vaulted it himself. The three of us tore off down the narrow drive, staying in the shadows as much as possible. The cab sat waiting on the next street. We heard sirens in the distance.

Our driver got us inside and racing down the street before he would answer any of our questions. "Lived 'round here for a time, so I knew about that lane going clear through," he said of our escape route. "Car pulled up as you went inside, then backed a length and parked across the way. I'm ex-military. Caught my eye. Then I saw the passenger raise what appeared to be a gun and attach a silencer. Knew things could get dicey then. Phoned the police as I drove. You know the rest."

Jack said, "They likely escaped before the—"

"Here." The cabbie ripped the top sheet from a notepad suction-cupped to the windshield. "Got the plate number."

Ohmigod. I looked at the man's posted name and taxi license

number, committing both to memory. Thomas Banks could become my regular driver.

"Thank you so much," I said.

"Yes. Grateful for this," Jack said, raising the paper as a kind of mini salute. He glanced at the writing, then slipped it into his pocket.

At his flat, he told me to stay in the cab. "Scoot down below the windows. I have a go-bag packed. Be back in a tick."

He disappeared and I followed orders. Thomas kept his eyes roving throughout.

"Afghanistan?" I asked.

The cabbie nodded. He looked about forty, and from the little streetlight that hit inside the cab, I could see the start of gray at his temples and sideburns.

"Our shared countries appreciate you for your service."

He ducked his head a fraction.

"Thank you, miss."

True to his word, Jack yanked open the door right then and tossed in his bag. We reentered traffic and were on our way to Scotland Yard.

Superintendent Whatley slipped the sheet of paper Jack had given him into a file folder. "We will definitely follow up on this," he said.

Before the page disappeared, I saw the shooter's plate number and the street Cassie lived on written in Jack's strong hand. He obviously did more than grab his go-bag in the flat, and that meant he still had the number to follow up on via other channels. I just hoped the plates weren't stolen or fake.

Whatley pulled a small thin art crate from where it leaned between his desk and the wall. "I have this for you, along with documentation saying you're our representatives of the copy. I had them add your name as well, Miss Beacham, in case the two of you need to separate. This should cover any difficulties along the way, but don't hesitate to give my name if necessary. Not sure that paperwork will suit whatever purposes you have for this piece, but it should keep you both out of trouble with foreign authorities."

I noticed Whatley simply assumed we were going out of the country with the painting. A change from the quiet rebuke he once gave for our not sharing travel plans with him during an investigation. This made me wonder if Jack and I were subjects of discussions wider than we preferred. The superintendent raised a questioning eyebrow at the end of his statement, but neither of us voluntarily offered additional information. Jack's face remained firm as he responded, "That will do, thank you. Anything else we need...we'll handle."

"Very good," Whatley said. But he shrugged, so I imagined he was disappointed we weren't more forthcoming.

Couldn't be helped. Despite having let Whatley know a good part of what had gone on the last twenty-four hours, we still needed to keep anything secret about the job that we possibly could. Despite the fact our public targets status grew by the day.

"Do be careful, as I can no longer offer you a replacement on the print," Whatley said. "Officers are investigating, but it seems the second copy is no longer in the evidence lockup."

"Just one was taken?" Jack asked.

"I'm aware it sounds puzzling, especially since you've needed a copy as well." Whatley's face held an expression devoid of interest, but I recognized a fishing expedition when I saw one. "Apparently, sometime yesterday the other copy disappeared. I would have had difficulty getting this released to you, since it's the only one left, but word came down from upstairs with the okay."

I looked at my lap and whispered, "Cecil?" Out of the corner of my eye I saw Jack give a quick nod. His boss was as annoying as Max when it came to signing off on some of the expenses Jack required in the field, but when we needed help cutting British red tape, Cecil came through.

"We have no connection to anyone wanting the other reproduction, Superintendent," I said, smiling as I delivered my statement with a direct gaze. Then I risked adding to the information to shore up our façade of honesty. "But we will return this one as soon as possible. We are currently in receipt of the original of this work. The foundation I work for will be returning it to the true owner very soon. Our hope in having this copy is to learn who may have originally stolen the painting, and what plans may have been in operation for the Caravaggio in the near term. When we learned about the copies coming through Calais, it seemed a fortunate coincidence. Especially since the prospective owner of the copies appears to be nonexistent. We decided to pursue a few angles with a copy as bait."

I saw Jack tighten his jaw and knew he wasn't thrilled with my ploy. He wasn't averse to stretching the truth; he simply liked being the one spinning the facts.

Whatley reacted by first raising his chin, as if my words surprised him, then nodded. "Brilliant plan."

"For it to succeed," I continued, "we must work under complete secrecy. If word gets out that we have a copy instead..." I raised my hands, palms up, and shrugged for emphasis.

"Absolutely. All the paperwork lists the Home Office contact. The only reference to you and Hawkes is the letter," Whatley said. "I'll make sure the file copy stays safeguarded from the rest."

"Thank you."

As we walked back through the building to leave, Jack said under his breath, "Built quite the scenario there. All founded on truth. And went a long way to assuage his reservations."

"Of course. Why should I lie? You act like I have something to hide."

He chuckled. I smiled and linked my arm through his as we walked.

In the parking lot, we found Thomas's cab waiting for us under the protection of Scotland Yard security. I glanced at the trunk—I mean, the boot—and thought I might actually arrive at a destination with all my clothes this time.

Thomas dropped us at the Heathrow departures area, leaving with a generous tip and the possibility of extra work in the future.

The earliest available flight to Barcelona lifted off in two hours, so we purchased tickets and checked our bags.

"I wish there was less down time," Jack groused.

What he truly meant was he wanted us on the ground the least amount of time. "Nothing we can do about it," I said. "It'll take time to get through security. And we'll need to grab a quick bite to tide us over until dinner. We won't be able to get an evening meal in Spain until ten or after. By the time we finally make the gate it will almost be time to board the flight."

"Good point. Eating. We've been on the run all day and that fish was too long ago. Hadn't realized I was getting peckish, but you're right."

Some of us noticed, I thought, but I didn't say it out loud.

Security was a standard wait time, no problems, and from there we entered a quiet bar that served quick meals. While we waited on sandwiches, I phoned Cassie. She picked up right away.

"Everything still on track with Max?" I asked.

"Yes. We're heading back through Heathrow tonight, and Max will be in London until he gets the okay to return with the painting to New York. He's been in touch with legal authorities already, explaining he has a recovered masterpiece without naming it yet. Once he has it in hand he'll take the next steps."

"Try to stay out of it as much as you can. Don't let Max get you doing his heavy lifting."

"I agree. If I get sucked in it'll likely connect any contribution I make in the recovery with you, and throw a light on the London office that we can't afford at this point in the project. We need to keep all the attention on Max and New York."

Loved how quickly she caught on. "Everything is in the secure place we discussed last night," I said, not comfortable identifying it more clearly over the phone line. "I removed the smaller object from the protective case, since it isn't part of the recovery Max is aware of. I wrapped the second piece in one of your scarves and left it at the bottom of the hidden cache. The larger piece is still in its tube and in the space."

"Do I need to say anything about fingerprints?"

"Ah, good point." Thank goodness I'd been wearing my winter gloves when I removed the statue earlier. "No worries in that regard. If any of my prints appear on the outside of the case, they can be easily explained away. Gloves were always used on the contents inside." I hoped Clive was telling the truth when he said he hadn't investigated the items inside the tube. Had to chance it. "We're waiting for a flight now. To where we've been discussing."

"Got it," she said.

Our order arrived and Cassie and I signed off.

"All set?" Jack asked. He'd been working his own phone while she and I talked.

"Sounds like." I shrugged and picked up my sandwich, beef and Swiss cheese tucked into a large country roll. "We'll know soon. Max never hesitates to call if something I do doesn't meet his expectations." I nodded toward his phone. "Any new text whispers?"

He shook his head and set the phone down by his napkin. "Checking for messages, and I reviewed the internet boards Nico posted on. Nothing since the link you showed me this morning."

"I don't like this."

"Me either. But if this isn't what we fear and he needs help, he'll find a way to send an SOS."

I frowned. "And he has the funds to do it." I sighed. This really sucked.

I understood the situation, and the money thing had put my teeth on edge, but I wasn't ready to stop worrying about my gorgeous geek. I needed to talk to Nico before things went much farther, but I had no clue how to do so. Though, if I brought anything up and Jack tried to dissuade me, I wasn't sure how I would react. I'd never felt this conflicted, and I didn't want any negativity affecting the team.

I took a bite of my sandwich to keep from talking.

After the bar food and a scotch each, we were back to our normal irritating selves. Worry and exhaustion tended to do that to us. My body ached from not enough sleep and my head wished for the lovely Egyptian pillowcase it rested on at Marci's last night—well, early this morning.

"Just once, I'd like for us to not be on the run when we're heading someplace," I mused, taking the last sip of my scotch. "Eight hours sleep, regular meal times, is that so much to ask?"

"Evidently so," Jack said, pushing aside his plate and glass. "I'm not sure I remember what 'regular' is." He looked at his watch. "You ready?"

I nodded and we worked our way through the crowded restaurant space.

The gate wasn't far, and the flight was ready for boarding. As we filed in line past the clerk my phone rang. I looked at the screen. "It's Clara." I answered, "Hi, this is Laurel."

"I have some information," she said. "A few friends who know Miguel said the best place to locate him is at the Font Magica. Do you know it? The subway will get you there."

"Yes, I've been to the fountain several times. It's beautiful." People hurried by me on the way to the door of the plane. I stayed focused on the conversation, and Jack stayed close by. "Will Miguel be around on weekends, or is there a best day to see him onsite?"

"Weekends would be good. Lots of crowds." Then she asked, "And you know how he looks now?"

I thought about the carefully crafted short beard he'd recently shaved off. "I saw him last week, but thank you for reminding me."

"Very good. Maybelle said you spoke to her," Clara probed.

"Yes. We're all going to meet up when I return." She was fishing now, and I could tell no further information was coming my way. I slipped a hand through Jack's arm and we walked faster.

"Thank you, Laurel," Clara said.

I wanted to remind her there were no promises. But common sense told me I'd go above and beyond anyway, so it might as well be a pledge. I simply said, "You're welcome. And thank you for helping me try to locate Miguel."

FIFTEEN

A couple of hours later, we walked off the plane and through the arrival terminal in the Barcelona-El Prat International Airport. I couldn't help smiling and neither could almost everyone around me. There was a kind of vibe in the air. That was one of the things I loved about this city—along with the interesting, sexy, happy people, some of the most glorious food on the planet, amazing architecture, and Picasso's and Dalí's art. Big changes over the last couple of dozen years had made this one of the most pleasant, thriving, and livable cities in Europe, and I was a huge fan. Despite the late hour—well, early by Spanish standards—darkness falling simply meant the energy and events geared up stronger.

"You look energized," Jack said, smiling at me as we walked.

"I am. There's something magical about this place. Barcelona's sun, sea, sangria, and street food seduces me every time. I know we're here to work, but yeah, I'm feeling energized."

We climbed into the cab at the front of the taxi line.

"Well, it's not bikini temps, but better than England's presently," I said, glad to stuff my scarf in a coat pocket.

Jack chuckled and gave the cabbie the name of the hotel we'd decided on. Though both of us had been there before, our cabbie pointed out sites along the way, like Casa Milá, an organic and curvy apartment building resembling a hill full of caves with no color except for the stone's ochre shade, one of the many famous Barcelona buildings designed by Antoni Gaudí, the Spanish Catalan architect best known for Catalan Modernism. I hoped we'd have time to go by Gaudí's Sagrada Familia cathedral, too, still about fifty years away from completion but amazing from every angle.

Our hotel was just off La Ramblas. Jack got us a suite and we dropped off our bags. Before we left, however, I pulled a long black cashmere sweater from my suitcase and swapped it for my light-colored coat.

Jack rubbed my shoulder. "I like it."

"Because it's soft?" I asked, wrapping my arms around his neck.

"No." He pulled me closer. "Because you won't stand out like a beacon in the crowd like you would in that champagne leather number."

"But champagne and Barcelona go together," I whispered.

"That's cava, and I'll make sure you have any amount of sparkling wine you want." Our lips met, and it took a lot to remind us we didn't have time for romance.

"Later," Jack promised and sighed, his forehead resting on mine.

"Right."

We grabbed our keys and headed for the door, ready to scope out the scene and try to spot trouble before intercepting Miguel. Neither of us had noticed any tails, but it didn't stop our concerns. With just a short time before the fountain's evening show, we struck off down La Ramblas to watch for watchers.

La Ramblas was a street in the city center, about a mile long, still filled with plenty of authentic charm. With unerring precision, we headed for La Boqueria, the famous market that had been around since anyone could remember. We found a wine bar and grabbed a glass of sangria—it seemed the thing to do—and pretended to meander through the middle, fresh produce and seafood visible at every turn. I swept my gaze around constantly, encompassing all the people around us as we oohed and ahhed over the merchandise. No one looked familiar.

Jack spoke to one of the flower sellers. He'd said he knew a little Catalan, but tonight he spoke Spanish; I, on the other hand, kept a good language translation book in the Prada. The one thing I did see often in English were chalkboard signs warning "Beware of Pickpockets." Since we'd specifically come to find one, it seemed ironic.

When Jack turned around he had two red roses for me, the stems wrapped in a protective layer of damp paper towels and plastic wrap.

"Watch out for the thorns," he said.

"They aren't razored off?"

He shrugged. "She said it was good luck, and I figured we needed whatever we could get."

It was likelier good laziness, but the flowers smelled heavenly and nothing sharp bit through the wrapping.

"Have you seen anyone to worry about?" he asked.

"Not yet, but it will be interesting to see if anyone we've spotted here decides to take in the dancing waters, too," I replied.

Since the Liceu Metro Station sat under La Ramblas between Gran Teatre del Liceu—the Grand Theater—and the Mercat de la Boqueria, which was the market where we'd been shopping in the Barri Gòtic section, we were close to our objective. We passed Joan Miró's mosaic mural, the eye-catching masterpiece he crafted into the pavement. The street art always made me smile, and my gaze strayed to the tile that bore the artist's signature.

We bought our paper tickets and boarded the train to the Montjuïc neighborhood and the Font Magica, or Magic Fountain. Every city had its sights, and this was one of my favorites in Barcelona. Yes, I had a lot of favorites.

The fountain was an amazing sight at any time of the day, but arriving when it was fully dark was critical to gaining the best effect, and was why pickpockets like Miguel chose it as a location to ply their trade. Marks focused on the performing water jets, lights, and music and forgot to safeguard their valuables.

"Have you been here for La Merce?" Jack asked.

"Many times." I smiled, thinking of the late Septembers I'd spent in Barcelona when the city put on their *fiesta mayor*—La

Merce. During the "festival to end all festivals," as many as two million visitors swarmed into this city to celebrate living. The Font Magica remained the chosen site for the Piromusical, which blended the fountain masterpiece with fireworks, music, and a laser light show. If I'd attended this past year, instead of planning the Tahoe vacation that got scrubbed, I might have suspected earlier what Simon was up to, since he always attended. Before so many forgers were killed.

Of course, the biggest problem with trying to locate Miguel at Font Magica was twofold. First, no pickpocket liked to be interrupted during business hours, and two, the scene was unbelievably huge. The largest of Barcelona's ornamental fountains, Font Magica was designed by Carles Buigas and built in 1929 for the International Exhibition. In 1992, it was lovingly restored to help show off Barcelona when they hosted the Summer Olympics. The moving water jets performed a magic dance in coordination with the colored lights and music, the water unfolding, rising, falling, hiding, then bursting out to the delight of the crowds.

But tonight, it was a job. The Museu Nacional d'Art de Catalunya was nearby, and we joined the crowd heading for the Font Magica de Montjuïc, just down the steps from the museum. The four majestic columns beckoned the masses, as the lights shifted hues and shades, and the music swelled with the cascading water.

"Should we split up?" I asked. I'd already given him a description of Miguel.

"Not on your life," Jack replied. "There are too many people here, and too many ways I might lose you." As if to punctuate the statement, he took hold of my right hand.

The crowds were happy and thick. I kept a tight hold on the Prada, using my left elbow to secure the bag on my shoulder and against my body, holding the roses in the hand clutching the purse strap for extra insurance.

It was difficult searching for one person while also scanning for anyone else who might pose a danger to our operation. After finally returning too many times to the same group of people who posed no risk, I pulled Jack to the edge of the crowd and said, "I think it might work better if I just focus on Miguel, and you watch out for anyone who looks too interested in us."

He nodded.

"Sounds more efficient."

And safer, I thought. There was something about having too many targets that made my heart race faster.

The darkness around us deepened, and the sounds of awe from the crowds increased as the fountain truly shined in its perfect milieu. I pulled Jack along a couple of times when I thought I'd seen Miguel, but all it got us was the chance to say "excuse me" multiple times in Catalan or Spanish. He raised his watch finally, and I could see the show was nearing its finale.

"Guess we try again tomorrow night," he said.

We started to turn away, and the crowd parted. Two men scuffled near the edge of the fountain. One wore the uniform of the Mossos d'Esquadra, the police of Catalonia. The other man was Miguel. "Come on. Follow my lead," I whispered.

"Excuse me, is there a problem?" I asked, raising my voice as I ran up to the men.

The policeman used our interference to get a better grip on Miguel. "Step aside," he ordered us.

Time to let my blondness work for me. "But this man is our tour guide. Where are you taking him? We don't speak the language. He helps us find everything. Where are you going with him? We need him." I had no problem speaking ditz when necessary. I fluttered around and pulled at their arms, succeeding in annoying the already irritated authority.

Jack physically got in the police officer's way. They started arguing in Spanish, and I used the opportunity to communicate silently with Miguel. He signaled he didn't have anything on him, which meant he'd already passed the loot to his partner. What I would do now was clearly in the gray zone, but I had too many serious items on my to-do list to worry about staying on the high road. I reached out and tugged harder on the officer's sleeve.

"What has he done? Why are you taking him away?"

"Pickpocket."

Obviously, the officer only had a small working knowledge of English. Or he didn't want to humor me since I was obstructing his efforts with Miguel.

"Did you find something on him that doesn't belong to him?" I turned to Miguel. "Do you have someone else's property? This is just a mistake, I know. Show the policeman so we can get this straightened out."

The officer switched to Catalan, but Jack continued in Spanish, speaking louder. I didn't know if it was because he didn't know what the officer was saying or he didn't want to blow his advantage. The policeman tried to push past Jack while pulling Miguel, but he wasn't successful. I grabbed the officer's sleeve again to get him to pay attention to me. "He hasn't taken anything. Can't you search him and see?"

We had a nice little crowd hemming us into a tight circle, which had been my plan. Nothing like unwanted publicity to make the officer consider whether he wanted to tick off supposed tourists like Jack and me and everyone else. Granted, I wasn't sure Miguel would be happy with me by the end, since he was gaining far more attention than thieves preferred. When several in the crowd shouted out something I took to mean "search him," it seemed our luck had shifted for the better.

Minutes later, Miguel had turned out all his pockets and cuffs. Nothing was found. As the crowd took in the activity, they chanted something Jack whispered meant for Miguel to be released. I smiled. The policeman knew when he was beaten and gave Miguel a shove, pointing and shouting toward the street. We didn't stop walking until we were down the avenue and well away from the police officer's vision.

"Thank you, thank you." Miguel took my face in his hands and kissed both cheeks. "I had a long night ahead of me if you hadn't arrived in the nick of time, Laurel. I had no idea you were coming to Barcelona when we last talked."

"Neither did I. We actually came here tonight looking for you," I said, leaning against the light pole. "Do you need to be somewhere, or is there a place nearby where we can talk?"

Miguel chuckled. "Oh, I am finished for the night. Probably for a week or two."

I didn't know whether to apologize or tell him to get a real job and stop stealing from tourists. Since I needed to stay on his good side I tried a different approach. "I'd be happy to pay you for your time. We came to see if you could tell us anything else about the plans for the auction."

Surprise flashed across his face. "The auction?" Jack pulled out his wallet, but Miguel waved a hand. "No, no. If I know anything to help the information is no charge. You saved me tonight." From looking at the bruising around his chin and forehead, I didn't doubt we might have saved him a lot of additional injury.

"Let's go get a beer," Jack said. "Get off the street."

Miguel knew a place nearby, and in about fifteen minutes we were comfortably seated around a table in a noisy tapas bar that offered the best kind of privacy because we had to lean close to hear each other speak. After an annoyingly short time of repeating myself to each of them whenever I asked about anything, I yelled in Jack's ear, "I'm going to the ladies' and see if I can call or text Cassie for an update. You go ahead and ask Miguel anything we need to know. I think he has my number." I looked toward Miguel and shouted, "Do you have my cell number?"

He nodded.

"Okay, good." I stood up and waved a hand between them, bending over the table to add, "You guys talk. I'll be back."

I grabbed my purse and roses, then I headed for the ladies' room.

The cacophony followed me down the back hallway, but when I pushed through the heavy door and it *thunked* closed behind me, the sound lessened a tad. I went ahead and entered one of the stalls first. With the series of wrong turns this night had taken, there was no telling when I'd be around a bathroom again. Two women were at the sink, and I heard the door open twice while I was sequestered in the stall. When I stepped out minutes later, I was alone. Perfect.

I washed my hands and pulled the roses from where I'd stuck them in my purse, intending to dampen their cloth again. One particular blossom wasn't faring well under all the excitement of the evening. I was half tempted to toss them in the trash, but we were too early in whatever kind of relationship Jack and I were nurturing to know how he might react if I didn't return with his romantic gesture.

I unwrapped the stems and set them along the edge of the sink, planning to wet a couple of paper towels and rewrap them right before I left. I moved next to the window to gain better phone reception. Cassie answered on the first ring.

"Max just left with the painting," she said.

I could hear the glee in her voice. "So you're off the hook for the rest of the weekend?" I frowned at myself in the mirror. My hair needed work. One blonde curl kept flipping into my eyes.

"Yes, thank heavens. I'm going to relax and read tonight, then head into the office tomorrow and pick up where I left off."

"Do me a favor and stay in your flat this weekend. Find a new corner to rework like it's the nineteenth century again," I said. "Until Jack and I get back, I'd prefer you hide out while you're in London alone."

"Max is—"

"No help at all." I held the cell to my ear with my shoulder and rummaged through the Prada as I spoke. "If he wants you to come in to play second chair while he schmoozes the legal eagles, tell him he has to send a car service for you. I said so."

She sighed. "Actually, hunkering in for the weekend is starting to sound pretty great."

"Okay then. Do that. Order food and have it delivered. Play princess of the palace with sandpaper and shellac."

"That's not quite the combo I use, but okay, I get what you're saying."

I ran my wide-tooth comb through my curls. "And keep an eye on the bulletin boards, okay? There hasn't been anything since this morning—though it seems like days instead of hours."

"That's because you've been busy. If you'd had the day I've had you'd already have checked the boards countless time. Not that it made any difference, but I can truthfully say Nico hasn't added any new information."

"I hate when things are quiet," I said, pulling out my travel-size hairspray.

"At least there's no distress signal."

"Too true. Jack said something similar."

"Did you get things straightened out with the bank?" she asked.

The bank. I sighed and shoved the comb back into my purse. "It seems the money was withdrawn with Max's PIN code."

"That's impossible—Oh, god, no…"

"Yeah, I think Nico took it."

"So he…"

"I don't know yet." Okay, yes, I probably did. But Cassie needed to digest this information the same way I had and come to her own conclusions. "I told the bank to put a hold on the account until I got back to them. I want to see if something changes later before I raise any alarms."

"Shouldn't we mention it to Max?" she asked.

No. Yes. Probably. "For the moment, I want to make sure he didn't borrow it as a means of having money for an escape."

"That's a pretty hefty escape, Laurel."

"This is Nico, Cassie."

She blew out a long breath. "Yes, and he's just as capable of draining the main foundation account too."

"He could do that anyway. Could have always done it." I let the conversation hang.

"Okay, yeah," she said finally. "I won't mention anything to

Max. You're right. He could have done this at any time. We can give him a weekend, I guess. But what about the builder invoices?"

"I texted them already and said we were both traveling today and would process the invoices when we returned," I said.

"Got it. That's a viable excuse," she said.

I needed to finish up and get back before Jack decided I needed rescuing. "Look, Cassie, we've found Miguel and we're trying to get information from him. I'll call you if anything new comes to light."

"Sounds good. I'll do the same. Take care."

"You too. Talk to you soon," I said, then hung up, tossed the phone into the purse, and spritzed my hair with spray.

The door clunked as someone started to open it, and I stood face to face with the Amazon. I wasn't sure which of us was the most surprised.

But I was the one who moved faster.

I shot her full in the face with hairspray, then scooped up my Prada and grabbed the roses by their blossoms. She moved semi-blindly to grab me. I raked the sharp rose thorns across the top of her hand and up her arm. Blood instantly hit the surface of her skin. She yelped and I circled her to reach the exit. She came at me again. I emptied the spray in her face this time. I flicked the stems like two short whips and slashed at her cheeks. She backed off. I opened the door. But as I ran away, she grabbed my hair. My head jerked back. Now I was getting totally pissed off.

I sawed at her neck with the stems. She let go of my hair, and snatched the stems away from me, stabbing her own palm. She shrieked. I tried to punch her in the neck, but she moved and I grazed her ear instead. When she grabbed the strap of my Prada, I used her move to create a higher base for my body and jumped to kick her in the stomach. She slammed against the wall and let go of my purse strap.

I ran for the front. Jack and Miguel stood by the table, and I screamed at them to come and help me. Several strangers looked our way, but I raised a hand, palm up, signaling everyone else to not move. We raced back to the hallway, Jack pushing ahead when I said it was the Amazon.

"Where is she?" He stood in the middle of the empty hall.

I pointed to a nearby door to the kitchen. "My guess is she went out the back. She went down hard, but it didn't take her out."

Jack pushed the door as if to go after her, but I stopped him.

"We don't have a weapon. We have no idea which direction she may have gone either. She could hide and hit us with a rock and leave us for dead, or shoot us if she has a gun," I said. "We need to wait until we're on familiar ground before trying to run after her."

"Yeah." He leaned against the wall.

Miguel took the opportunity to hand me a card. Everything around us was still loud, so he spoke in my ear. "That is my address. I live in the Barri Gòtic. I will find out all I can and call you tonight or early in the morning, but this is my address if you need to find me." He pointed to the card.

"Thank you," I said, figuring he read my lips more than heard me. He nodded and waved, then left back through the public area.

I turned to Jack. "I think we've worn out our welcome here."

"Yeah." He wrapped an arm around my shoulders and pulled me close. "I can't take you anywhere without you creating a scene."

"At least the flower stand lady was right," I said. "Rose thorns are good luck."

SIXTEEN

A taxi ride and a recommendation from the driver got us to a restaurant right on the water, with a view of the amazing yachts. I stood on the deck while Jack secured us a table. Looking out at the Mediterranean, I could see larger vessels anchored far out and off the coast, away from the noise and ready convenience, yet with civilization and the harbor a few minutes away. A full moon in the dark sky not only lit up the heavens, but bathed the sea in light as well, the rippling waves appearing to bring the luminescence to shore. Jack joined me a few minutes later and pulled me close. I think I could have stayed there forever, in the quiet moment of not feeling danger for the first time in days.

The hostess called and we were led to a table by the wall of glass. The dark water, the sparkling lights, and the stellar marine scene all framed in the window brought me back around to asking exactly what we were trying to do as just a two-person team. We hadn't worked this shorthanded before, and it wasn't something I ever wanted to do again. But as I opened my mouth to voice concerns, our waitress arrived and the moment was gone.

"The sea bass?" Jack asked and I nodded. He ordered in Catalan. The waitress smiled and left. He'd ordered a bottle of cava too, and she hurried back a few minutes later with the lovely sparkling wine. The champagne of Spain.

"Are we celebrating?" I asked. "Or just buoying our spirits with the bubbles in the wine?"

"Well, we did find Miguel. That's a success. And you escaped the Amazon without any help. That's toastworthy."

"I wouldn't have managed without my hairspray and your roses. May not have been a lethal combination, but eye-burning chemicals and blood-letting thorns succeeded in throwing her off her game. Anything I contributed has to be credited to Leif's training."

"So no arguments in keeping it up?"

"What? Until this week I've made my daily appointments." I leaned closer. "Want to test me?"

"I just want you safe."

I sat back and crossed my arms. "You want me wrapped in cotton wool."

He shook his head wearily. "Don't get defensive."

"Then don't say something that gets me started."

I played with the candle in the middle of the table, running my fingers back and forth across the flame. "So who was she following? Or why was she in Barcelona?"

"My guess is she has our credit cards flagged," he said. "We may have to start working strictly in cash."

"No." I pulled back my hands. "She was surprised to see me in the ladies' room. When she opened the door, she didn't expect to see me any more than I expected to see her. I saw it in the expression on her face. In fact, that's truly what helped me get away, because I recovered from the shock faster than she did. She's here for some*thing* or some*one* else."

Jack rubbed his chin. "I didn't see anyone else in the bar I recognized. I just assumed..."

"Yeah, so what else can we assume?"

"What do you mean?"

I held up a hand. "Stay with me for a minute." Ricocheting threads spiraled in my head. "That bar was probably the closest one to the fountain."

"Okay."

"When we spotted her in Rome, it was at night and at the Trevi Fountain. Who's to say she wasn't part of the crowd at the Font Magica?"

"You think she saw us there and followed us to the bar?"

I shook my head. "Maybe. No. I don't know. If that is true, then she'd know I was in the bar, so it wouldn't have surprised her to run into me." I caught up a wayward curl and poked it behind my ear, irritated to be bothered by it as I tried to think out loud. "If she didn't know I was there, she wasn't following us. If she wasn't following us, why was she there? Does she have a fountain fetish of some kind? Or are water features her go-to when she stakes out major cities?"

"Or she was there to meet someone."

"Someone who was in the main room with you and Miguel, and who heard me scream for the two of you when I needed help? Or someone who hadn't arrived yet and heard about the scene later?" I picked up my glass and took a long sip. "So much for us staying under the radar. Now the Amazon and whomever she was with knows we're in town."

"Since she got away," Jack said. "She would have told her accomplice anyway. Though, you're right. Even not pre-booking the flight didn't help."

"It may have bought us some time," I said. "Doing anything differently could have been catastrophic. We barely kept Miguel out of jail as it was. If we'd missed him at the fountain tonight, we'd have missed our chance entirely."

"Yeah, small favors."

"Did he say anything important while I was in the restroom, before the Amazon showed up?"

Jack shook his head. "We kept the conversation down to what information you and I needed from him. He'll get in touch with us when he knows any new details."

We had our phones on the table, and mine started vibrating then. I recognized the number as the one Miguel had given me earlier. Jack held out his hand. "Let me have it and I'll go outside. Less chance of being overheard than in here."

"Tell him to be careful, too. Maybe sleep someplace else tonight. We don't know that the Amazon won't decide to tag him."

"I will."

He answered the call, walking toward the door. Our sea bass came soon after, along with a basket of bread. I used my fork to brush some of the roasted garlic cloves off the top of the fish. I loved garlic, but it was too late in the evening for me to even contemplate so much with my dinner. Not to mention I'd be diving for breath mints for dessert.

The bass smelled heavenly. I hoped the guys' conversation ended soon, or I was going to do the unmannerly thing and start on my dinner without waiting for Jack. I buttered a warm slice of bread and stared out at the water while I munched. A waiter came up soundlessly beside me and refilled my wineglass with cava. "Thank you," I said. He smiled and walked away with the bottle.

Jack arrived back as I was finishing my bread.

"The auction is on a yacht out there." He spoke softly and nodded toward the dark water. "Starting at two in the afternoon tomorrow. He apparently knew that much information before, but said he's been working since we left to get options for joining the festivities." He placed his napkin in his lap, then looked at me and realized I hadn't tasted my food yet. "You didn't have to wait on me. Go ahead and eat."

"I munched, I'm fine." I picked up my fork and flaked off a good-sized piece of the fish. Jack did the same. "Tomorrow doesn't give us much time. Did he know the name of the yacht?"

"Yes, it's the *Faux Foe*. Had a devil of a time trying to figure out what he was saying. He finally spelled it out."

"What could that even mean?"

"I long ago gave up the challenge of figuring out why people name their boats the way they do. Especially rich people and yachts."

We each reached for our glasses, but while mine was full, Jack's was still nearly empty. He reached for the bottle in the standing holder beside him. I gasped.

"What's wrong? Are you choking?" He started to get up, but I waved him back to his seat.

Staying calm was difficult when I wanted to whip my head around to see the entire dining room at once. Jack was curious but kept quiet once I raised a finger to signal I needed a minute. I didn't see the helpful waiter anywhere.

"A waiter came by and refilled my glass with cava. I didn't think about it when it happened, but my brain recognized he walked away with the bottle. Except it wasn't our bottle. You have ours." I pulled my Prada close, digging to find the small bottle of liquid Jack gave me to use to see if a drink was tainted. I found the bottle and kept my hand hidden in my lap as I painted the end of my longest nail.

"Did you drink any of it?"

"No. I'd drunk enough of the glass you poured, along with the beer at the bar, and decided to get food on my stomach. The sea bass and bread arrived before the fake waiter came. I snacked on the bread until you returned."

"Thank goodness."

Everything went back into my purse and we waited for the nail to dry. Minutes later, we had our proof. The tip of my fingernail changed colors. The wine was drugged.

Jack's face turned thunderous. "Don't eat anything else. Let's see if we can find him in the kitchen. And stay right beside me."

Like he had to tell me that.

I scooped up my Prada with one hand and cradled the wineglass with the other. "For evidence," I said.

"Good thinking."

The young man had left minutes before. He'd probably been watching us and realized we knew. The restaurant manager gave us the waiter's name but could provide nothing else. He also offered another meal, more wine, a better table, but he could not tell us how to find the absent waiter. He tried to get our contact information, but Jack said no. We would handle things from this point.

I asked for a to-go cup to pour the tainted cava into something transportable with a lid. One of the kitchen help scurried away to find what was needed. I wandered over to the trash and saw a mostly full bottle of cava sitting at the top.

"Jack, we probably should take this, too." I pointed at the open bottle. He grabbed a towel and lifted it from the bin.

Later, in the cab, I said, "And to think, I felt so calm when we arrived there. Someone obviously followed us from the bar."

"I think we need to forget calm for a few days." He'd stuffed the end of the towel into the opened mouth of the bottle and was doing his best to not touch the wider end where I saw the waiter holding it. After a stop at the nearest police station to tell our story and give the waiter's name, we headed back to our hotel. Neither of us had any real appetite anymore.

In our hotel suite, we snacked on Cokes and Toblerone bars out of our mini-fridge and relished the fact that since Spain was still part of the EU the chocolate triangular lovelies carried the candy's original shape, despite the change in the brand bars for U.K. customers.

"I still need to write Toblerone officials a complaint letter," I groused. "If I didn't travel so much, I probably would."

Jack laughed.

"What else did Miguel say?" I asked.

He blew out a breath and grabbed my phone from the coffee table. "He said he'd email or text us further information, but there's nothing here yet. I told him to stay vigilant. Might need to call back and tell him our further adventures."

"You're getting off topic. Tell me what he said," I repeated, taking back my phone too.

"He gave me the yacht and the time. He's going to try to get me onboard in some capacity—"

"Us. I go wherever you go."

"No way." Jack set his Coke a bit too heavily on the tabletop and liquid flew in droplets. "Your picture will be on the phones of any security guys there, or any of the stooges sent to close out whatever transactions the criminals are making."

"I'll wear a disguise." I uncurled from my spot on the sofa and walked into the bedroom to rummage through my bag. A few minutes later, I was back with Liza Minelli hair and brown contact lenses covering my blue irises. "See?" I posed. "And I don't even have to have a stylist change the color back later."

"Interesting." He pulled my arm and I landed in his lap. "Never thought of you with short hair. Brunette or otherwise."

"I have a lot of surprises in my bag of tricks, Mr. Hawkes."

"I'll just bet you do."

He tried to kiss me, but I pulled back. "Let's keep on-topic, buster. You know I'm not staying out of the play. I've been doing this job without you all this time, but we both know our strength is in teamwork. Keep treating me like a partner, Hawkes, and not some fragile masterpiece. Or else."

"You're right. Even if I can get police support, I'm going to need someone beside me who knows the other players in this farce. I don't like it, but I'm going to have to learn to accept this as status quo."

I held his gaze. "If you can't work with me without mother-henning me, then we can't be together like this. It's that simple. I worry about you the same way you worry over me, but we're both damned good at what we do. Protect each other? Sure. That's what backup is for. You worrying too much about me risks putting yourself into greater danger and threatens any plan we have in place."

"I get it."

My phone vibrated from a text, and I held the screen so we could read it together. It was from Miguel.

"He's got you a server's uniform for tomorrow," Jack said.

I smiled. Miguel knew better than to think I'd agree to be benched. I read the rest of the text. "And you're on the guest list under a strange name. John Leeds. Short and sweet, but can you get by using it?"

"Yes. I have a passport with that name and gave it to Miguel when we spoke in the bar."

Wonder what other secrets he hadn't told me yet, I thought.

Aloud, I said, "Alrighty then. Guess I need to start searching out ways to get the yacht's blueprints."

"You can do that?"

I patted his cheek. "Baby, I can do anything."

SEVENTEEN

We spent most of the night working our individual sources to see what information we could get and what additional reinforcements we might be able to count on. Jack woke his friend in Italy's military police and carried on a long conversation in Italian, while I searched under every internet rock for blueprints of the *Faux Foe*. I worked backward from its registration for info on who owned it and found a shell company that had me naturally thinking of Ermo Colle. Eventually, I found the factory specs of the yacht from delivery to its original home in the Bahamas.

"Be back in a second," I whispered while Jack continued a call, this time with someone in the U.K. "I'm going downstairs to see if I can make some copies."

"Just a minute—"

"I'll be fine," I interrupted. "This time of night I should be the only person there besides the desk clerk."

He nodded, and I was glad the argument ended so quickly. I didn't want this to start becoming a problem, no matter how much I understood his reaction.

The wireless printer at the desk quickly made friends with my smartphone, and I was back upstairs with the copies in less than ten minutes. Jack was at the elevator when I hit our floor.

"I finished my call. Thought I'd take a walk."

I grinned. "Come on and memorize the major points on five decks instead."

"Five?"

"Yep. It's a mega."

"I guess I'm not surprised."

I wasn't either, but it would mean a lot of studying to make sure we didn't get turned around if we needed to escape quickly. Plus, the yacht was three years old. Plenty of time for the owner to think about changing up the factory setups, no matter how custom-built it had been on delivery.

"There's been some chatter about a big gun delivery," Jack said once we were back in the room. "No names associated with it, but my Italian friend thinks this auction could be the means of transferring ownership. My Home Office contacts share his opinion."

"Using art as payment?"

"And the fact it will be off land. Nothing like the high seas to conduct illegal business. Did you get anything from the yacht's ownership?"

I shook my head. "Shell company. I'd need Nico or someone like him and a lot of time to dig any deeper."

"So it could be Colle."

"Or Moran. Or any number of Asian conglomerates or Arabs with lots of money and yachts of their own. It's registered in the Bahamas, but that doesn't mean the owner actually lives there."

"Which means we wait and see who we recognize."

I nodded.

We took over separate areas of the room. Jack requisitioned the desk and made notes, working up ways he could get on and off the boat without relying on measures afforded to other auction participants. I took over the loveseat and coffee table, studying printouts of the blueprints until lines started crossing with my eyes. I remembered the contacts and removed that phase of my disguise.

A phone rang as I reentered the sitting room from the bedroom, and Jack answered. It seemed like every time a call came he spoke in a different language. The words became a kind of white noise while I worked. As I looked at him then, however, taking control of the operation side of things, I wondered again about his relationship with the government and his own father as an MP.

There hadn't really been time to talk about this and how it impacted our jobs and...us. It seemed the deeper we moved into this project, the greater each of our histories became involved in everything we were doing.

He finished up the call and noticed me looking at him. "Something wrong?"

"Just watching you in action," I said, smiling. "I..." I caught my lower lip with my teeth. "I like that confidence."

"I'll remember that." He rose and started moving my way, but another call stopped him. I received a shrug and a grin as he answered in French.

Moving back to my own abbreviated office space on the loveseat, I resumed my own specialized work. I spent the next hour scrutinizing the plans and making notes on the prints where I feared changes might have been made, so we'd remember to check before we needed to use any of the fixtures or architectural features.

Then I rescanned everything again from stem to stern, comparing floors and composing mnemonics in my head to remember what was on each floor. I finished the tick list I wanted Jack to memorize of the public spaces where the auction likely would take place and any staterooms or storage areas that appeared irregular.

I closed my eyes for a minute, just to rest them and get the gritty feeling on my eyeballs to go away, but woke up hours later in the bedroom. Alone in the bed. My clothes laid neatly across a chair.

Voices in the sitting room led me to crack the door before I slipped on a robe and stepped into view. It was Jack's friend from the Italian military police.

"Hello, Giuseppe," I greeted the stocky man with the trim mustache. "It's good to see you again."

"Happy to see you as well, Laurel." He shook my hand.

I turned to Jack. "Are you going to get any sleep?"

"I crashed here on the sofa for a couple of hours," he said, waving a hand to encompass the about five-foot couch measuring a foot shorter than he was.

"That couldn't have been comfortable." I fisted my hands on my hips.

"I'm used to it." He handed me the room service menu in English. "Why don't you order all of us some breakfast. I promise to try to nap afterward."

I was starting to feel like "the little woman" again, but I didn't want to argue while we weren't alone. Figuring if I ordered the food and kept quiet, I might better learn intel than if I asked either man anything directly. Pick my battles.

Speaking of battle, one thing I did notice was the gun on the table. Jack hadn't tried to bring a weapon into Spain because of their strict laws forbidding foreign parties transporting firearms. Even if the person was law enforcement. I assumed Giuseppe managed this one somehow. Frankly, I didn't care. I was just glad Jack would be armed.

By the time the full breakfast I ordered arrived, they still hadn't switched from Italian long enough for me to know what was planned. I finally asked.

"You're going on the servers' launch with Miguel's contact," Jack explained. Something I already knew. "I'll follow on a hired craft I arranged a short time ago. Giuseppe is going to be coordinating with the Cuerpo Nacional de Policia, the state police here in Barcelona. He has a contact in the CNP who works with the division for international crime. We can't get full police support because we have no proof a crime is being committed. But they've heard their own chatter and are going to work together to see what they can do."

Which meant we may have reinforcements, or we might be on a yacht with lots of guns and pretty much on our own.

"The big thing is," Jack continued, "if you see Colle or Rollie, try to get off the boat or hide somewhere. Be sure and wear your charm bracelet in case I have to find you later."

Nico fixed me up weeks ago with a special charm that looked

like a camera but could track me wherever I went. He and Jack had an app on their phones keyed into the GPS of the charm.

"It's in my purse. I'll make sure to have it on. But if Nico has his phone, he has the app too."

"We'll have to take that risk," Jack said. "Tracking you via a GPS hack on your mobile is the greater risk."

We finished eating, and I went to shower and dress. I still needed to go by Miguel's apartment and pick up my uniform for the day. As I pulled out a pair of jeans and a long-sleeved white blouse, I called and made sure he'd be ready for me.

"Yes, I'll be here all morning," he told me.

When I came out of the bedroom, I grabbed my sweater and the Prada and said, "Giuseppe, would you mind going with me to Miguel's so Jack can get some sleep?"

Jack started to rise from the chair. "I'm going—"

"No, you're not, my friend." Giuseppe put a hand on his shoulder to keep him in the chair by his plate. "Laurel is correct. Get some sleep. I will escort her and keep her safe."

To reassure him, I pulled the charm bracelet from my purse and put it on while he watched. "There. You'll be able to track my movements until you conk out from exhaustion."

"Take the battery out of your mobile."

"Already have." I held up the two pieces, one in each hand. "Satisfied?"

"Okay. But I'm really not tired."

Except the yawn that nearly split his jaw belied his words. I kissed him goodbye and followed Giuseppe out of the room.

The morning was cool but comfortable with my sweater, and the walk to the nearby Gothic Quarter would have been pleasant if my companion hadn't been in recon mode. I couldn't blame him. With all the talking he and Jack had been doing I assumed he expected a bad guy around every corner. For me, going in disguised as other people at the auction kind of set my teeth on edge anyway. I would have much rather snuck in. Easier to sneak out. Besides, I was used to being served, not having to handle trays and be the server. My grace under pressure skills weren't always available when needed.

We entered the Barri Gòtic. It was easy to see the historic Moorish influence in Barcelona, but particularly so in this section of the city. The area was a system of narrow lanes and courtyards that kind of created mazes in the Gothic Quarter. Giuseppe jumped when we turned a blind corner and surprised two lovers either saying good morning or kissing goodbye. I noticed he quickly re-hid his gun under his jacket.

"Is the whole place like this?" Giuseppe asked after we left the pair still necking.

"I know it can feel like a rabbit warren, but honestly, this is one of my favorite places to wander on foot. There's so much history and character all around us," I said.

"The twisting lanes are confusing," he said. "And it makes for easy places to hide people."

"Another part of its uniqueness."

He gave a kind of snort, and I assumed he didn't agree with my compliment.

This neighborhood of connecting buildings, with courtyards that almost formed a labyrinth, usually charmed me. Yet, as we entered gates and walked past painted wrought-iron fences which blocked and delineated the public space, I caught some of Giuseppe's anxiety.

My goal was an apartment in a back hall on the second level about halfway down the next block. The way inside remained clear, and I told myself to relax. We climbed stairs and walked along an open hallway—actually, a breezeway—to get to the door marked with Miguel's apartment number. Giuseppe followed close behind and kind of whistled under his breath. I shook the tension building in my neck and shoulders and quickened my steps as I drew near the door. I knocked, but no one answered.

"He said he'd be here," I said. Then I noticed the door wasn't latched. I pushed it open.

Miguel sat on a beat-up brown couch, staring our way but not seeing anything. The bullet hole in the middle of his forehead took care of that.

"Get down, get down," Giuseppe yelled.

I hit the floor and bullets sprayed through the window. Glass peppered my head. Giuseppe motioned for me to crawl with him to the door. Obviously getting pinned down in the apartment was a bad idea, but with only a half-wall for the breezeway outside, I didn't see how leaving would help either. Beside my hand was a cell phone, and I grabbed it. I didn't know if it was Miguel's or not, but it seemed prudent not to leave the device behind.

Giuseppe duckwalked into the open hallway and quickly sighted in on a shooter on the next roof. He shot and we heard a cry, then he waved for me to run. I followed orders, and he was a pace behind me. I headed for the stairway down, but another gunman stood in the shadows, starting up toward us when he realized I'd seen him.

EIGHTEEN

"We have to go up." I grabbed Giuseppe's arm and pushed him back toward the other set of stairs. There was no way to block access once we'd made it to the rooftop—no lock on the door and nothing nearby to wedge under the knob. What we did find were huge concrete bunker-looking blocks we might be able to use for protection, probably hiding HVAC and other utility needs. As the gunman opened the roof door, he shot wide. We ducked behind a bunker and Giuseppe fired back, driving the gunman behind the door to reevaluate his options. We didn't stop to wait and see. We ran to the next large object, making our way to the edge of the building, opposite from the side where the other shooter stood.

At the roof's edge, I crammed the confiscated phone into my purse and leaped across the opening between the buildings. Giuseppe followed a second later. The Prada messed with my trajectory, and I didn't make the distance. I grabbed the short wall ledge along the top of the building. Hitting the apartment building knocked the air from my lungs, but I clung tight and took shallow breaths. The gun screwed Giuseppe the same way, but when I looked over he hung on with one arm, and turned to fire when the gunman tried again.

We heard a cry.

"Got him. Not that it's going to do us much good now," Giuseppe said, panting.

I focused on all muscle memory I'd ever used to climb rock faces. The toes of my boots searched out every crack or crevasse I could find for upward movement. There was no way I could talk, so I hoped Giuseppe knew what to do or was strong enough to pull himself up. When my head cleared the short wall and I managed a temporary one-armed hold, I slung the Prada over, letting it drop to the roof so I had all hands free. My fingers ached for gloves, but I ignored the scrapes, pain, and broken fingernails, focusing on my goal. Close by, Giuseppe scrabbled like me up the rough exterior of the wall. I worked my feet and used my arms to pull myself up inch by inch. When I finally cleared the top, I hurried over to help Giuseppe.

"Take the gun," he cried. "Be ready to shoot if someone else comes."

His words were prophetic. A third gunman arrived, banged open the roof door of Miguel's building, and fired as he ran. I pulled Giuseppe on over and handed him back the weapon. In the seconds he returned fire, I grabbed my Prada, then stayed low and did a one-eighty sweep to see what options offered escape.

None.

There was a door into the building, but it was locked. I didn't have time to pick it and there was nothing big enough to use to break the lock. Giuseppe followed me to the far end of the building, watching to see if the gunman tried to jump as we had. So far, this new baddie relied on bullets. We needed to keep something between him and us whenever possible.

"Should I shoot the lock on the door?" he asked.

"If you do that, he'll shoot you while you can't shoot back." I pointed down. "If we can drop to the balcony below, we can go through the window into the apartment. It's just one floor. Unless he jumps, he'll have to run back down to the street to shoot. We'll have the building between us and him."

Another shot hit close, making the decision clear. I went first, holding onto the top of the building. Giuseppe returned fire.

The balcony was only a couple of feet wide, and I hit the side instead of dead center, hugging the railing to stay vertical. Again, I had to pull myself up and over, but it was easier this time.

Standing by the railing so I could block for Giuseppe, I shouted, "Come on."

He took another shot, then slipped the gun into his shoulder holster and followed my lead. He knocked against me as he fell, but I was ready. We didn't go over the side.

I pushed on the window. Locked. Cupping my hands around my eyes, I couldn't see anyone.

"Move!"

Giuseppe grabbed the small iron plant stand at one end of the balcony and hurled it through the glass. We knocked the bigger shards inside and leapt through the shattered window, just as footsteps sounded on the roof above us. The shooter had decided to jump too.

The apartment was a blur. We ran through to the hallway, found the stairs, and almost flew down both flights. We exited the building and broke cover at the courtyard, running full out. Zigging and ducking through shadowed lanes and leaping past wrought-iron gates. We heard shots from above and behind, and bullets zinged around us. I felt something bite into my thigh, and I stumbled but kept moving forward, limping as my energy flagged. Giuseppe cried out a moment later but kept pace with me. I was out in front, headed for an open portico in the eastern area. I turned to the right, trying to gain cover there instead of the open avenue to the left. My thigh burned. Giuseppe panted behind me.

I caught movement to the side. A hand grabbed our collars, jerking us back a step. "I've got you. Come on."

NINETEEN

My sight was blurred, but from the corner of my eye I saw Giuseppe reaching for his gun. Our captor noticed too.

"Wait, no! Laurel, it's me, Nico. I have a car. Come on."

Suddenly, my knees gave way. From relief or shock or the gunshot in my thigh, I didn't know. Both guys grabbed me. We ran in tandem to the banged-up Peugeot Nico pointed to sitting at the curb along the avenue. We piled in and Nico floored the beater.

In the backseat, Giuseppe immediately called his contact at the CNP and began feeding him information in Spanish. I had a feeling he never mentioned he had a gun.

However, I had other personal—and greater—questions on my mind. I punched Nico in the shoulder.

"How in the hell—" I began.

"I've been monitoring your charm bracelet."

"But you're here. We saw you on the video with Rollie. Heading for Switzerland. The message you left on the internet board. Were you kidnapped? Or...I can't even say it."

Nico gave a rueful laugh. "No, I didn't turn into a new Simon. Rollie thought I was working for him, but that was never the case. But my cover is blown. I won't be able to go back."

Oh, we obviously had tons to discuss.

"Did you know they were going to kill Miguel?"

He shook his head. "I only learned last night they were feeding him bad information to get to you. He didn't know it was coming from Rollie. It was all a front. Miguel was an innocent all along. Well, except for wanting to work pickpocket on the luxury yacht."

"So Rollie is trying to kill me."

"He says no, but his actions say otherwise."

"Do you know why?"

He gave me a sad smile and nodded. "Do you?"

I sighed. "Probably. But I'd prefer to have substantiated proof."

Still, what did I gain either way? Be the daughter of a master criminal moving guns and forgeries who'd pulled a gun on me? Or be the daughter of the apparently only good guy in a family of thieves and killers who died shortly after my mother? Likely by actions of that other possible father figure.

"We're staying at—"

"I know where you're staying," Nico said. "Call Jack and tell him to meet us on the street. Rollie knows where you're staying too."

I put the battery back into my phone. I had to redial twice before Jack woke up to answer, and by then we were almost to the hotel's parking lot.

"Leave our stuff," I shouted. The volume on my brain seemed short circuited. "We have to cut and run. Rollie had Miguel killed and gunmen shot at us. Nico grabbed us."

"Nico?" Jack seemed to fully wake then. "Are you hurt?"

I chewed my lip. "We could both use a doctor."

"I'll kill him."

"You'll have to stand in line," I said.

Nico said, "Tell him I'll go to the front desk and take care of the bill. Just get out as quickly as possible."

Oh, it's nice to have my right-hand geek back, I thought. Then I passed out.

I woke up in the ambulance the CNP officer sent when Giuseppe said he and I had been shot. Saying I was fine did no good since Jack was there.

"You've lost blood, you're likely suffering from shock, and I'm going to wring Nico's neck for not heading straight to hospital instead of coming for me. I would have gotten away, dammit."

"You were asleep. You had no clue." While I did feel woozy, I hated to play the helpless female role. But getting shot after little sleep, sporadic and bad food, a whole lot of overnight tension, and a boot camp workout strenuous enough to keep me out of the gym for a month was making me kind of glad I was lying on the gurney.

I needed stitches, but Giuseppe said his was nothing and made them just clean and cover his wound with a bandage. Luckily, the bullets caused no major damage. Giuseppe's passed cleanly through his arm, mostly a flesh wound. The one in my thigh didn't hit bone, but I was warned I'd need to have physical therapy if I didn't want lingering pain. I hated PT, but I hated lingering pain even more, so my future was set.

Though I argued, I was admitted to a hospital room. It was a boring, much too beige room, but I figured it was the authorities' way of making sure I stayed there until someone could come and get a statement from me. At least the room had a coffee station down the hall.

Giuseppe told me the dead and wounded at the apartment house had all been rounded up after he told them where to look for everyone. But Rollie wasn't one of the felons caught up in the delayed dragnet.

"Did Rollie have visual on the takedown?" I asked Nico when he brought in coffee for us.

He gave me a lazy look and a shrug. "He said he was going to, but I wasn't the only one Rollie had working technical duties. My guess is he watched the whole thing from a distance. I wouldn't have even known about it if one of the shooters hadn't slipped up and said something when they were getting ready to leave. I hacked their phones then and pieced together what lies were told and what plans were being carried out. When I saw from your charm bracelet signal that you were in the center of things, I stole the car and got there as quickly as I could."

Jack disappeared by this time, as had Giuseppe's gun and

shoulder holster. I hoped he was just getting rid of the firearms and not doing something stupid. I was beginning to think I needed to plant another bug on Hawkes.

"Where is he, Nico? I don't need Jack to go all cowboy on me and singlehandedly take off after Rollie," I said.

"Rollie is in the wind. We need to watch out for him, but he's not back today. However, I did find a cache of rather explosive treasure, and Jack and the CNP were very interested in that."

"Rollie's team left it behind?" I asked.

"I may have secured the room with a computer lock with a twenty-digit code, making it difficult for anyone to get back in and get the merchandise."

"Was there ever an auction?"

"Yes, originally," he said. "But you were right in thinking we messed up those plans. The original idea was to trade the Caravaggio to settle a debt for inventory. The auction was a fast, hush-hush maneuver to pull it off. Make the payoff with a bunch of other masterpieces run over the auction block. The time and place have been changed now. They'd originally confirmed the details at a restaurant in London, and Miguel stayed to eavesdrop when he heard about a big money event in Barcelona and happened to catch a reference on the painting. He remembered you talking about the work. But when he became too interested, Rollie used his curiosity to his advantage."

I sighed. "If I hadn't pushed for extra information..."

"It wasn't your fault. Miguel was a thief," Nico said. "He was doing it as much to try to get his own payday at the auction as to find out details for you. He believed the wrong people."

What Nico said made sense, but I still felt badly about what happened. "I grabbed a cell phone when we were in his apartment and put it in my purse. The phone was on the floor. Can you take it please and see if it's his, and if he had any family I can contact?"

"I'll take care of it," he said, patting my non-wounded leg.

Barcelona would never have the same kind of memories for me after this trip.

TWENTY

While Jack wasn't at the hospital to offer him support, Nico played babysitter to me and used the time to explain how when Rollie contacted him on his return from London he put into play a plan he and Jack had concocted behind my back. I'd resisted the stronger pain meds, but due to the fact sleep had been a luxury I couldn't afford for the past several days, I had trouble staying alert as he talked. After I'd zoned out the third time, he said, "Why don't you sleep a little. We'll fill you in later when Jack gets back."

I wanted to argue, but a nap sounded too good right then. I played patient and stored up my anger for when I could unload on the two of them at the same time.

"Okay," I said. "I can wait."

Nico was no fool though and knew my quiet demeanor didn't bode well for either of the males on my team. Once my short nap was over, and Hawkes came back flush with success over his and the CNP's joint recovery of a battalion of automatic and semi-automatic weapons, Nico immediately snuck off again pleading the need to make arrangements for our return to London.

By the time we took off, I had my plan in play, and when I had them as a captive audience and we were thirty-thousand feet from an escape, I made my move. "Exactly what moment did I become impeached as head of the Beacham London team?"

Nico had booked us passage on a practically empty plane, so I had room to stretch out my leg, despite not being in first class. But more importantly, with the ambient sound of the engines and the air-filter system, there was little likelihood of being overheard. Jack and I sat across from one another in aisle seats, with Nico in the seat ahead of Jack, but he sat sideways to talk to the two of us.

Nico initiated the back pedaling. "Jack and I talked before about what I should do if anyone previously associated with Simon tried to coerce me into working with them. He felt that was a calculated risk, and he was right."

I turned to Jack. He shrugged, saying, "It's what I would do. Think out of the box."

"You can think outside the box all you want," I said, looking each in the eyes. "But if I'm ever kept out of the loop like this again, you'll find yourselves manning your own entire team. Because you won't be on mine. I will not be treated like someone who has to be protected at every turn."

One of the flight attendants approached with a cart. "Would you like something to drink?"

"Three Cokes," I said. "Just leave the cans, please."

She smiled and handed over three cups of ice and cocktail napkins and opened the three cans. When she left, I figured we had a half hour before we'd be bothered again.

Looking directly at Jack, I said, "From what I know you heard from Giuseppe, I showed my ability to perform in stressful situations. Anyone could have gotten shot and passed out. I stayed standing and scrambling at all critical junctures."

"You're right, and I'm sorry," Jack said. "Nico and I had unfounded concerns." But his contrite manner didn't completely convince me.

My mind cast back to one of the first conversations he and I had at a fish and chips meal in London, when I was trying to figure out who Hawkes was and we were on the run from Moran's guys. Jack made a comment then about not having "a Nico" working for him, and I smarted off that Nico would never work for Jack because my tech wizard didn't tolerate smartasses. But now, though the epitaph fit him like a bespoke suit, Jack was much more, and I couldn't stop vacillating between my anger over his setting this up without telling me and awe in how he set everything up so perfectly

I never realized I, too, was being out-maneuvered. Leaving me to wonder at his apology and whether I was still getting played.

Nico started talking again, and I tuned back in to the debriefing story.

"I received a phone call when I was in Paris. Just after you boarded the Chunnel train on Thursday morning," Nico said. "Very lucrative offer Rollie presented. Simon apparently extolled my talents on numerous occasions, exactly as Jack figured. Rollie's current project had been derailed and needed me to provide digital backup for his team. I told him I'd think about it and call him."

"And you called Jack." Obviously, I'd been wrong years ago about Nico's tolerance for smartassery. I stopped trying to think in two directions at one time when he made the next revelation.

"Yeah, to get everything set up like we'd talked. The idea was to get me in to feed info back from the inside. But we didn't count on him being as paranoid as he is. I can get back in, except the digital operation randomly changes entry codes every twenty-four hours. What I know today will be useless tomorrow."

I looked at Hawkes. "So you already knew all about this at the same time I had Nico on speaker three days ago and made my big confession about the Caravaggio."

"Sort of," he said. "Nico and I didn't have the chance to talk about the full spectrum until after he got back into London and temporarily rid himself of Rollie. We talked after the conference call."

"Of course. That was why you looked guilty when you shoved your phone in your pocket Thursday morning when I came out of the restaurant bathroom after talking to Marci. You hadn't been talking to your boss. You'd been talking to Nico."

He shrugged, then had the courtesy to offer a sheepish grin. "I did talk briefly to Cecil before the call from Nico. And Cecil did call me in for a briefing."

Nico jumped in to fill the conversation then. I had no doubt it was due to the look on my face. I tamped down my anger to listen to his words.

"When I realized we needed to move quickly, I called Patricia," Nico said. "The group was in Berlin, and I connected with them from Paris to return in their plane to London. You could have blown me over when I learned Rollie was the one who originally planned to transport the Caravaggio to the auction as a scheme to get onboard to meet with the secondary gun purchaser."

"He told you that on the phone when he called with the job offer?"

"Not exactly," Nico said. "He said he had to revamp, and his idea was to use me to hack into some of the computers and get him entrance without the painting. I learned this the second time I talked to him, after I'd made it back to London with the group. By then, of course, he knew the Caravaggio was no longer available. I'm sure he was notified soon after we left the facility grounds. He just didn't know I'd taken part in its recovery. He was concerned about the people running the auction. He needed capital to pay off the guns he'd already taken receipt of, since he could no long produce the painting. He wanted me to trick the system. His understanding was their computer setup was foolproof."

I couldn't help smiling. "But not Nico proof."

"Goes without saying." He shrugged.

"Yet, you say he has a top-grade computer structure," I said.

Nico nodded. "And two of the organization's computer experts recently left Rollie's employ."

"Voluntarily?"

"From the body language of the guy who whispered it to me, I would say their termination was the permanent kind," Nico said.

Wow. Did they try to leave and he didn't want them to? Did their consciences weigh too heavily? Or was the fact I'd seen Rollie's personality evolving to the dark side something they'd noticed and worried about too? "You have no clue why?" I asked.

"No, just the same thoughts you're likely processing," Nico said.

He knew me too well.

"So the Caravaggio was never the objective on the forgery and heist side of things? It was all to give the gun runners their preferred payoff?" I asked.

"Yes and no," Nico said. "Well, for Rollie anyway. Granted, I only knew the sketchiest of details about the copies, as Rollie pulled me in soon after, and anytime I mentioned Caravaggio forgeries I received blank looks. The copies could still be a duplicate maneuver by Ermo Colle."

"How did Rollie contact you next?"

"He and two cronies entered the Tube car I was in seconds before the doors closed."

"From Heathrow," Jack clarified.

Nico nodded. "He had no luggage, and he wouldn't answer when I asked where he'd arrived from. I can only conclude I was spotted in the airport, and he was notified. He had to either have been in Heathrow already or at least London. Customs went quickly, then I ran into a friend and talked with him in the bar until his flight was called. Someone could have been keeping me in sight and reporting to Rollie if he was in transit."

"But no one actually tried to detain you," Jack said.

Nico shook his head.

"Could your friend have been in on Rollie's plan?"

"No, I..." Nico's brown eyes widened in comprehension. "I don't know. But I will do some digging."

"Did Rollie take you away from the train? Or did he give you a meeting place for later?" I asked.

"He wanted me to go immediately, but I said I couldn't. I had a toothache. The dentist was getting me in for an emergency appointment. Before the dentist worked on my tooth, I called Jack, so I could be sure the phone line was clean."

Well, well. A toothache was why he cut off the conference call. It wasn't just to jerk Jack's chain like Cassie and I had thought. Now that I had the fuller picture, I had to marvel at Hawkes's performance during and after the conference call and hang up.

"Where did you meet later?" Jack asked.

I crossed my arms and frowned, noticing Mr. Home Office

didn't ask if Nico notified authorities about Rollie being in the country. He apparently felt his knowing was enough. Though, to be honest, I would have done the same thing.

"Heathrow. He had us booked on multiple flights, depending on when I arrived back. But I found a tracker one of his goons slipped into my jacket on the train. That's why I couldn't call you, Clive, or Patricia, and why I turned off my cell phone. I might have been followed or the call overheard. I figured Clive would contact you when I didn't show for the pickup."

I nodded.

"I left the tracker in my coat," he said. "To stoke their confidence. But I can reverse the frequency."

Jack raised an eyebrow. "That could be handy."

"As could the little presents I left hibernating in their computer files," Nico added, grinning. "However, with their over-paranoid system, once activated we will have a limited timeframe before either method is noticed. If they catch one, most likely they will ramp up defenses and soon detect the other one too."

"Good to know," Jack said.

"And good work on getting the bugs planted," I said.

I leaned toward Jack and whispered, "I know you can't tell me anything, but I have to ask—was Rollie's gun shipment part of the bigger thing...you know...or is he just trying to play with the big boys?"

"Nothing can be determined until the shipment is traced."

"And you can't tell us anyway." Nico frowned.

"Regardless," Jack said, "gaining the shipment is a success. We don't know what new information will fall out of the evidence trace, but if anything relates to art I'll be able to bring that over."

Nico nodded an acknowledgment, but since I knew we weren't going to learn any sensitive info, it was time to poke Jack again. "None of this explains why Cassie and I had to be kept totally in the dark."

Jack cocked an eyebrow. "Aren't the pain meds supposed to knock you out? Or at least mellow you?"

"They probably would if I'd taken them, but I plan to stay awake this entire flight," I said, raising my own defiant eyebrow.

"It was a solid plan," Jack tried again.

"The whole scheme between the two of you feels all 'boys' clubby.' It would have been nice to not be sick with worry over Nico."

He pointed a finger as I spoke. "That's exactly why neither of you could know. I tried to soften the stance some when we took the conference call with Cassie because I felt guilty about you thinking someone else had changed sides, but you both needed to be convinced he had it in him to turn."

"And the money?" I asked Nico.

He shrugged. "Already back into the Beacham account. That wasn't Jack's idea, but it probably went a long way to magnify your concerns. Right?"

I nodded.

"It was important I show Rollie I was taking the assignment for selfish reasons rather than monetary ones," he explained. "To make him believe the facts I presented: I was underappreciated, I was ready for new challenges, and I have no allegiance to Beacham. Or for whatever reason his suspicious mind thought up. I showed him my bank account didn't need his money, but I let him know I expected top dollar because that is what I am used to."

"The money was a loan to make you look flush," I said, then turned to Jack. "And Cassie and I couldn't know in case Rollie had someone watching and so we would act appropriately female."

Jack did a calming motion with his hand. "I get that you're mad—"

"Mad does not begin to cover it." I leaned close and my tone was quiet. Too quiet. Nico's eyes widened; Jack's narrowed. I said, "You aren't taking this seriously enough. You may have both done all of this with the best of intentions, but neither of you thought it through. Just because you worried Rollie would be watching—"

"Which from the way circumstances occurred, we can only conclude that he was," Jack interrupted. "We needed you both to react as if you believed Nico was gone. Or at least didn't know where he was and what he was doing."

I counted ten in my head. "So the messages on the boards—"

"Was Nico playing rebel."

Nico's expression darkened. "It didn't seem right to not at least let you know I was unhurt and felt like I could eventually escape. Since Rollie believed I'd signed on for the big payday, I didn't want him to think I had contact with you so I could keep the tactic going. I didn't know you'd need the money before the weekend, so I didn't expect you to worry I'd stolen from the account. But I counted on you checking out the boards and seeing our code."

"The hardest thing I ever did was not catch a plane for Basel as soon as Cassie called about the message," I said.

"Proving my point," Jack said.

I ignored him and asked Nico, "When did you leave Basel for Barcelona?"

"Everyone cleared out Saturday morning. When I had the run of the place, I did some digging. Then Rollie called and told me to join them in Barcelona, as he felt he needed me there instead. He sent a helicopter for me."

"Think he just wanted to keep an eye on you?"

"Most likely. But he did need me to add security at the warehouse where he housed the guns. Unfortunately for him, I made them non-accessible to Team Rollie."

We all smiled, then Jack asked, "What about the copies from Calais? Did anyone in the group mention them?"

"When Rollie finally mentioned them at all, he said something about Ermo Colle. But nothing conclusive," Nico explained. "He didn't say a lot about Colle or any forgeries, but what he did say points to a big rivalry going between the two. Moran seems to be out of the loop on this, which substantiates the belief that Rollie is working toward a coup."

"Did he mention getting a forgery of the Caravaggio stolen from Scotland Yard?" Jack asked.

Nico shook his head. "I heard nothing about him securing a

copy. If he had, I don't know why he brought me in. Or..." He looked at both of us in turn, then finished. "Maybe I wasn't supposed to survive either."

"Don't know." Jack massaged the back of his neck, sending a message much louder than his words. "We need to think about this."

Yeah, like no one had better do this again.

"And the Amazon?" I asked, hoping I could learn why she was on my tail. "Was she in Barcelona to help Rollie? Or was she there on an assassination run?"

Nico shook his head and blew out a long breath. "No one would talk about her. I even asked direct questions a couple of times, but the subject was immediately changed."

"Rollie is a master at the silent technique when he doesn't want to reveal anything." I thought back to the car ride and the time he'd spiked the wine. "So at the restaurant last night. He paid the waiter to come by and pour wine to drug me?"

Nico said. "I only learned about the wine incident this morning, but I assume he will keep it up unless he no longer views you as a threat."

Jack looked at me. "That proves the Amazon works for Rollie, since we didn't see him in the bar, and the restaurant wine incident happened so soon after. When she ran away, she reported our location and we were followed. Only possible conclusion."

"I agree," I said. "Can't I just tell him I don't want to take part in his grandfather's filthy business? I'll hire a skywriter and make a completely public profession of the statement."

"But Moran's the problem, right?" Jack looked at Nico. "Rollie has figured out his grandfather has reservations about leaving him the business, regardless of whether Laurel is related to the family or not."

Nico nodded slowly. Jack and I frowned.

The only way we were going to solve this was to get Moran's grandson locked up. Preferably soon to keep me from being sidelined while we worked on the next phase to stop the heist.

At least our goal hadn't changed, even if Rollie's priorities had. The bigger question of the moment was "why?"

"Humor me for a second, guys." I winced as the plane hit a succession of air potholes and the jiggling made my leg scream. I took a sip of soda to cover the pain, then said, "Why would Rollie switch from trying to get me as an ally to trying to kill me?"

"Because his grandfather is seeing what a psycho he is?" Nico said, then rolled his head to crack his neck. I could never stand when he did that, but it was all a side effect of the stress he felt from his loathing of air travel. "Anyone can pretend to be sane for a few months before the crazy starts to show."

I pulled gum from the Prada and offered him a fresh piece. "Maybe," I said. "Or did he really try to have me killed?"

Jack snorted. "Don't tell me you've forgotten the bullet the trauma doctor took out of your leg? Or the follow-up questioning by the Barcelona police?"

"I promise not to roll my eyes at what you say if you promise not to make scoffing noises until I finish with my thought," I said.

He gave me a sheepish grin. "You're right. I apologize. Again."

Oh, this was going to be a fun trip, I thought. Plowing forward, I said, "Look at it from a different perspective. Could it be instead that I was to be kidnapped, with Giuseppe being shot in the apartment, and I got caught in the crossfire?"

Then I thought about all the crossfire. Three different gunmen. Why send that many for what they presumed was one or two unarmed people? I shook my head. "They planned on killing someone, but they had too much manpower for what they would have presumed to likely be a simple job if I, an unarmed female, went to see Miguel."

"But you still got away from them," Jack said. "They were exactly right not to underestimate you."

I felt heat in my cheeks. "Only because I had Giuseppe and his weapon as my wingman. Given the stiff Spanish laws about foreigners with firearms, they couldn't have known he'd have a gun, even if they had intel pegging him as Italian law enforcement.

They'd already put an entire takedown team of men in place, and they'd killed Miguel before we arrived."

"What are you saying?" Jack asked.

I absently stroked my wounded left thigh, the leg stretched out into the aisle. There were a couple of things I needed to say, but I wasn't sure exactly how to say them. "We weren't hit until the end. How could all three gunmen be less than expert shots? Moran has never been sloppy, and I can't imagine his grandson doesn't have the connections to hire the best. When we came across Miguel's body..." I stopped for a moment and took a couple of small breaths to force back the memory so I could speak. "In the apartment, I instinctively moved toward Miguel, to make sure he couldn't be saved, while Giuseppe checked out the windows. He's the one the gunman on the opposite roof saw. Giuseppe was the one who instigated the shots if it was based on sight. But if the gunman was supposed to shoot anyone who entered the apartment, he could have shot us in the open breezeway before we entered Miguel's front door. Why didn't the gunman do so?"

"There was nothing beforehand?" Jack asked.

My mind cast back to the bullet-riddled apartment we raced out of. Giuseppe saved my life by telling me to get down when he saw the gunman on the roof across the way. But while I had used the window for light, I wasn't in the gunman's view inside the apartment. Only Giuseppe was. Spraying the bullets to hit him risked hitting me, sure, but the guys with the guns were likely mercenaries, rather than rocket scientists.

"No, nothing happened to warn us before we saw Miguel." I leaned against the headrest and closed my eyes. "We had no interference until we set foot in the apartment. As if we were supposed to see that Miguel was killed. Then the bullets followed us as we made our escape. Giuseppe shot from the breezeway and hit the gunman on the roof. That was the only way we both escaped. We heard a cry and didn't see him again. Then the second gunman, the one at the stairs, took over the chase."

"And you went up instead of down."

"Yes, using the roofs over the maze below to keep moving in the direction away from each gunman. But was it also the way they'd wanted us to go if we left at gunpoint? Seriously, the more I think about it, the greater my feeling we were herded along the route. Like our running away was part of the plan."

Nico chuckled. "I cannot believe the gunmen planned to take the very difficult route you took them on. No one is such a masochist."

"I'm not saying it was their first choice, but when we saw the gunman on the stairs we ran the other way. Why didn't they have a man in place to stop us from going up? Pin us down right there in the hall if they wanted to take us out?"

Jack frowned. "Good point. So you think he sent the gunmen to kidnap you instead of kill you?"

I shook my head.

"I think he sent the gunmen there to take us. You and me, Jack. No way Rollie would know Giuseppe would go with me instead of you. I think they were trying to kill Giuseppe because he didn't fit the job schematics. But Rollie wanted me to know first that my friend was dead. Dead because he worked with me. I also believe the shots I experienced were just to keep me off-balance instead of kill me. We always moved in a direction away from the gunmen, sure. But it felt like we were directed toward a specific point, like it was the same direction we would have gone if we'd left at gunpoint."

"Toward the avenue." Jack's eyes narrowed again. "Where they could have a vehicle."

"Still, all those gunshots," Nico said. "Everyone heard. The police were called."

"Because it was the reserve plan. Not their plan of choice," I said. "This is just a hypothesis, I know, but it makes sense once you consider all that happened and in what order. And while it seemed like Giuseppe and I were in the middle of it for hours, it couldn't have lasted longer than five minutes. An eternity for those of us running away from the bullets, but a very short amount of actual time. And worth the risk to Rollie. Especially if it meant capturing me—and you, Jack, if Giuseppe hadn't gone instead."

Jack nodded. "Makes sense based on the police report. The time the calls came in. When they arrived. What they found. How many would you say Giuseppe shot and do you think any of the gunmen were killed by his gun?"

I massaged my forehead with my fingers. "One guy didn't get up after he was shot, but I think Giuseppe only wounded the other two."

"Yet when the Mossos d'Esquadra swept into the Gothic Quarter and processed the area, three gunmen lay dead. Two shot with two different caliber bullets," Jack said.

"Sounds like a cleanup job to me," Nico responded.

"Yes, and all of the men were in the Interpol system. Arrest records, fingerprints, everything," Jack added.

I tugged on a lock of hair to focus my thinking. "Did Rollie leave them because there was no time to get them out? Or because he didn't care if they were identified?"

"If they couldn't talk, it didn't matter if they were identified or not, I imagine," Nico said. "My question is who made sure the other two were dead before the police arrived?"

"Do you think Rollie would do the job himself?" Jack asked Nico, and he received a shrug in response.

But I knew who was on the scene for exactly that kind of corporate cleanup. "No, killing and tidying up afterward is why the Amazon was in Barcelona. She was there to eliminate any loose ends."

"Then why not have her in the building when you arrived, to take you and Giuseppe at gunpoint with the other mercenaries?" Jack asked.

"Because she's never Plan A," I said. "Think about it. She's always around after the fact. To clear away any problems that might plague her boss when something gets messy."

"Unfortunately, knowing she's Rollie's version of crime-scene cleanup doesn't make her any less dangerous," Nico said.

"No," I replied. "However, knowing she's not first-string offense could come in handy someday soon. We might be able to better manage options and risks."

TWENTY-ONE

Max left London ten minutes before we touched down at Heathrow, taking the Caravaggio with him and leaving my team to sigh in relief.

Jack immediately jumped into the official side of things, staying busy with meetings and paperwork involving the gun confiscation. With multi-country interest in who had jurisdiction on everything, I didn't envy him. However, we both shared in the frustration over the only physical evidence retrieved was the guns and the dead guys. Rollie disappeared into the wind again.

The fact Hawkes couldn't discuss anything about the situation didn't help either. While I spilled whatever intel I could provide, he stayed tight-lipped due to the constraints of the Official Secrets Act and its rules and regulations that would put us both into a U.K. prison if we talked about anything of substance. Or at least land us in even more trouble than we were already in. We knew the guns tied peripherally to the art crimes I worked, and I remained forthcoming as circumstances arose and he needed historic specifics on some of the copies confiscated. But he couldn't reciprocate at all. Not a shred. I had to believe him, even though the quiet voice inside me whispered something else in my ear. Let's just say the personal trust issues meter hung around the red zone, but I had to pretend all was green and steady.

Worse, nothing tied to Rollie, and we knew from Nico the copies didn't originate with Moran either. This meant no evidence to hold him if we did find him. Plus, circumstances indicated Ermo

Colle was still in business—whether Daddy Dearest ran operations from a hospital bed with a new face or from the grave with proxies.

The Rollie concern, however, kept me tossing and turning at night. Due to the guys' back alley scheme Nico was as much at risk as I'd been all along. Rollie had to know he'd been conned, and no way he would simply forgive and forget. Too much pointed to a bullet in Barcelona having been reserved for Nico—and the bullet was still out there. When I mentioned this to my tech wizard he shrugged, but his face remained sober. I put a hand on his arm. "You know you probably saved my life. I'll always be grateful. But I never want you to risk your own life like that again."

He shrugged and grinned, trying to level the tension with a bit of gallows humor. "The next time Jack wants to do out-of-the-box thinking, I'll make sure I look for ways I might get caught in the box and buried."

"Don't even joke about it, Nico."

He laughed and walked out of the door. I had no idea where he was going or when he'd be back.

Thanks to my bullet wound, by Monday I was hobbling too much because I couldn't sit still, but had already tired of crutches. We'd given up on the office space for the time being, since I couldn't handle the requisite stairs. Operations moved to the sitting room of my hotel suite. When housekeeping came by to make my bed and change the towels, the maid surveyed the room—wide eyed—and I could imagine the silent screams. I made a snap decision. "Leave the towels and don't worry about the bed until the sheets need changing. I'll take care of everything else while I'm using the room for work."

I think Cassie's whiteboard was what truly sent her over the edge. My assistant had moved into notetaking hyper-mode after returning from Paris, and the poor board looked like someone had vomited multi-colored Post-its all over the surface.

"I'll be back later if you need me," Cassie said, pulling on her coat. "My friend at the V and A—"

"Oh, right." I nodded. She'd set up the meeting before she left for Paris, and in all the excitement I'd forgotten. The man was a visiting expert to the Victoria and Albert Museum, known for his abilities to identify forgeries and the forgers who created the works. Cassie hoped to get some insight into the paintings that surfaced in the coffee table book she'd discovered over Christmas and sent up a steady stream of red flags. She was also taking the forged Caravaggio that traveled to Barcelona and back with us.

I added, "Hope he can tell you something. If he asks to keep the Caravaggio for study, you'll have to clear it with Whatley."

She flipped her collar into place and said, "If anyone can provide information, he'll be able to. Just the fact we know for certain the paintings in the book are forgeries, and the originals are still safe, will make him interested enough to take a closer look."

"But you know—"

"Don't tell him too much," she finished before I could complete my warning. "Believe me, I want as few people as possible to know anything."

"Attagirl." I reached for the folder on the desktop that held the photos. "I don't know why I bother saying anything."

She raised an eyebrow. "Maybe because we're all feeling guilty about how too many people who've tried to help us ended up dead?"

For a second, I counted the most recent fatalities: Roberto in Rome, Miguel in Barcelona, and likely Nelly here in London. Plus, Giuseppe was shot. All of them just in the past month. To get the real total, however, I had to go back to the previous fall and the Greek courier of the snuffbox that started this misadventure. And the forgers we'd found in the morgue files along the way. While I didn't know for sure that Nelly was attacked due to her scruples toward helping me, the fact she'd been killed—or been ordered to be killed—by the same person who'd murdered so many forgers already made me consider she might have balked at the last minute about switching the tapestry she was restoring for the foundation with a fake. Then there were forgers like *Il Carver*, Nico's source in Rome who'd noticed the fatal trend and was already on the run before he met any of us. Too many people were no longer around to answer our questions because they'd made contact with us or Simon or Rollie or Ermo Colle.

"Yeah. There is that," I said.

My phone rang mid-afternoon, and I expected Jack at the other end. "Hello."

"Interest you in a late lunch or early dinner?"

I pulled the phone from my ear and looked at the caller ID. Lincoln Ferguson. Damn. "Oh, gee, Linc, I..." Something made me just stop and think *oh, the hell with it.* "Sure. Where do you want to meet?"

"The restaurant at the top of the Tate?" he asked. "We can mix talk with art."

The Tate Modern used to house public utilities. Its enormous exhibition hall once displayed ten fully functioning turbines. Today, about three hundred works of art graced the multi-storied structure. Including one of my favorites in Room 9, a later impressionistic water lilies painting by Monet on long-term loan from the National Gallery. The view out the café windows was also one of the best views of St. Paul's Cathedral across the Thames. However, all of that would have to come another day when I could walk without assistance.

"Sounds lovely, but could we meet somewhere at street level? I've had a slight mishap, and I'm on a restricted-movement regimen."

"What happened?"

"Oh, I zigged when I should have zagged. Not a biggie."

"How about your hotel?"

For a fleeting second, I almost took him up on it. Then common sense reminded me I didn't want to let this professional snoop any closer to my life than necessary. I may have been meeting him out of gratitude and guilt, but he was still technically persona non grata in my closemouthed world.

"No, I—"

"Or we could go white tablecloths," he interrupted me. "Whatever you prefer."

While London boasted over forty Michelin-star restaurants in a ten-mile radius, I wanted to keep things low-key. Fine dining too often included pictures or write-ups later in the media. Besides, I figured I might have to pick up the check as part of my penance for socking him in the nose. This needed to stay cheap. "What's your favorite pub near the BBC offices?"

He named one I'd only passed by but never stopped in to try, and I agreed to meet him in an hour. Then I called Jack.

"Anything wrong?" he answered.

I sighed. "That's what it's come to already? I call you in the middle of the day and you want to know what's wrong?"

"Ah...Didn't realize this was that kind of call. I'm on my way."

"Cool your jets, cowboy, it isn't that kind of call either." I couldn't help grinning.

"Damn."

One of us had to remain professional. "Wanted to let you know I'm meeting Lincoln Ferguson at four at a pub around the corner from the BBC."

"You need me there?"

"No." *Yes. Maybe. No.* I continued, "It's just Cassie and Nico are both gone, and I thought I should let someone know why I'm not in my hotel room."

"Good call. Going alone might not be in your best interests—"

"I'll be fine, Jack. The doorman will help me with a cab, and when I leave the meeting I'll make sure Linc gets me another taxi before I set foot outside the pub."

"No, I'll wrap things up and come by there about five. You can give me a sign if you want me to stay away, in case you need to finish anything up with him. I don't want you leaving alone."

One part of me wanted to argue out of habit, but as I felt the smile on my face grow broader, I said, "Sounds perfect. Thank you."

"Wear your charm bracelet."

I raised my left arm and looked at the silver bracelet with its tiny little camera which stored the device Jack could track on his phone. "Check your app. I have it on right now."

The pub was dark paneled and noisy, exactly as I'd hoped. After a less than nimble exit from the cab, I crutched my way inside, happy to find Linc not yet in attendance so I could ungracefully pick my own way through the semi-crowded tables to the best available reconnaissance spot. A booth near the back seemed perfect, no one sitting directly adjacent but enough people laughing and talking around to mask our discussion. I was getting my coat and crutches settled on the black leather seat beside me when the door opened again and the reporter was backlit by the outside sunlight.

"Hallo," Linc said after crossing the room, pointing at the crutches before he shucked off his coat. "You weren't kidding."

I deflected by commenting on his nose. "You're looking much better than the last time I saw you. Almost no trace of the black eyes either."

He touched one side gingerly, a small bandage still in place. There was bruising, but most of the swelling was gone. "Another week before I can be on camera."

"I really am sorry."

He waved a hand. "Given the situation, your reaction was perfectly natural. I'm just glad I was there."

Okay, now I felt really guilty.

"You want something?" He pointed to the bar. "Beer? Sandwich? Wine?"

"Just mineral water, thanks. Maybe some chips."

"Oh, right, you're still on pain meds," he said and walked away.

Actually, I'd already weaned myself off everything other than paracetamol, but his allusion could work in my favor if I decided things became too difficult. No better reason to cut and run than the need to take a fake round of meds.

He wore another brown suit. Couldn't someone tell him to liven up his wardrobe? As I watched, the skinny barman looked my way, then said something to Linc. I had the feeling of being assessed.

A minute later, Lincoln was back with our drinks and settling into his side of the booth.

"I thought getting together to do some pre-interview work would be beneficial to both of us," he said.

"Oh, I assumed this was the dinner I owed you."

"I was talking out of my head that night." He laughed. "Or, rather, out of my nose. Forget anything I said."

What was he up to? Yes, it could have been over-obsessive thinking on my part, but given my previous dealings with this reporter, I dared not discount my instincts. I never liked it when someone's objective seemed to be focused on making me feel too comfortable.

After pulling a small notebook from an inside pocket, he flipped a couple of pages then searched for a pen. "Damn."

"No worries." I pulled the Prada closer and withdrew from a side pocket the gold pen Max gave me last Christmas. "Here you go."

"Thanks." He shook his head and the light from the kettle lamp above the table brightened his brown hair. "What does it say about a reporter who forgets his pen?"

"At least you didn't forget your notes." I couldn't read the upside-down scribbles, but there were a lot of them on the pages of his moleskin pad. "That's always more important."

He pointed my pen at me and nodded. "Absolutely." Then he folded his hands together, so his fingers held my pen as they also hid the open notebook. "But I don't want to barrel in asking questions."

I waved a hand as if this type of thing happened every day. "Ask away. We'll get all this business stuff over with, then we can talk."

His head gave a tiny jerk, as if I'd surprised him. Good.

He smiled and pulled his hands away to look at the notebook. "Terrific. How about discussing what a typical day is like for you."

"No day is typical." I chuckled. "Seriously, every day is both mundane and unique in its own way. Sounds cliché, I know."

A waitress passed by and slipped our basket of chips onto the table. As she moved out of earshot, Linc ratcheted things up. "You've made quite a name for yourself in recovering stolen art."

Though truly wanting to grimace, I smiled. "A lot of it's luck. Our foundation also has a network of contacts to help if we call. But mostly I have a great team."

"Ah, yes, tell me about your team." He flipped to a clean page and kept the pen poised over the paper, but his gaze never left mine.

Careful, Beacham, this was too choreographed. Keep it simple. I broadened my smile. "Well, Cassie Dean is my brilliant right hand. She has several degrees, including expertise in art restoration, so she's invaluable to me in the office."

"Yes, she interned at the V and A last year."

I raised an eyebrow. "You did your homework."

"Fatal flaw," he said. "And you have another member of your team."

"Nico, yes. He works independently, but—"

"No, I meant Jack Hawkes."

I felt my smile tighten, but I was too fixated on breathing to relax. I reached for my glass and took a sip of water. Then I squeezed the lime that floated on top so I could concentrate on the glass instead of the reporter. I said, "Jack doesn't work for Beacham."

"But he does work with you. Has for several months. You've even traveled together."

"My, my, Lincoln. You really have been stalking me." I laughed to further the pretense of teasing and was pleased when it sounded natural to my ears. "However, your information is incorrect. Jack Hawkes doesn't report to me. We've had a few instances where our job needs dovetailed. Nothing else."

"I'm simply surprised your boss wants you associating with someone whose reputation isn't the most..." He trailed off, like he couldn't bring himself to say the word. Then he offered a kind of aw-shucks look and said, "A bit of a cipher is your Mr. Hawkes. Some interesting pieces to be found, but larger chunks of expected data missing. And rather a lot of interesting informational avenues peter off in the end. But I do hear Hawkes has a habit of showing up as things head off-track."

Why was the conversation going sideways? What was this all about? I decided to keep it playful and cocked my head to one side as I said, "Are you trying to tell me something, Linc? Or just fishing?"

"I guess I'm saying be careful. I wouldn't want your boss to think you were consorting with unsavory people. Things have gone missing after Hawkes leaves a scene. People too."

Obviously, Ferguson stumbled upon a few of the "colorful backgrounds" Jack had alluded to. I wanted to ask if someone had a vendetta, but couldn't risk raising the interest level. I also considered the line Tony B said to me months ago in Florence, before he got Jack arrested. The line I'd never completely worked out or been able to push out of my memory. *I'm doing you a favor*, Tony B kept telling me, and he added that Jack *isn't who you think*. I didn't like the uncomfortable feeling of déjà vu I experienced at the reporter's words. I thought I'd made my peace with the previous uncertainty, but my inner suspicious self apparently had additional work to do.

"Well, I appreciate the heads up, but we only work together when our individual projects mesh. And to be truthful, it was my boss who first assigned me to work with Jack, so it all falls back on him."

"Head of the New York office, Max—"

"Yes, exactly." I caught my lower lip between my teeth before I said anything troublesome. Letting him get to me was not something I could risk.

"And what project did you work together?" His smile was

friendly enough, but the look in his eyes said he knew he had me. "Or has there been more than one? You've been seen together often the past months."

I refused to break eye contact. "Hmm." Raising the glass to my lips, I took another sip and pretended to think. "Must have been the seventh-century sword. Yes, that's it." That was the first time, and I didn't intend to trot out any bonus information. There was no reason to keep those facts secret. Too many people had been involved in trying to authenticate the piece for us to possibly bury the information from the U.K. press. "Unfortunately, it was proven to be a very well-made fake."

He flipped a couple of pages back in his notebook and feigned reading. "Quite right. I remember jotting a few things down about the report."

I'll just bet you did, I thought.

"And earlier this month," he said, flipping back to his previous page, "the art restorer you found dead in her London flat. I believe it was the same day your office was broken into."

I ignored his punchline and focused on the part about Nelly. "She was still alive when Cassie and I arrived. She lingered in the hospital for a day or so, but she did kill her assailant in the flat. And Hawkes wasn't on the scene at all. He wasn't even in the country that day." I crossed my arms and leaned back. "Let's cut the crap here, Lincoln, okay? Stop sounding like you're looking for an exposé or this interview—or whatever it is—is over." I shifted in my seat to straighten out my coat and pull it from under the crutches, preparing to leave if the conversation didn't change immediately.

"Laurel, I—" he began. His phone started a crashing ringtone. "Damn, that's my boss. Just a minute."

He fished the cell from a pocket and answered, his face turning pale under the bruising as he listened. "Right. I'll be there." He hung up and said, "I have to go. Stay. Please." He made a "stay" motion with one hand, as the other grabbed his coat. "Finish the chips. They're already paid for. This isn't the way I wanted this to go."

I weighed my options, deciding no comment was my best response. My silence seemed to work.

"Please meet with me again." He scooped up his notebook and shoved his hand in his coat pocket. "Please."

"I'll see what my schedule allows," I finally said, but his deflated expression told me he understood what I wasn't saying. It all depended on how I assessed the risk later of having a reporter like Lincoln still too interested in me and what my team did.

As he left, I looked at my watch. Almost thirty minutes before five o'clock. Deciding I may as well eat Linc's chips and make notes while I waited on Jack, I reached for a napkin.

"Damn." Ferguson took my pen.

But it was worth losing one of the only nice things Max had ever given to me to get the reporter out of my life—at least for the moment.

"Versatility, thy name is Laurel." I pulled my phone and accessed the notes app.

"Ah, we do not need that," a French-accented voice said, as my phone was removed from my hands. Rollie slipped into the seat Lincoln had vacated. "I thought he'd never leave. Good thing I have media connections in this city."

"More people on your bribery payroll, Rollie?"

And who should step back through the door at that moment? Yep, Mr. Nosey himself, smiling and holding up my pen as he took a couple of steps back into the pub.

I made a grab for my phone, and Rollie reacted as I'd hoped, pulling it farther out of my reach. That allowed me to *accidentally* let my arm catch the chip basket and my half-filled glass, and knock them loudly to the floor. "Oh, look at what I did. I'm so sorry." I spoke toward the barman.

As Rollie's attention stayed directed toward the mess on the floor, I shook my head at Lincoln and held up a hand. I saw the reporter squint at Rollie's profile. Moran's grandson spoke to the waitress who came to our table with a towel. I hoped Lincoln didn't recognize this nice-looking guy with the long brown hair sitting across from me. He already thought Jack was a hood. No telling how I'd be categorized if he pegged Rollie too. This was the same young man who ordered the deaths of at least three people this past weekend in Barcelona and was responsible for the bullet hole in my leg.

It wasn't only a desire to avoid being the source to an uncomfortable fact-finding mission. I didn't want to risk what might happen if the reporter or anyone else approached the table. When Ferguson did as I'd mimed and backed out of the door, I finally breathed again.

"See there." I pretended to slap Rollie's arm playfully, while I directed my words toward the waitress. "He was playing keep-away with my phone and this is what happens. Give it back now. Fun is over and you owe this nice person a very big tip." The waitress smiled at us, and I held out my hand. Rollie frowned, but realized how it would look if he didn't cooperate while we had an audience. I took the phone, pressed the record option, and put the device in my lap, then tried to figure my next move.

The waitress finished the cleanup and moved away. Rollie leaned over the table and said, "Let us go."

"I haven't rested enough since I got here," I said, leaning closer. "News alert—I'm recovering from being shot in the leg."

"You should stop such risky pursuits." His dark gaze locked on mine.

"I thought I was just going to visit a friend."

"A friend who was a thief." He *tsk*ed. "Not so good company."

"How did you know he *was* a thief?" I said, hoping he would incriminate himself further. Though I doubted the phone's microphone was getting anything through the surrounding noise. Worth a try.

He sat back, but continued speaking softly. "I will not argue about this, Laurel Beacham. Come with me or you may not like the *conséquences*."

"I don't understand why there have to be any consequences, Rollie."

He laughed silently. "You are much too smart for me to believe this."

"You don't have to worry about me. I don't want to be part of anything."

"Ah. So you do *comprendre*."

"I only know what I've surmised," I said. "And I wouldn't even know that if you hadn't given back the things belonging to my mother. If you didn't want me to know anything, why return the items?"

He scratched his left eyebrow with his thumbnail. "Their return was not up to me."

I figured as much. Moran wanted me to have everything, just like he'd said in Baden-Baden. "I do want to thank you for returning them. They gave me wonderful memories of a mother I almost don't remember. And I think I better understand now about my rocky relationship with my...my father." I frowned. I couldn't help it. Even knowing I had to say the words as subterfuge, I stumbled over the term.

"And you want to walk away from..." He shrugged. "Everything?"

"Why would I want to do otherwise?"

"Why indeed." He shook his head, turning for a moment toward the bar.

I kept watch on the door while he was occupied, worried Lincoln might decide to return—and worried he wouldn't. My options were narrowing by the second. "Look, just tell your grandfather—"

"Tell my grandfather?" He laughed, but there was no humor in the sound. "My grandfather does not listen." He slid out of the booth and stood beside me. "Come along. We need to go."

"I can't—"

"Come with me *immédiatement*, or I will make sure you recognize what an *erreur* you've made. If I don't leave London with one blonde *la demoiselle*, I will leave with another."

Cassie. He meant he would take Cassie if I didn't cooperate.

I reached for my coat and crutches.

It was exactly like we'd talked about in the conference call. Any of us would do anything for another member of the team. Even leave with someone who likely wanted me dead.

TWENTY-TWO

The Marylebone section of London was busy with people skipping out of work before five, but not busy enough that I could use it to any advantage. We passed All Souls Church, with its brave pointy steeple fighting for prominence against the city center skyscrapers that circled it. I sent up a silent prayer I could somehow get away despite my gimpy leg, load of fatigue, and zero available options. Rollie kept a firm hold on the upper part of my right arm.

"There's no point in holding on to me, unless you want to help me walk," I grumbled. "It's not like I have any chance of running away. You took care of that in Barcelona."

He grinned. "Your escape was *incroyable*. I see now why so many people underestimate you."

"Thanks, I think."

This made him laugh. "Oh, Laurel, if only we were on the same side of things. How you say? Cousins in crime?"

"Unless you know about a paternity test I've never been informed about, there's no proof we have any bond beyond a common one over art. You like to steal it, and I prefer to recover it."

He laughed even harder. A woman walking toward us smiled at Rollie, assuming, I supposed, we were on a friendly date. But he did at least drop my arm. Not that it mattered. My flagging energy levels hovered in the danger zone.

"Why wasn't I just killed in Barcelona?" I asked.

"Because you weren't supposed to be. You and your friend Jack were supposed to come together. The change made for...alternative plans."

Which meant my supposition on the plane was on target. But what constituted his end game, and how could I get him to tell me? I took the offensive. "What more do you need to hear? Unless you force a test, I certainly won't. I want no part of anything you're involved in."

"A test is no longer necessary." He gazed straight ahead, but he stayed close beside me.

"What do you mean?"

He shrugged but didn't elaborate.

I spotted a bench and headed for it. He pulled at my arm again, but I shook him off. "Let me go. I have to sit a minute. Unless you want to throw me over your shoulder like a caveman, my leg needs some rest."

"The car is close."

"Unless it's parked beside that bench, it isn't close enough."

He put his hand into his coat pocket and I felt the barrel of a gun press into my side. I wanted to scream in frustration, but stopped walking instead and kept my voice low, saying, "Go ahead. Shoot me. Shoot me right here in the middle of central London. Great game plan, Rollie."

"You know I can."

Actually, I didn't truly know if he was capable of the act. While I was positive he could order someone be killed, from the evidence collected and hypothesized, the Amazon likely did most of his wet work. I had no idea if Rollie pulled any triggers himself. Regardless, it was a sucker's bet, but I was beyond caring as long as he didn't go after Cassie. I resumed my hobbling trek toward the bench, just me and my risky shadow.

"So, do you know if Ermo Colle is alive? Have you heard any scuttlebutt?" I asked. Might as well try to get my own questions satisfied if my hours were numbered.

"He survived, yes. But he already looks different, and not just because of your baton prowess."

Damn.

At the bench, I hopped on my good foot, using the two

crutches for support as I turned around to seat myself. Rollie remained standing. I patted the seat. If I acted friendly, maybe I could change his mind about killing me. Or at least slow him down with my fake confidence. "Sit and rest with me. Whatever you have planned for later today can't work without the two of us."

He gave me a crazed look and shook his head as if in wonderment. Well, that part of my plan seemed to be working. Now to figure out what to do for the next stage.

"What is it you want, Rollie? Give me a chance to negotiate. You might find everyone comes out ahead." For an instant, he smiled and seemed once again to be the genuinely nice guy he'd pretended to be when I first met him. Before I learned his family connections. Even after I found out about the familial ties, he'd still acted friendly all through the fall and into the start of winter. It was just this past month I kept glimpsing a hidden monster. Now this. "What happened? I thought we were friends."

And the nice-guy mask disappeared completely. "The guns. I will offer you in trade for the guns."

Yeah, but would he let me go if he got what he wanted? No matter, since the guns were tied up in international red tape and there was no way anyone would trade them for my life.

Then I saw a frightening sight. Lincoln Ferguson stood across the road, shooting video of us. Shit. Now I had to find a way to keep from getting him killed too.

Rollie also saw the reporter. He jerked me up by my arm. "Move."

"I'm trying."

"*Non*, you are not trying hard enough. Hurry."

My chest felt full of tears. Not from fear, but of frustration. No way though was I going to let either of these Neanderthals see me cry—and I definitely wasn't letting someone get it on digital high def. I didn't look at Lincoln, but I could tell from Rollie's curses the reporter continued to shoot video as we walked. The gun remained firmly in my side, and I received a bonus jab whenever I didn't hobble quickly enough.

Suddenly, I heard rapid movement behind us. I kept walking, but Rollie looked back. He cursed again and turned so the gun left my ribs. I moved sideways a step, just as Jack leapt on the bench and used the seat to launch himself at Rollie. My vision tunneled, and I only saw the gun pointed at Jack.

I let one crutch drop and grabbed the other before it fell, swinging overhand to slam Rollie's gun hand as he pulled the trigger. He fired wild. I screamed. The bullet entered the grass near the edge of the pavement. Jack's fists took over from there. I had no idea where the gun went.

Rollie gave as good as he got. While Jack was angry, Rollie was crazy. Never a good combination in a fight. I used my remaining crutch to help me reach the fallen one.

I kept one under me for balance, then got close enough to swing with the other if I had an opportunity. Rollie gave an almost primal cry, then jerked and tried to push Jack onto his back. That's when I saw the gun. It had been hidden under Rollie. And now he had one hand scrabbling to try to reach it.

"Jack! He's after the gun!"

I swung the crutch, banging at his arm, trying to knock the gun away from his body. Rollie caught the crutch and it flew from my hands. He hit Jack upside his head with the metal side. As Jack fell back from the blow, Rollie turned to better see the gun.

That was when I used my best two-handed back-handed tennis return to knock Rollie in the face with the business end of my remaining crutch. The second broken nose I delivered in one week.

As he fell back, I dove for the gun. A second later I felt Jack's strong arms helping me stand.

"You're lucky I'm giving him the gun," I said to Rollie, as Jack exchanged my other crutch for the weapon and trained the gun on our prisoner. "He won't shoot you unless you try to flee. But I would. I'd shoot you for Miguel. And I'd make sure the pain was excruciating."

Superintendent Whatley arrived then, and he and his DS took charge of Rollie and the gun. Jack winked at me and I grinned. We really did make a good team. Even if I did almost have a heart attack every time. Of course, he swore I nearly gave him heart attacks too.

Lincoln jogged over while Jack and the Scotland Yard men cuffed Rollie and stowed him into the back of the unmarked police car. I pointed at the camera. "If I see any footage of me tottering down the sidewalk on the news tonight—or ever—I swear you'll be the one who gets the next beating with these crutches."

"But you want a copy of the footage, right?" Linc grinned.

"Damn right, I do."

"And don't worry. I'll make sure your face and Hawkes's are pixelated."

Better than the alternative, I guessed.

Ferguson left then, just as Jack headed my way. "Why'd he run off? I was going to thank him for calling me."

"He called you?" I turned and watched Lincoln's departing figure. "I'd assumed you homed in on my bracelet."

Jack wrapped an arm around my shoulders and helped me back to the bench. "I did that as well, but I'd have never known anything was wrong if Ferguson hadn't called me with the tip. He didn't like a look you shot him when he went back to return something."

"My pen."

"Right. When he described the guy with you, I recognized it was Rollie right away and notified Superintendent Whatley. He monitored the GPS on my phone while I monitored your bracelet."

But Jack still beat Scotland Yard. Why did that not surprise me?

"You did threaten Ferguson if he put the video on the news, right?" Jack asked.

"Our faces will be abstract pixels."

He laughed. "Kind of like Rollie's is right now."

As Whatley's car pulled away, Rollie's battered profile appeared in the window. Amazing what a crutch could do to a nose. He turned and shot us a dark look as the car merged with traffic.

TWENTY-THREE

First physical torture session was Tuesday. Less than a week since I was nimble enough to scale a sixteenth-century French chateau. Now, only five days later, I had trouble climbing stairs. Between a therapist with the soul of a gestapo agent and the overexertion of the previous day, by four that afternoon I was feeling whiny about life in general. I compensated by eating my way out of the tormenting pain, devouring a Mars bar with my sore leg propped up on a chair. When the room phone rang, I thought seriously about ignoring it. My leg hurt that much. Hell, my whole body ached. But the bell was so loud and annoying I didn't want to have to listen to it anymore. At least I knew for sure it wasn't Lincoln. He'd sent me the copy of the original video—the proper pixelated one running in news hours as promised—and pledged to leave me alone until I cooled down. His words, not mine. The man was obviously an optimist.

"Hello."

"Laurel Beacham? This is Margarite. I am in your hotel lobby. Jack Hawkes said you would love to talk to me."

Ohmigod, yes. It was hard to believe that only Thursday I'd asked Jack about meeting with her. Too many things had happened in the meantime.

I started to say I would meet her downstairs. Then I thought about what I wanted her to tell me and changed my mind.

"Would you mind coming up here?" I asked.

"Not at all. What room?"

A couple minutes later, I was opening the door for her. She

breezed in with the same cosmopolitan flair and Sophia Loren looks and grace that drew me to her the first time we'd met. As I hopped away, she asked what happened.

"Occupational hazard," I said. "Nothing that won't be right as rain soon enough."

She laughed. "There is plenty of rain outside today in London. You shouldn't have long to wait."

Since she was a coffee drinker like me, I made us each a cup before we got too far into the conversation. I started things off by congratulating her on having such a terrific son as Dylan.

"I hadn't known until last week the two of you were related," I said. "But once I did, I realized I wasn't surprised. I think I'd recognized it subconsciously already because your eyes are so much alike."

She smiled. "Yes, is so true. As is the way you look much like your dear mother."

Well, that was as good a segue as any, I thought. I hobbled over to the room safe and opened it to remove the jewelry case, the compact, and everything each of those items contained.

"I've been receiving gifts lately from a relative of Paul-Henri Aubertine," I said.

"Moran?"

I nodded, opening the jewelry case to withdraw the large photo of my mother and Aubertine. "Was their affair ongoing? Or..."

She sighed. "Your mother was so young when she agreed to marry your father. They were engaged when she and Paul-Henri met. It was..." Her hands wiggled as she raised them from her waist to shoulder height. "Electric. No two people had ever fallen in love so quickly."

"But...?"

"Paul-Henri was honorable and Catholic, and though he loved your mother, his family was quite...angered by his brother's business. And your mother was promised to someone else when they first met. They were in similar circles of friends and saw each other several times a year. Paul-Henri tried to deny his attraction, and when willpower disappeared he told her about Moran and the family's empire. He loved her, but he wanted no secrets. She listened and understood. She was also conflicted because both of your grandfathers were in business holdings together, and she knew any indiscretions on her part would impact her own father's fortune. Paul-Henri felt guilt and she felt guilt. He thought his words would drive her away. And they tried again to stay apart. Many, many times."

Margarite stood and paced the room as she talked, moving her arms gracefully with her words. "Your grandparents wanted an heir. Both sides. The Beachams especially. Also, your mother's parents pressured her against divorce. She thought giving her husband a child would make things better, and she truly wanted to be a mother. She tried hard to get pregnant and not miscarry. The miscarriages happened four times, each more heartbreaking than the last. She thought a baby would make everything right. But it never worked out and she had all but given up. Even tried those painful fertility treatments and surgery options, but nothing was successful. Then, out of the blue, she was pregnant with you. And she was so happy at first."

"At first?"

"Oh, she was happy about you, don't misunderstand. However, she counted back, and began to worry. She'd gone off for a weekend during the time, and..."

"She slept with Paul-Henri and my father around the same time I was conceived."

Margarite hurried over and took my hands, sitting beside me. "Don't think badly of her. She was such a wonderful person, and so very unhappy too much of the time. But she smiled and pretended. Everyone loved her."

"Do you believe her death was an accident? Or Paul-Henri's car crash? It happened in a similar manner. Do you think it was too similar?"

She shook her dark head, but the look on her face showed frustration and anger, rather than uncertainty. "Your mother asked for a divorce. That bas—I'm sorry. But he said if she left she had to leave you behind. Never would she let such a thing happen. She would stay and do everything possible to keep his cruelty from touching your life. She told him this. She'd stay, but only because she didn't want unhappiness to touch you."

"How long did this conversation occur before her accident?" I asked.

Margarite shrugged, but it was a shrug of resignation rather than ignorance. "Maybe three weeks."

I thought about so many things in a millisecond. How I couldn't remember not having Grandmamma beside me at every turn. How soon after my mother's death my grandfather secured my protection with my faithful Bruno and the ever-vigilant Kelly. Maybe there were rumors of potential kidnappings in our social circle. Maybe there was something more. Throughout this time, I missed my mother, though I didn't remember her. Yet I never felt unhappiness until my grandparents both passed away.

"Thank you." I reached over and hugged her.

She clung to me as she spoke. "I should have told you sooner. But how could I?"

"I understand."

"I'm sorry, but I can't give you the information you want to hear."

Pulling back, I smiled and said, "I honestly don't know what I do want to hear. But you have given me a wonderful gift. You told me about the times my mother was happy. The times she was with Paul-Henri. And while hearing she gave up future happiness with him to keep me from being hurt is sad to hear—"

"It did not help anyway."

"But it fills my heart to know she loved me that much," I said, squeezing her hand.

"Are you going to keep trying to find out who your father is?" she asked.

"I honestly don't know. Probably. It all depends on whether I can get the means to test a sample from one of the men whose genes can definitively be matched to mine. I can't see Ermo Colle or Rollie and Moran willingly take the test. It could have been easily accomplished years ago when I didn't have a clue about what the outcome would have meant. Art runs through my veins as surely as does anyone else's blood. And art is a connector between me and all of these men. Regardless of who I'm related to, for me to recognize what I want to choose to do, I must see the outcome as a true bond instead of some forgery concocted for their own means. The thing they each fear from me the most isn't something I've brought to the party. If I continue with this, I need to find a way that not only keeps from masking the truth, but won't bind me to a conundrum they've created themselves. No matter whose daughter I truly am, I'm still my own person. Their names, their plans...can't dictate my future."

Tears glistened in Margarite's dark eyes, and I knew similar tears shined in my own. Eyes exactly like my mother's.

"Did Margarite tell you what you needed to know?" Jack asked when he arrived for dinner that evening. He'd been involved in Rollie's interrogation at Scotland Yard, but he gave me enough information to assume there was still much they needed to know. They were at least able to get him remanded into custody, despite a high-priced solicitor turning up to pitch for bail.

I'd napped after Margarite left, trying to keep myself from thinking too hard about what we'd discussed. Just before Jack arrived, I ordered room service and requested champagne. I put on a long black velvet party gown to hide the repairs on my leg and added a pair of my mother's chandelier earrings to keep attention on the part of me that wanted to smile.

"She told me things I needed to hear," I said. "No great revelations. No absolute truths. But I do recognize I want to keep going with this investigation on her death. If you'll help me, of course. I want to know the truth about her death. If one—or other— parties should be blamed, I want them to pay for their deeds.

However, if accidents truly happened, I want to turn it over to karma and brush the residue of memories and regrets from my hands."

We sat at the small round table in the corner of the room. Jack poured the wine and handed me a glass. A plate of artichoke and stuffed mushroom hors d'oeuvres sat between us, and the steak and potato main course stayed warm in the heated container on the cloth-covered shelf of the rolling cart I'd left by the door. I wanted food to warm and strengthen me tonight.

"You realize," Jack said, taking a sip of the wine, "even if no one is guilty of your mother's death, if we reach a conclusion on the heist mission we're on now, one of the men your mother knew and cared about will be in jail. Whether it's Ermo Colle, or Paul-Henri's relatives."

"*Que sera, sera.*"

"You're sounding very philosophical." His teal eyes held my gaze. Frankly, I didn't want to look away.

I sipped from my glass. "I'm just realistic." I smiled.

Jack frowned. "You know, that song always bothered me. The way a happy feeling and melody was put to such ambiguous words."

"There's a lot of ambiguity and bittersweet aspects to life. Like the Caravaggio painting Nico and I set out to return to the owner, only to see it start a chain reaction that ended up with more people hurt—or worse. However, the family whose plight started the whole endeavor, the ones who hadn't had the painting in their home for several generations, they'll receive back the gift originally stolen from them. Dozens of family members have been born since the painting disappeared and never knew its tie to them. Other older ones died years ago without knowing what happened to the masterpiece. And though they'd missed seeing it for years, it will again hold a place of honor and make family members smile every day."

"Despite the fact you risked your own life and reputation to return it to them."

"It was the right thing to do."

He grinned and said in his Southern Charmer voice, "You can give a guy a heart attack always doing those kinds of right things."

I laced the fingers of my left hand with his. "Much like art, the interpretation of acts depends on who is looking at the pictured events." I raised my glass and smiled. "Let's toast to happiness. I think my mother would like that."

Our glasses made a lovely tingling clink.

"So you're happy?" he asked.

"I'd be happier if you'd spend the night."

"I believe that can be arranged." He stood and pulled me into his arms. Dinner could wait.

Duty, however, could not. His phone rang and I returned to my chair.

"What? How?" he asked.

I heard loud chatter over his phone, but I couldn't make out the words. On the other hand, Jack's rapidly darkening face was easy to read.

"Yes, right. I'll be there as soon as possible."

He hung up the phone and began apologizing.

"It's fine, I get it." I held up a hand. "This kind of thing goes with the job."

"You don't understand. Rollie is gone."

"His lawyer got him released on bail?"

"No, he apparently had help within the police department."

Who needs bail money when bribery works so much faster? Before we had a chance to talk further, my phone rang.

"Would you mind handing it to me please? It's on the lamp table." I pointed.

Jack glanced at the screen. "It's Max. You sure you want to take it?"

"If I don't answer now, he'll just keep calling." I held out a hand. "Hello, Max."

"Why did you let me think this Caravaggio is an original? I trusted your judgement and now I look like a laughing stock!"

I let him rant on for another half-minute, but the upshot of the conversation was the Caravaggio in the tube that he took back to New York after cutting through miles of red tape was the second copy that disappeared ahead of us gaining the one we took to Barcelona. When he emailed me a picture of the forger's mark that appeared near the lower right corner, the confirmation was complete.

"Max, it had to be switched sometime after you got it from Cassie's. It hadn't been out of my possession except when it was in the hotel vault. The copy you have was stolen from Scotland Yard last Thursday. It obviously didn't leave the building, and the switch was made when you were there."

"You're sure?"

"Yes. Superintendent Whatley told us about its disappearance out of property on Friday, just before we flew to Barcelona."

Max spluttered. "It wasn't out of my sight either, and locked up in a safe otherwise. How could this have happened?"

Jack and I stared at one another as I said, "You had to go to Scotland Yard with the painting, right? And to offices of several government officials?"

"Yes."

"I have to assume whoever stole the copy from Scotland Yard used one of your meetings to switch the Caravaggios."

"Impossible."

"Did you ever leave the painting alone in a room? Or were you distracted at any time the Caravaggio was accessible to another person?"

"Hmm...I need to think about this. I may need you to do some investigation from your end as well. Let me make some calls."

"Fine. Talk to you later, Max," I said, then I turned off my cellphone. I looked at Jack. "He'll likely try to call me all night. I'm going to have the desk hold any calls I get on the hotel line, but I'll tell them to put through any from you."

He nodded. "The question is, did whoever helped Rollie escape also switch the copies? Or are there two Moran moles we need to find in Scotland Yard and/or British government?"

"My guess is the latter."

"Unfortunately, I agree."

Jack never returned or called, but when I went downstairs the next morning to go for coffee and a donut, the Serbian desk clerk smiled and handed me eighteen phone messages from Max saying "call right away." I handed the stack back to him and said, "Please throw these in the trash."

Two children and their mother sat on one of the sofas in the lounge area, giggling and pointing out the front window. My newspaper reader was gone.

"The older dark-haired man..." I pointed toward the sofas. "Did he check out?"

The clerk nodded. "Yesterday evening."

I'd never even talked to him, but for some reason I missed him. Just seeing that recurring presence, I supposed.

TWENTY-FOUR

About two weeks after Barcelona, I was back in the office and going over construction invoices when I received a phone call from Danny Williams, Jack's techy friend. It amazed me the people I could get to know because of Jack, and know them even better when he wasn't leading the conversation. Even learn they had a first name.

"Hi, Danny, what's up?"

"How you moving, Blondie?" he asked.

Okay, maybe getting to know some people better wasn't always the best idea. Especially when they're young and cocky. "I'm off crutches but staying away from heels."

"Balance still suck?"

"Is this some kind of pep talk? Because if it is—"

"I just want to make sure you can get to the Tate without falling down." He chuckled.

"What? Why?"

"The face you gave me is moving. Entered the front door two minutes ago."

"I'm leaving now."

"Call me when you get close to the museum, and I'll give you an updated location."

"Will do." I was already pulling on my coat and hurrying as fast as I dared down the stairs. My slower-than-normal pace allowed me to use the taxi app at the same time, and once I got to street level I only had a few minutes' wait time in the frigid February temps.

"The Tate Modern," I told the cabbie. "And please hurry whenever possible."

"Will do."

Once I started thinking about everything that happened, how Rollie disappeared as well as the Caravaggio, I began shifting puzzle pieces to try to determine who was behind the vanishing acts. I located photos of various suspects. Some I could get online, others from security sources, and I went by Danny Williams's command center one afternoon to get reacquainted with the sharp-eyed guy and see if I could get him to do me a favor. There was one picture in particular I felt played the biggest behind-the-scenes role in what ultimately occurred.

When Danny ran that photo through one of his facial recognition programs, he confirmed my hypothesis. This person became The Face, and Danny spent the last week and a half watching to see if the person showed up anywhere in London on CCTV.

The cab moved through the surge-and-stop traffic, and I cursed my luck this happened in the middle of the day. The Tube would have been faster, but too many long walks and flights of stairs kept me from trying to use the system yet. I'd only been back in the office two days. As soon as I could see the Tate building in the distance, I phoned Williams.

"Is he still there?"

"He left the building, but he's outside watching the river."

"Great. Keep an eye on him until you see me in the shot too." I sat up high in the seat, trying to look over cars to see if I could spot my objective.

"Are you kidding me?" Williams laughed. "Of course I'll keep you in sight. Hawkes would kill me otherwise. He might do it just because I called you today. I'm assuming, of course, he doesn't know where you are."

"He's busy with an assignment. I don't want to divide his attention. It's my Valentine's Day gift to him."

"Somehow, I think he'd prefer sex."

"That's my backup plan," I said. "I see him!" I tapped the driver's shoulder. "Stop here."

"Sex before or after he gets pissed off about you confronting a criminal?" Williams asked, as I tossed pound notes toward the cabbie.

"Both, probably," I said, hurrying quicker than I should down the sidewalk. "But I'm not confronting him. I'm just going to talk. See if I can get some answers. I've never been in danger talking to him before. Nothing to make you or Jack worry."

Williams laughed. "Yeah, tell that to Hawkes. I'm sure he'll think it's completely fine then."

"I'm hanging up now, Danny. Thank you."

"Don't you da—"

I shoved the silenced phone into my pocket.

As I approached, I noticed his hair under the fedora was back to gray. The hat wasn't the same one as he wore in Germany, but it was similar. He didn't wear his glasses either, since he wasn't reading. He was watching something or someone either in or across the river. I got closer and he spoke first. "You must be tired. Why don't we go and sit over there?"

Moran took my arm and led me to the bench under a bare-limbed tree. I wondered how long I had before Danny had a Met police car cruise by. I said, "I get the feeling you expected me."

There were plenty of people around. I felt safe in the open like this, but my phone vibrated and I knew someone didn't share my belief.

"Eh," Moran said, shrugging. "You're smart. I knew you'd figure it out."

"Not until you checked out of the hotel. I missed seeing the quiet man with the newspaper. Once you were gone, I started remembering things I'd missed in those busy days. I got security to give me a picture and a friend helped me locate you. Why were you there? Did you know what was going to happen?"

He chuckled.

"How could I know? I just needed a vacation."

"So you decided to spend it in the lobby of the hotel where I lived?" A boat on the water tooted its deep horn.

"It was quiet. Good light there for reading," he said. "For watching people."

"You also spotted when I brought in the Caravaggio too. Did you see the video?" My phone began vibrating again. My gaze swept the roof eaves and lamp poles, trying to see if I could figure out which camera Danny watched us from, but it was no use. He probably zoomed in. I pulled my cell from my pocket and held it high, so he could see when I turned it off completely.

Moran chuckled, but ignored my actions and answered my question. "*Oui*. You have distinctive movements and marvelous talent. I've had my suspicions about you for years. Too many things have been stolen from thieves or wealthy men without scruples and returned to original owners. The video was simply confirmation."

"And that was when you decided to *vacation* in my neighborhood of London."

"Perhaps."

A Met police car crawled by. I smiled and waved. The car moved on. "But you didn't give the painting to your grandson, despite the fact he'd paid for it and scheduled a pickup so he could take it to Barcelona."

"If..." He sighed. "If my grandson prepared to use the art to gain other art, or even money, I would have aided him in his efforts. However, after he called and raged about the midnight theft, and sent me the video link, I took other measures."

"And I assume an informant in Scotland Yard lets you know about any art-related confiscations, which gave you the added advantage of learning about the copies confiscated in Calais."

"Your mind is *très* young and brilliant."

I felt heat in my cheeks. "Which all means I must admit to my boss the original work disappeared in my care, out of the hotel safe where I thought it was better protected than in my room. Instead of being stolen after he'd acquired it. I never dreamed the nice man who sat in the lobby each day, and who had logical access to the safe room just like me, would spirit away the painting. Max has been blaming a mole at Scotland Yard."

"Let him continue." Moran shrugged. "What does it matter really when it happened? It would have been one place or the other. Trust me. Once I knew where the masterpiece was, the Caravaggio would be taken. Maybe by me, maybe by someone else. It is the nature of our business."

"Your business," I said. "Not mine."

I was sorely tempted to do as the old man said. Maybe if I told Max that Moran confirmed he had an informant in Scotland Yard, then let my boss draw his own conclusions... No, this would take some thought—and a stronger sense of courage. However...

"One has to love Caravaggio. He was such a scoundrel," Moran said, changing the subject. His smiling face shone in the surprising February sunlight.

I couldn't help grinning at the fact I'd said almost exactly the same thing many times. Talk about the bad boy of the art world. And here I was sitting beside a septuagenarian of the same personality. "He's one of my favorite artists. His works always walked the edge between acceptable and...maybe not."

"At least not in the eyes of the Church," Moran said.

"Especially when he'd made them prepay a commission, then they had to turn down the work after he added something intolerable that he wouldn't change."

"So he would sell it a second time to a noble and make double the rate for the piece," Moran said. "Which is your favorite of his?"

"I like them all. But I love how he hid the tiny self-portrait in the wine decanter in *Bacchus*. Almost like a secret Easter egg."

"You know, that painting was lost for hundreds of years. Too many works like this. A tragedy. Shipped off to storage like some warehoused merchandise," Moran complained.

"Yes," I said, pulling my coat tighter around me. The wind off the water was sharp, despite the sunshine. "*Bacchus* was rediscovered in Florence in 1917, when a museum worker stumbled onto it in an Uffizi Museum storeroom."

"Lost art people cannot see for generations because it is stored away and someone forgets where it even is."

"I had a similar discussion with your grandson in Germany," I said. "It's frustrating, true, but such instances do not provide a reason for art to be forged or even just copied later. The original public works should stay available to the public. Like the original Caravaggio you substituted for the Scotland Yard copy. The family is disappointed a second time because the painting still isn't coming home."

"I am not a good guy. I am not a bad guy. I am a thief." He stood up. "I should go before one of your policemen come by again and arrest me for loitering. That is the only crime they can hold me for today. You, however. There is proof of who actually held the Caravaggio. Video proof."

I probably should have felt alarmed, but logic told me not to bat an eye. Confidence was respected. I smiled instead. "You may have seen the proof you needed, but I'm not concerned. No one at the French facility wants the video link part of a court case. Too many others would suffer far greater risks. But I will keep looking for the Caravaggio, and I will someday return it to the family home where it truly belongs."

He laughed and tipped his hat. "*Touché.*" He turned to walk away.

"Before you go," I said. "What do you want from me?"

He gave me a puzzled expression and rested a hand to lean against the back of the bench. "I want nothing from you. You arrived here seeking me."

"I mean..." I stopped and took a breath. "What do you know? And what have you told your grandson that makes him see me as a threat?"

Moran shook his head and moved his shoulders. "I've told him nothing to view you like that. He has asked for things he cannot have, and he may have misinterpreted—"

"Please tell him for me..." I stood up and faced him, the bench between us like a means of dividing worthy opponents. "Tell him I do not want *anything* associated with the name Aubertine. I want to make this clear. I want nothing. And please understand this yourself. I want nothing."

"You are very clear, my dear." Moran frowned. "I must leave now before your secret policeman has me detained."

"This isn't over, Moran."

"Why would I think otherwise? *Au revoir.*"

RITTER AMES

Ritter Ames lives atop a high green hill in the country with her husband and Labrador retriever, and spends each day globe-trotting the art world from her laptop with Pandora blasting into her earbuds. Often with the dog snoring at her feet. Much like her Bodies of Art Mysteries, Ritter's favorite vacations start in London, then spiral out in every direction. She's been known to plan trips after researching new books, and keeps a list of "can't miss" foods to taste along the way. Visit her at www.ritterames.com where she blogs about all the crazy things that interest her.

**The Bodies of Art Mystery Series
by Ritter Ames**

COUNTERFEIT CONSPIRACIES (#1)
MARKED MASTERS (#2)
ABSTRACT ALIASES (#3)
FATAL FORGERIES (#4)

Henery Press Mystery Books

And finally, before you go...
Here are a few other mysteries
you might enjoy:

ARTIFACT

Gigi Pandian

A Jaya Jones Treasure Hunt Mystery (#1)

Historian Jaya Jones discovers the secrets of a lost Indian treasure may be hidden in a Scottish legend from the days of the British Raj. But she's not the only one on the trail...

From San Francisco to London to the Highlands of Scotland, Jaya must evade a shadowy stalker as she follows hints from the hastily scrawled note of her dead lover to a remote archaeological dig. Helping her decipher the cryptic clues are her magician best friend, a devastatingly handsome art historian with something to hide, and a charming archaeologist running for his life.

Available at booksellers nationwide and online

Visit www.henerypress.com for details

TELL ME NO LIES

Lynn Chandler Willis

An Ava Logan Mystery (#1)

Ava Logan, single mother and small business owner, lives deep in the heart of the Appalachian Mountains, where poverty and pride reign. As publisher of the town newspaper, she's busy balancing election season stories and a rash of ginseng thieves.

And then the story gets personal. After her friend is murdered, Ava digs for the truth all the while juggling her two teenage children, her friend's orphaned toddler, and her own muddied past. Faced with threats against those closest to her, Ava must find the killer before she, or someone she loves, ends up dead.

Available at booksellers nationwide and online

Visit www.henerypress.com for details

MURDER IN G MAJOR

Alexia Gordon

A Gethsemane Brown Mystery (#1)

With few other options, African-American classical musician Gethsemane Brown accepts a less-than-ideal position turning a group of rowdy schoolboys into an award-winning orchestra. Stranded without luggage or money in the Irish countryside, she figures any job is better than none. The perk? Housesitting a lovely cliffside cottage. The catch? The ghost of the cottage's murdered owner haunts the place. Falsely accused of killing his wife (and himself), he begs Gethsemane to clear his name so he can rest in peace.

Gethsemane's reluctant investigation provokes a dormant killer and she soon finds herself in grave danger. As Gethsemane races to prevent a deadly encore, will she uncover the truth or star in her own farewell performance?